Flowers for the Living

by

Sandra E. Johnson

Texas Review Press
Huntsville, Texas

Printed in the United States of America

FIRST EDITION

Requests for permission to acknowledge material from this work should be sent to:

Permissions
Texas Review Press
English Department
Sam Houston State University
Huntsville, TX 77341-2146

ACKNOWLEDGEMENTS:

I thank God for my life that, though at times has been hard, has always been precious. I am forever indebted to my parents, George and Mary Johnson for their love and support. My gratitude extends to the rest of my family including my church families at HOPE Baptist and Mt. Elon Baptist.

Trey Pruitt, Martha Irvin Jones, Janie Durham Phillips, Brenda McClain, Scott Sharpe, Diane Hahn Hall, Joanne Derrick, Karen van Heerden, Kathy Morganelli and Rachel Elizabeth Hall have been rays of light when the way was dark.

Paul Ruffin is a dream of an editor. I appreciate him and the rest of the staff at Texas Review Press. Thanks, too, to Karen Peluso for her friendship and lovely photography, and to Nancy Parsons for such a gorgeous cover design.

May God bless and keep each of you.

Cover Design: Nancy Parsons, Graphic Design Group

Library of Congress Cataloging-in-Publication Data

Names: Johnson, Sandra E., author.
Title: Flowers for the living / Sandra E. Johnson.
Description: Huntsville, Texas : Texas Review Press, [2016]
Identifiers: LCCN 2015047404 | ISBN 9781680030839 (pbk. : alk. paper)
Subjects: LCSH: African American mothers--Fiction. | Mothers of murder victims--United States--Fiction. | African American teenage boys--Crimes against--United States--Fiction. | Police-community relations--United States--Fiction. | United States--Race relations--Fiction.
Classification: LCC PS3610.O3763 F58 2016 | DDC 813/.6--dc23
LC record available at http://lccn.loc.gov/2015047404

Flowers for the Living

CHAPTER 1

White calla lilies meant forgiveness. That was what Emma Jennings had read somewhere in a magazine. Well, if there ever came a time when she needed to show someone she forgave them, she had plenty of flowers for the occasion. From just three bulbs, they had multiplied to spread around her gardenias and now threatened to invade her bed of lantanas. The creamy whiteness of the lilies with their deep golden throats blended nicely with the sunshine-yellow lantanas, but they were becoming too much of a good thing, at least in this particular place. Balance. That was the secret to good gardening. There had to be the right balance of colors, textures, shapes, sizes, and fragrances. Otherwise, a garden could get out of whack as badly as the rest of the world.

Sitting back on her heels, Emma yanked her bandanna from the pocket of her faded denim shorts and mopped away sweat. Lord, she was hot and tired, but looking over her front yard made it all worthwhile. With the exception of the lilies, she had gotten everything exactly the way she wanted. The freshly pruned roses displayed lush blossoms that were as wide as her palm. The hollyhocks, delphiniums, salvia, gerber daisies and black-eyed Susans stood as neatly as little soldiers, and the crape myrtles stretched their sculpted limbs to the clear blue sky.

Judging from the sun's position, it was probably close to noon. No wonder it was so hot. It had been in the mid-eighties when she started working at dawn, but no telling what the temperature was now. She had planned to work only an hour or so—just long enough to add shredded cedar mulch to the flower beds—but she ended up pruning the roses, clearing away brush that had sprung up near her magnolia tree, and repotting the bright red geraniums on the steps leading to her front porch. And because her husband Otis couldn't seem to tell where the grass ended and her flower beds began, she had mowed the lawn too. She vowed to call it quits after replanting the lilies. Years ago, she could work in the yard all day no matter how brutal the weather, but she was sixty-one now and knew her limits.

She took a long swallow from her water bottle and loaded the lilies into a battered wheelbarrow and rolled them to the other side of the house. Not a bit of shade there. The heat felt heavy enough to be measured by the pound instead of by degrees. When was this doggone heat wave going to end? The temperature had hit over a hundred degrees for twenty-nine days straight—a record for the city. By midday, it was almost unbearable to do anything outside. It was the kind of heat that made folk act crazy, and the local police department's shooting of yet another black man already had the city on edge. The aroma of dark, fertile soil floated up to her as she pulled away mulch from where she wanted to plant the lilies. Mmmmm . . . It was only one of the reasons she loved gardening. Yes, it was a lot of work, but it gave her so much more in return. For one thing, it helped free her mind. It made it easier not to think about things like whether the police were telling the truth when they said the shootings of the black men had been justified, that they'd been forced to fire in self-defense or to protect innocent bystanders. Emma had known the latest man the police killed—Maceo Wilson. He had lived only a few streets away and used to shuffle past her house on his way to the liquor store nearly every day so she had vivid memories of his matted afro, scraggly beard, and pee-stained pants. That vacant stare, too. It was as if something had robbed him of his mind and left him with only a shell of a body that barely functioned. Making it to the liquor store and stumbling back to the rundown shotgun house he shared with his elderly parents seemed about the only thing he was able to work up enough energy to do during the twenty-some-odd years Emma had known him, so she was shocked to hear the police department's claim that he'd gone berserk during a backyard cookout and tried to kill one of his nephews by chasing him with a piece of metal pipe. The cops shot him dead in front of his whole family.

Emma shook her head. That was a sad, sad situation—too awful to think about. She didn't want to think about her job at the county hospital either, especially how she and the other nurse's aides had to do the most work for the least pay, how their minimum-wage wages and their black skin made them invisible. She wished she didn't have to go to work the next day. That old biddy Lucy Caulfield was sure to still be there waiting to be shipped to a nursing home. She was one of the meanest patients Emma ever had. Not only did she make it a habit to cuss Emma out, including calling her a nigger, but she'd also heaved a tray of food at her, turning her plain white scrubs psychedelic with splattered meat loaf, gravy, green beans and stewed tomatoes.

More sweat streamed down Emma's face, forcing her to reach for the bandanna once again. Realizing that she couldn't last much longer, she quickly planted the lilies, rearranged the mulch around them and gave them a good soaking of water. She couldn't help but to take a moment to run the tip of her finger up the side of one of the lilies. It felt like touching the skin of a newborn baby which reminded her of Marcus, the youngest of her five children. When she called him her miracle baby, she wasn't exaggerating. She was forty-five years old when he was born, and he arrived so prematurely that the doctors held little hope he'd live to see his first birthday. He had, though, exactly as she prayed, and now he was a fifteen-year-old growing faster than a wild weed and getting to be about as hard to handle as one, too. The stubborn streaks her other children flashed during their teenage years paled in comparison to his. It was getting to where talking to him was like talking to a brick wall. She'd be glad when he got through this phase and was back to being her sweet, adorable son.

The phone began ringing from inside the house. Assuming Marcus would answer it, Emma kept looping the long garden hose on its holder, but when the phone kept ringing, she abandoned the hose and went inside.

By the time she reached the phone, she was nearly out of breath. "Hello?"

"Sister Jennings! How you doing, honey?"

Emma winced at hearing Clara Mae Robinson's voice. She could never get through a conversation with the woman, who was the wife of Emma's minister, without getting pressured into doing some kind of volunteer work at church.

"I'm fine, Sister Robinson. And you?"

"Blessed, honey! I'm just trying to stay out of this heat. It's already hot as all get-out."

"I know. I've been working in the yard," Emma said, fearing what request lay in wait once the pleasantries ended.

"Honey, you keep your yard looking like something from a magazine. Matter of fact, somebody ought to call *Southern Living* or one of those other magazines so they can come and take pictures and write you up like they did in the paper."

It had been one of the proudest days of Emma's life when the local newspaper did a small article earlier that spring about her and her yard. Her pride had not only been for herself, but for her neighborhood. For once, there was something positive in the news about Waverton instead of how bad it had become since the black lawyers, doctors, teachers and other professionals who used to live there either died or moved to wealthy white suburbs.

"Being out amongst my flowers and trees puts my mind at rest, makes me feel closer to the Lord," Emma said.

"Hallelujah!" Sister Robinson shouted. "That brings me to why I'm calling you, sugar. You know we've got the prayer breakfast coming up this Saturday."

"Yes, ma'am." Emma's chest tightened.

"Well, you do flowers so pretty, I was wondering if you'd mind making a few arrangements for the tables, say a big one for the head table, a couple of medium-sized ones for the tables with the food, juices, and coffee, and then about four smaller ones for the other tables where people will be sitting. However you want to fix them is fine with me."

Emma's tension melted away. This one was easy. The last time Clara Mae Robinson got hold of her, she ended up having to get in front of the congregation and introduce the new officers of the Women's Auxiliary. She'd known nearly everyone in church for decades, but she was still so nervous about speaking in front of them that her voice shook and her hands trembled as she read the names.

"I'd be happy to do that. Would bringing them about an hour before the program starts be okay?"

"That would be fine, honey, mighty fine. I knew I could count on you. Thank you, Sister Jennings. See you Sunday."

"Yes, ma'am."

After the phone call ended, the only other sound in the house was the steady humming of the air conditioner. Emma frowned and put her hands on her hips. Where was Marcus and what was he doing? He'd better not still be in bed, not when she'd told him over an hour ago to get up and clean his bedroom.

She climbed the stairs of the house she and Otis had bought thirty-eight years earlier. Though modest, it was still the best one in Waverton, and she was glad that she and Otis at least had something to show for all of their hard work and had something to pass on to their kids. A lot of people in Waverton weren't able to leave their kids anything but a stack of overdue bills.

Marcus's door was closed.

She knocked on it. "Marcus."

Silence.

She rapped on the door one more time and opened it. With the window blinds closed and the drapes drawn, it was so dark she could barely make out her son's thin form buried beneath the quilt she hand-stitched for him last winter. The bedroom was like a cave, and its dank odor made her suspect rotting food was somewhere amidst the piles of junk covering the floor and chest of drawers. She'd fussed at him about leaving dirty dishes in the room, especially since he already knew she didn't like how he had started eating in his room instead of at the kitchen table with her and Otis. He acted as if he couldn't stand being around them long enough to even eat the simple meals she prepared for them.

"Marcus!" She snapped on the bedside lamp and yanked back the quilt, revealing more of his scrawny body. He wasn't eating enough anymore to keep a bird alive despite her pleading and making a special effort to cook his favorite foods.

Raising his hand to shield himself from the light, he blinked at her as if she were a stranger.

That made Emma even madder. "If I have to tell you one more time to get up and clean this nasty, filthy room . . . "

She let the unfinished threat dangle in the air. Maybe both of them would believe it this time.

"Yeah, in a few minutes," he muttered and tried to pull the quilt back over his head.

She yanked it away again, trying to ignore how horrible his breath smelled. God, was she going to have to begin getting on him about brushing his teeth, too? "That's what you said over an hour ago."

He muttered something under his reeking breath.

"What did you say?"

"Nuthin'."

Flinging the quilt completely off the bed, she glared at him. "Don't you sass me, boy."

He returned her glare with an intensity that chilled her.

This, she decided, was the reason why it went against the natural order of things to have a child so late in life. Old women like her didn't have the stamina to deal with teenagers the way younger mothers did.

Three more years. If she could just hang on until then, Marcus would be in college and out of the house because she'd make sure he'd live on campus. Unfortunately, he had to make it through high school first, and his freshman year at Waverton High had been so awful that both of them dreaded the start of his sophomore year, which was only a few weeks away. It seemed like she spent the entire last school year meeting with his teachers, guidance counselor, vice-principal, and principal trying to figure out how to turn the sullen teen who ignored them and their assignments back into being the straight-A student he'd been in elementary and middle school.

Three more years. *Lord, help me,* she silently prayed. *Help the both of us.*

"Get up," she told Marcus in her sternest voice, "and do what I told you to do."

"All right, all right," he said, not moving.

She put her hands on her hips. "Now."

He sat up.

That he was at least upright gave her some relief. To encourage him, she added, "The sooner you start, the sooner you'll finish."

"Yeah." His tone, though, made it clear he thought what she said was about the lamest thing he'd ever heard. She reined in the temptation to fuss at him about it, that he ought to be more respectful, but she was tired. Thirsty, too. Her tongue was nearly glued to the roof of her mouth.

"Let me know when you're finished," she said, walking toward the door, "and I'll fix you lunch. You've slept through breakfast."

"Okay," he said with not much more enthusiasm than in his last reply.

Emma sighed, went to the kitchen and drank an entire glass of ice water. With her thirst quenched, her curiosity arose about what the weather report would say. Would it include a prediction about when the heat wave would break?

She settled on the couch and turned on the midday news.

"At the top of the news," said the perky blonde news

anchor who wore a little bit too much makeup, "a rally was held thirty minutes ago on the steps of City Hall to protest the latest in a string of killings by the police of black suspects. We've got more on the story."

A reporter appeared on the screen. In contrast to the news anchor, the reporter was an African-American man whose expression was as somber as his dark gray suit. In the background, a small crowd of other African-Americans milled around the front of City Hall. Some held signs, but Emma was sitting too far away to make out what they said.

"Several dozen people have gathered here at City Hall to protest last week's shooting death of Maceo Wilson, a fifty-four year-old African-American man from Waverton with a history of alcoholism," the reporter said. "Here with me is Rev. Curtis Brown, president of the local NAACP chapter, the group sponsoring this event."

The camera lens widened to show the middle-aged black man who visited Emma's church from time to time to talk about community issues and to make pitches for them to join the NAACP.

The reporter turned to him. "Rev. Brown, what do you think this rally has accomplished?"

"For one thing, it put this police department on notice that the African-American community will not tolerate any more of this open season the cops have declared on our men here in this city. We demand that it stop and we demand that there be a federal investigation into this department."

"So you think the recent incidents are the result of racism in the department?"

"Of course they are," Rev. Brown said, as if it were obvious. "All you have to do is—"

Emma cut off the TV. "The No Good News News Show." That's what her daddy used to call it, and he was right. Watching it made it easy to believe that the world was just one big cruel place. She'd watch the weather report later. For now, she'd finish rolling up the garden hose, then take a nice cool shower and relax the rest of the day.

She went outside. After the coolness of the house, the heat felt even more vicious. She'd barely begun rolling up the garden hose before sweat was streaming down her face. "Whew," she said, wiping it away.

"Hey there, Emma!"

Emma twisted around to see Dottie Peters, her best friend and next-door neighbor, waving at her with one hand and leaning against the porch railing with the other.

Smiling, Emma replied, "Hey! How you doing?"

"Oh, I'm making it." A gust of hot wind blew by, causing Dottie's white cotton dress to billow around her knobby, arthritic knees. Using her cane, she hobbled over to an old recliner she kept on the porch and eased into it. "Lord have mercy!" she said, resting her arms on the recliner's frayed dark brown and gold polyester fabric that clashed with a bright blue metal glider that added to the clutter on the small porch. "I bet you it's a hundred degrees already."

"Probably so. I would've watched the news long enough to find out, but they kept going on and on about that demonstration for Maceo Wilson."

"Shaquice said he wanted to go to that, but he had to take his girlfriend to the food stamp office," Dottie said of one of her great-grandchildren.

Emma sat back on her heels. "I don't know—seems like folk ought to let things be. All the protesting in the world ain't going to bring that poor guy back."

"Too hot to be protesting anyhow." Dottie fanned herself with a church fan that advertised a local funeral home. "You could have a doggone heat stroke marching around and carrying on if you ain't careful."

"Ain't that the truth. Once I finish with this hose, I'm going inside for the rest of the day. You ought to get out of this heat, too." Emma couldn't help but worry about her friend. Dottie was getting close to eighty and had open-heart surgery earlier that spring.

"Uh-uh. I got to be out here so I can watch what everybody's doing. I can't be nosy cooped up in the house."

She and Emma laughed. One of the many things Emma loved about Dottie was the pleasure she took in owning up to what many at church considered sinful—she dipped snuff, played bingo every Thursday night, and she lived to gossip.

Emma looked along the street and didn't see anything happening other than some kids riding bikes. "Not much going on now."

"Yeah, but you should've been out here last night. Rev. Stanley brought Tanya Hampton home and what I saw them doing in his car didn't have nothing to do with no religion."

"What?!"

Dottie nodded her head with firmness. "They were slobbering all over each other like dogs in heat."

"Good God almighty! In front of her house for everyone to see?"

"I guess the only someone they was worried about is her husband, and he's down in Florida working on that construction job."

"What a mess."

"It's a bottle of hot sauce, for sure," Dottie said, and obviously cozying up to the subject of local ministers cheating on their wives, she started telling Emma about one pastor who was running around with his sister-in-law, of all people. She was right in the middle of telling about how his wife caught them at a motel when Marcus appeared.

"You finished cleaning your room?" Emma asked him.

"Yeah," he said, walking toward her while hitching up his baggy pants. Otis hated the way he dressed—declared it made him look like a thug—but Emma did her best to make him stop badgering Marcus about it. She knew how desperate he was to fit in with the other kids, and starting high school had been hard enough without him having to dress in a way that set him apart more than he already was because of how shy and quiet he was.

Emma didn't raise her hopes that his bedroom was really clean. After fussing at him for days about it with little effect, she doubted that today would be any different. He'd probably only shuffled the dirty stuff around to make it look like he'd done something. It had become another of their long-running battles.

She thought he was going to say whatever he came

out to tell her from a few feet away, like he normally did, but he drew closer to her with breath scented with mint toothpaste and tenderly kissed her cheek.

Shocked, Emma laid her hand against her cheek. She couldn't remember the last time he'd kissed her.

"What was that for?" was all she could think of to say.

"Because I love you, Momma." His dark brown eyes looked like they held all the sadness in the world.

She touched his cheek. "Baby, what's the matter?"

The faint softness on his face gave way to the hardness that had been there almost constantly for the past year. "Can't I tell you 'I love you' without something being wrong?"

"Awww," Dottie cooed at him. "Ain't you the sweetest thing? I wish my boys were like you."

For once, Emma wished Dottie would hush and go inside. Something was wrong.

"C'mon, baby," she told him. "Let's go in the house and I'll make you whatever you'd like for lunch." *And we can get to the bottom of this.*

But he pulled back. "No, I've got to go."

"Where?" He hadn't even wanted to leave his bedroom lately, much less the house.

"To meet a friend."

"A friend?" Emma asked, even more surprised. He had none as far as she knew. "Who?"

Digging his hands into his deep pockets, he kicked the ground. "Uh . . . you don't know him yet, but you will."

"Quit answering me in riddles," Emma said as he started walking away. "Tell me exactly where you're going and who you're meeting."

He turned to her. "I told you—you don't know him. You'll meet him soon enough, though."

Emma crossed her arms. She was too old for this, way too old.

She watched as his jeans and T-shirt flapped against him in the hot wind. "Who Feels I Knows It" was spelled out on his shirt over a picture of a man with hair shooting out in all directions. Bob Marley. That was the name printed near the bottom of the shirt. Marcus had played one of his CD's for her, but she hardly understood a single word.

"You'd better be back by the time I put dinner on the table," she called after Marcus, but he just kept walking away.

CHAPTER 2

"Goddamn it!" Russell "Rusty" Carter, Jr., whacked one of the air vents in his police cruiser, but only hot air kept spewing out. Of all the times for the Crown Victoria's A/C to go on the blink again—right during the city's worst heat wave. No doubt it was well past one hundred degrees now, and Rusty was only an hour into his ten-hour shift. Finishing the rest of it was going to be hell.

He turned off the useless AC and rolled down the windows which only let in more hot air. Thanks to strains in the department's budget, he was driving the same cruiser his father had before he was forced into retirement eight years earlier. The cruiser hadn't been in good shape even then. Rusty remembered his dad calling it the "Blue Bomb." There was always something going wrong with it—a fan belt breaking, a head gasket cracking, a fuse blowing, and the AC conveniently waiting until summer to start screwing up. Yet instead of junking the car, the brainiac over the department's fleet of vehicles kept getting the cruiser patched up. Rusty was sure that it would've been cheaper over the long run to have bought a brand new one, but he was just a rookie cop, so who cared what he thought about it?

As a way to try to take his mind off the searing heat, he considered what he and his buddy Scott, who was also a cop in Rusty's unit, might do after their shifts. The idea of knocking back some ice-cold beers at the Silver Spur held an appeal, especially since the local honky-tonk was running a special on Buds, and with any luck, better looking chicks would be there than when they last stopped by the place, which was about a month ago. At that time, what few women were there were so scrawny and mangy looking that Rusty suspected they were hooked on meth. The last thing he needed was to connect with women like that. His love life sucked enough as it was. He was twenty-two years old and had yet to have a serious relationship. Still living at home with his parents wasn't helping, but things were bound to get better once he saved up enough money to get a place of his own.

Continuing his patrol of downtown, he tried the A/C once more. Still nothing but hot air. "Damn," he muttered. He wondered how his dad had managed to put up with the unreliable contraption for so long. He also wondered what his dad was doing now. He glanced at his watch: it was a little past noon. Nevertheless, Russell Carter, Sr., was probably already on his second beer for the day, one of a six-pack he would probably finish before nightfall. Despite being eight years into his forced retirement, he still wasn't adjusting to it well. Perhaps things would be different if he had started a second career, but being a cop was all he'd ever wanted to be, and since that was no longer possible, he passed the time stretched out in his recliner, slurping beer and watching mind-numbing talk shows and re-runs of old Westerns. He normally didn't stir to life until Rusty returned home and relayed what happened during his shift that day and who was doing what within the department. Russ, Sr. latched onto each detail like a drowning man grabbing a lifeline. While Rusty was proud he could provide such details, it saddened him that his dad was so desperate for them, that eight years had done nothing to ease his longing for what used to be and his bitterness that it was no more.

And Rusty's poor mom. She acted like she didn't know what to do other than share her husband's smoldering anger at the police department and occasionally suggest to him, in ways that he always ignored, that he cut back on his drinking and find more constructive ways to make his days go by. At least she had her crocheting. Surely she held the *Guinness Book of World Records* for the number of afghans, mufflers, caps, sweaters, booties, mittens, tablecloths, dish rags, and doilies that she had crocheted, although considering all the years she had worked the yarn looms at a textile mill, anyone would've thought she'd never want to see another strand of yarn after she retired.

Rusty hoped her crocheting kept her from worrying about him too much. Her feelings about him following in his father's footsteps into the police department were a mixture of pride and anxiety, and the recent killings of black suspects by Rusty's white coworkers brought back too many painful memories of what led to her husband's highly publicized ouster from the department. Although Russ, Sr., had taken the brunt of the punishment, she and the rest of their family had gone through hell with him. Rusty could still remember the hush that fell throughout a steak restaurant that he, his parents, and his sister, Charlene, had gone to shortly after the media coverage began to flare about what his father had done. It suddenly became so quiet that a George Strait ballad could be heard playing softly from the kitchen, and Rusty sensed everyone staring at them as if they were space aliens. They weren't able to stay for more than thirty minutes before his mom couldn't take it anymore—they left with their just-served meals in carry out boxes.

But like the string of days that the temperature shot past the one hundred degree mark, the tension that had the city in its grip over the killings would end sooner or later. Patience—that was what it would come down to. He wished he had more of it, especially with the damned Crown Vic's A/C.

He maneuvered the sedan onto a downtown street near the city's main bus station. The exhaust belching from the buses parked along the street mixed with the heat rising from the asphalt to create shimmering waves of soot.

Dozens of people, nearly all of them black, tried to shield themselves from the glaring sunrays by sitting beneath an overhang that offered a thin strip of shade.

Rusty glanced across the street and scowled. Damned if Theo Willis wasn't there wildly gesturing with a fistful of rags in one hand and a spray bottle in the other as he spoke to an elderly white lady who was shrinking away from him. While Rusty wasn't close enough yet to hear Theo's words, he knew what the gist of them was—to pressure the woman into paying for a "specialty car wash" which consisted of Theo merely squirting some water on a windshield, wiping away a bit of dust, then demanding ten dollars for his efforts. Of course, he would claim he was doing it only to keep a roof over his head but in reality, it was to feed his unrelenting crack habit. Rusty had warned him to quit bothering people like this, but Theo was obviously ignoring the warnings and risking yet another trip to the county detention center, a place that he had turned into his home away from home.

Rusty parked the cruiser and climbed out of it. "Theo!" he yelled.

Theo whirled around. "What'choo want?"

"To do what I tell you to do and quit harassing people."

"I ain't 'harassing' nobody," Theo grumbled.

"Oh, yes you are," the old woman said, clutching her purse to her chest and sidestepping to her Chrysler LeBaron. "You ought to be ashamed of yourself!" She turned her attention to Rusty. "Isn't there a law against this sort of thing?"

"Yes, ma'am. For one thing, he's disturbing the peace."

"I'm just trying to run my bid'ness," Theo said. "If anybody's being harassed, it's me." He glared at Rusty. "I'm sick and tired of you dogging behind me all the time, and I ain't got to put up with no mo' of your shit. This is America! I knows my rights!"

"You tell 'em, bro!" someone shouted from the bus station across the street.

"Yeah!" someone else added.

Rusty scanned the crowd. Too many people were shooting furious looks at him to guess which of them had hollered out in support of Theo. They had witnessed the same scene as he had, and yet in their eyes, Theo was the victim.

Niggers, Rusty heard his father's voice in the back of his mind, *they'll stick together no matter what.* Damned if he wasn't right.

Sweat streamed down Rusty's face. He wiped it away while keeping one eye on Theo and the other on the crowd, especially the young thug who was fully outfitted in gangsta-style regalia all the way from his baseball cap pulled low over his forehead to the high-topped sneakers that probably cost more than what Rusty earned in a week. It wasn't so much his pointing at Rusty that was alarming, but how he then shielded his mouth with a hand while leaning over to speak to another young guy. What was he saying? It had to be something he didn't want Rusty to figure out through lip-reading, as if Rusty even knew how to do such a thing. "We oughtta kill the motherfucka," Rusty imagined him saying. Time for backup.

He pressed the button on his shoulder radio unit. "This is Five Adam," he said, identifying himself. "Got our ol' buddy Theo Willis disturbing the peace on—"

"I ain't disturbing no peace!" Theo hollered, cutting Rusty off as the old lady dashed to her car and drove away.

Trying to ignore him and the increasingly hostile looks from across the street, Rusty continued, "On the corner of Butler and Washington streets. Need backup ASAP."

"What for?" Theo demanded to know. His expression twisted into a smirk. "You ain't man enough to handle me by yo'self?"

Rusty grew even hotter beneath his sweat-soaked dark blue uniform. "Shut up and put your hands behind your back. You're under arrest for disturbing the peace."

Theo jammed his hands into the pockets of his faded jeans. "I ain't got to listen to you, you muthafuckin' cracker."

That drew whoops and jeers from across the street.

Goddamn it, Rusty thought, fighting to keep his spiking anger and jumpiness in check. After drawing in a deep breath, he said, "Fine—have it your way. I'll add 'resisting arrest' to what I'm hauling you in for."

A squad car appeared from around the corner, and Rusty was relieved to see that one of his buddies, a seasoned veteran who knew how to deal with assholes like Theo Willis in his sleep, was behind the wheel.

Apparently recognizing the no-nonsense veteran too, Theo's defiance melted quicker than ice on a searing sidewalk. "Aw, man," he grumbled. Clasping his hands behind his back, he stood meekly as Rusty recited the Miranda law and wrapped Flexicuffs around his wrists.

After booking Theo in at the detention center, Rusty was back in the Blue Bomb and patrolling the southeastern side of town.

"Attempted robbery reported at 678 Greg Avenue, corner of Greg and Wallace," the dispatcher announced. "Caller states he forced unarmed suspect to flee premises of which he is owner. Whereabouts of suspect presently unknown. Caller gave his name as Sam Brayboy."

Lifting his hand mike from its holder, Rusty spoke into it, "This is Five-Adam, Central. In route to investigate."

"10-4, Five-Adam."

678 Greg Avenue. The high chain-link fence enclosing it made it stand out from the other brick bungalows on the quiet, tree-lined street. So did the large "Beware of Dog" sign on the fence's front gate that was latched with a heavy metal chain and a bulky padlock. Someone must've known Sam Brayboy and what he possessed to make venturing into such a fortress worthwhile when there were more accessible homes nearby.

After notifying Central Command that he had reached the address, Rusty honked his cruiser's horn to alert Brayboy of his presence. He stood at the gate for several moments waiting for someone to come and unlock it. When no one did, he noticed that although the padlock linked the ends of the heavy chain, it was unfastened.

He removed it, unwound the chain and opened the gate while keeping an eye out for dogs. From the looks of it, Brayboy was the type to have a Doberman or two. Fingering the collapsible steel baton and canister of pepper spray at his side, he walked to the house and rang the doorbell.

An old man opened the door. "It's about time you got here," he snapped.

"The dispatcher reported your call less than five minutes—"

"Come in," the man said, cutting him off. "Your excuses can wait. I can't." Leaning on an aluminum cane, he tottered into a musty living room that was frozen in the 1960's with its wood paneling, mangy shag carpet, and couch and club chairs upholstered in puke-green vinyl.

"Are you Sam Brayboy?" Rusty asked.

"I most certainly am." The old man sank onto the couch, smoothing back a thin strand of graying hair that probably was dishwater blond when he was younger.

"I'm Officer Carter with the city police. I'm here about the attempted robbery report you called in."

"Why else would you be here?" Brayboy shot back.

"You fucking asshole," was what Rusty wanted to say, but instead, he drew in a deep breath and released it slowly. *One...two...three.* He took out a small notepad and pen. "Tell me exactly what happened, sir."

"Just a little while ago some goddamned, low-down, conniving son of a bitch came here trying to rob me blind! I ran him off with my cane." He held up the cane in one of his gnarled hands.

"Ever seen the guy before?"

"No, but I know who sent him."

Surprised, Rusty asked, "Who?"

"The county," Brayboy said, spitting out the words. "They sent him out here to do their dirty work."

Now I've heard it all, Rusty thought. "What makes you think the county sent him?"

"Because he gave me this." He yanked an envelope

from his breast pocket and shoved it at Rusty.

Opening it, Rusty began reading aloud. "Dear Mr. Samuel Brayboy, this letter is to serve as final notification that due to nonpayment of property taxes for—"

"Why the hell should I pay property taxes?" Brayboy cut in. "If they want more money to pour into those fancy-schmancy schools that only teach kids how to become juvenile delinquents, they ought to get it from their parents, not poor old pensioners like me."

Thoroughly disgusted with the jerk, Rusty said, "We all have to pay taxes, Mr. Brayboy, whether we like it or not, so if you want to keep this place, I'd suggest you pay the taxes you owe on it."

Brayboy's expression turned meaner. "And if that's the only thing you can tell me, I suggest you get the hell out of my house, you damned bastard."

Rusty nodded curtly. "Have a nice day, sir."

The dispatcher and other cops on patrol had a good laugh when he called in to report what happened.

A sergeant came on the air. "Aw, Carter," he drawled, "you know you should've arrested that tax collector like that old geezer wanted. Better yet, seeing as how you're a young guy with no responsibilities and all, you should've offered to pay those taxes."

"Yeah, right," Rusty grumbled. "I tell you what, the next time Brayboy calls, he's yours."

He wished the Police Academy had given more training on how to deal with all the goofy calls that came in. He was still in his rookie year and had already responded to calls from more nuts than he knew lived in the city. There was that lady who complained that her neighbor cut his grass with his shirt off; another lady who wanted the couple in the next apartment arrested because she said they got too loud while having sex; an owner of a small business who said some angry customers were casting spells on him; and a high school student who wanted his parents locked up because they made him walk a half-mile to school instead of chauffeuring him there. And all those had been just during his first few weeks on the force. Still, he wouldn't trade his job for any other kind, if nothing else than for the pride it gave his dad. Russell Carter, Sr., hadn't been the best father in the world, but he'd been good enough, and Rusty loved him for it.

Stopped at a downtown traffic light, Rusty scanned the street, then glanced at his watch. Six more hours left on his shift. It was going to be a long, long day.

"Attention all units," the dispatcher's voice crackled through the radio. "Armed robbery in progress at the 7-Eleven at the corner of Guinyard and Oak."

In Rusty's distraction, it took a moment for him to realize what the dispatcher said. Guinyard and Oak—that was almost across the street from where he was.

"Suspect is teenage black male, approximately five-ten, weighing approximately one hundred fifty pounds, wearing baggy blue jeans, multi-colored T-shirt, white tennis shoes. Be advised that suspect is armed. Suspect with black handgun."

"Holy shit," Rusty whispered and grabbed his hand mike. "10-4, Central," he said as his heart pounded and his mouth went dry. "This is Five-Adam. Location within sight. Need immediate backup. Repeat—need immediate backup."

"In route to scene, Five-Adam," he heard his friend Scott say. Other voices echoed Scott's words, and sirens began to wail in the distance.

With the store's plate glass windows nearly covered with ads for beer, soft drinks, and snacks, Rusty couldn't see much of anything inside the place. There were two cars parked near the store's entrance and another at a gas pump, but no one was visible in any of them. Whoever came in the vehicles must've gone inside the store. Since Central Command had made no mention of the armed robber having left the scene—he was probably still in the store with those who had the bad luck of being at the wrong place at the wrong time. Rusty wiped away sweat. Shit, it could easily spiral into a hostage situation.

After quickly checking for oncoming traffic, he shot across the street in the cruiser and skidded to a stop in front of the store. "10-23, Central," he said into the mike. *I've arrived.* "Five-Adam awaiting backup." Knowing that at least three or four other officers would come within moments eased the tension that gripped him like a sharp talon.

He climbed out of the car. At the same moment, a black kid who appeared to be in his early teens stepped out of the store. He looked as if he had the worst news to tell Rusty, but couldn't find the words.

That made Rusty's heart jolt again. What the hell had happened? He said, "Hey, dude. I'm with the city police. What's happening here?"

The kid didn't answer. Instead he took a step closer, closing the distance between them to only a few yards. His arms hung at his sides and he gripped something in his right hand.

With total disbelief, Rusty realized what it was—a black semi-automatic. And for the first time, he also noticed what the kid had on—a wildly colored T-shirt, baggy jeans, white Nikes. This child was the armed robber.

"Drop your weapon and put your hands up!" Rusty yelled. He yanked his Sig-Sauer from its holster and flipped off the gun's safety. A chorus of sirens wailed but they still sounded distant.

The kid took another step, holding the gun at his side.

Rusty pointed the Sig-Sauer at him and hollered, "I said drop your weapon and put your hands in the air! Now! Now! Do it now!"

But with that same sorrowful expression, the boy took a deep breath, raised the gun and aimed it straight at Rusty.

An explosion rang in Rusty's ears, and the boy fell to the pavement with a soft thud.

"Holy shit!" Rusty yelled and raced to his side. The kid lay sprawled on his back, his arms outstretched, his hands empty. His gun lay scattered in pieces. Plastic. Nothing but thin black plastic, Rusty realized. It had been just a toy.

He looked down into the boy's soft brown eyes and shrank back. *This can't be,* he thought wildly. This has got to be some horrible nightmare. He shook the boy hard. "C'mon, man! Get up!" he yelled. "Get up, goddamn it!"

A squad car screeched to a stop beside them. Josh Tomlinson got out with his gun drawn. "Carter! You okay? What happened?"

Rusty could only raise his head in response. *An explosion. There had been an explosion.* He couldn't corral his racing thoughts enough to reply.

"Carter?" Josh said.

A black woman ran out of the convenience store. She gaped at the boy and screamed.

Two more squad cars flew into the lot. Scott jumped out of one and rushed over to where Rusty knelt by the boy.

"What happened?" he asked Rusty.

Rusty could only stare at him.

"He shot him," the woman said, pressing a hand to her heaving chest. "I saw the whole thing. That boy came at him with a gun so he shot him down."

"Call an ambulance!" Rusty yelled. "We've got to get this kid to the hospital!"

Scott knelt beside him and put his index and middle fingers alongside the boy's neck. "He's gone."

"Gone?" Rusty said blankly. *This is getting crazier by the minute.* "What are you talking about? He's right here and he needs help."

Josh gripped him by the shoulders. "Rusty, he's dead. This kid's dead."

"No." Rusty didn't so much say the word as it escaped from him like the last bit of air leaking from a balloon. He peered again into the boy's unseeing eyes.

How could he be dead when there wasn't any blood on him? Rusty stared at the boy's T-shirt. No, not one drop. Then he noticed something else. "Oh, Jesus, no," he moaned. But there it was—the small dark hole his bullet made when it pierced the boy's shirt, right between an image of Bob Marley and the words "Who Feels It Knows It."

CHAPTER 3

Emma tamped down the soil around the last of the calla lilies, settled back on her heels, and wiped her face again with her bandanna.

"Oooh, Emma," Dottie said from her porch, "those flowers sure look mighty pretty there. You got your yard looking beautiful!"

"Well, you know how much I enjoy it," Emma said. She gazed at the lilies. Their stalks were so elegant and slender that they looked sculpted. Hard to believe something so beautiful could be so tough. But the lilies could take the heat and just about anything else that came at them. If only she could say the same about herself. She held the sweat-dampened bandanna against her forehead. "Lordy, I've just about had it."

"No wonder, girl!" Dottie fanned herself. "You been working so hard you're even making me tired. Get yourself out of this heat."

There was nothing Emma wanted to do more. She was worn out, drenched in sweat, streaked with dirt and sure that she smelled something awful. Good thing Dottie wasn't sitting close by.

As she forced herself to one knee, trying to summon the strength to go inside, a police cruiser pulled up alongside the curb in front of her house.

"Oh, no, not again," Emma muttered. This was the third day in a row that a cop had stopped by. No doubt this one was going to ask her and Dottie the same questions the other two had about the ransacking of the house across the street that had happened earlier in the week. How many times did she and Dottie have to tell them that they hadn't seen or heard anything? It wasn't because they didn't want to get involved; it was because it was the truth.

Dottie scowled. "These doggone cops is getting on my nerves."

"Shhhh!" Emma said, fearful that Dottie—who was never one to bite her tongue—would get herself into trouble.

Both of them watched as a white cop emerged from the cruiser. Emma guessed he was in his late fifties, much older than the two cops who had been by earlier that week. He seemed much more somber too. She noticed how he paused and drew in a deep breath before slowly trudging toward her.

"Excuse me, ma'am, but are you Emma Jennings," he asked her.

"Yes, sir."

"Mrs. Jennings, I'm sorry, but I've got some terrible news. It's about your son Marcus."

"What?" Emma said. She leapt to her feet. Surely she hadn't heard him right. "Did you say this is about my son Marcus, Marcus Jennings?"

He came closer, so close Emma could hear him swallowing hard before he said, "Yes, ma'am. He was shot by a police officer today while holding up a convenience store. I'm afraid he died instantly."

"Oh, my God!" Dottie shrieked. She jumped up from her recliner and braced herself against the porch railing.

Emma glared at the cop. She was hot, exhausted, and already sick of this man's foolishness. "Sir, I don't mean no harm, but you're just as wrong as wrong can be. My boy's over at a friend's house. He just left here a little while ago. And he ain't no robber. He ain't never done nothing to nobody."

"Ma'am," the cop said, "I'm mighty sorry, but your son tried to hold up the 7-Eleven on the corner of Guinyard and Washington less than an hour ago. He was killed when he threatened a police officer. Marcus Abraham Jennings. He had his Waverton High ID card in his wallet."

That was it! Emma thought. Someone had either stolen Marcus's ID or hoodooed Marcus into giving it to him. Since he had it on him when he was shot, the police assumed he was Marcus. Somewhere there was a family that would have to hear heartbreaking news today but they weren't going to hear it until she got the mix-up resolved. There was only one way to do it. She took off her gloves. "Take me to him," she said.

He walked beside her down the corridor leading to the morgue. Considering that she had spent most of her adult life working on the floors above, Emma thought it ironic that it was her first time on the corridor. She never had any reason to be there before. Whenever one of her patients died, a couple of the orderlies would come with a stretcher, load the body onto it, and whisk it away. That was the last she saw of it.

At the end of the hallway, an orderly she'd known for years pushed an empty stretcher through a pair of swinging doors.

"Hey, Emma," he said as he came toward her. Noticing the cop next to her, he looked back at her with concern. "What you doin' down here?"

"Getting something straightened out," she said. "I'll tell you about it when I come to work tomorrow."

"Okay," he said and rolled the stretcher past them.

Cold air enveloped her as she followed the officer into the morgue. It seemed strange to find several staff people in the large room either typing on computers, talking on the phone, or scribbling in charts just like they would if they were upstairs. Unlike the rest of the hospital though, there were no patients to be healed in this place.

She tried not to look at what lay on the metal exam tables in the center of the room—two bodies draped with white sheets. A foot stuck out from beneath the sheet covering the smaller body. The petite foot appeared gnarled from arthritis and its papery white skin was wrinkled and spoiled with age spots. That made the color of the nail polish on the toenails especially unexpected—it was a vivid lime green. Emma couldn't help but wonder if the woman—and it was certainly a woman under that sheet—had known she was going to die when she did, would she have painted her toenails a more sensible color or was she the type who didn't give a damn if she went to glory with her toenails looking like small neon lights?

Gesturing toward a man scribbling in a chart, the cop said, "Mrs. Jennings, this is Bruce Richards, the coroner for this county."

Bruce Richards closed the chart, laid it on a counter and lightly touched Emma's shoulder. "I'm so sorry for your loss, Mrs. Jennings."

She jerked away. "I ain't had no loss. Y'all talking crazy. My boy ain't here. Somebody else's is, but not mine. He's at a friend's house."

"I'm afraid you're wrong," the coroner murmured.

"I ain't!"

With a gentle voice, the cop said, "Mrs. Jennings, I know I asked you this on the way over here, but are you sure you want to see your son by yourself? It might be better to have somebody else with you, a family member perhaps. If you'd like, we can wait until someone can come down here to be with you."

"No," Emma said firmly. "I don't need nobody with me for this."

She caught him giving the coroner a look that said, "I tried." She hated it, she hated him, and she hated the coroner as he shrugged in an apparent sign that he saw her as yet another person unwilling to accept the truth of what had happened to a loved one. She had never felt such hatred before in her life. She had never imagined herself having the capacity for it. All of this was insane. She couldn't stand another second of it.

"I want to see the body," she said to them.

"Yes, ma'am," Bruce Richards replied. He pulled back the sheet covering the other body.

Emma's heart stopped. Marcus. So perfect. So beautiful.

This can't be happening, she thought. *This – this is a horrible nightmare.*

With a trembling hand, she touched his cheek. It was as soft as when she had touched it earlier that afternoon.

"Marcus," she called to him quietly. She leaned closer to him. "Marcus." This time her voice quavered. She slid her hand from his cheek to his chest. But he lay still, perfectly still.

She backed away from him, fighting for breath. "No," she whispered, then screamed, "No!"

Her legs buckled and the men had to grab her to keep her from collapsing to the floor. "My baby!" she cried. "Why, Lord, why?"

The smooth whir of the air conditioner and her weeping were the only sounds in the Crown Victoria on the way back home. The bandanna that had been damp from her sweat was now soaked with her tears. She struggled to think, to string one coherent thought to another. Marcus was dead. Shot. A policeman shot him after Marcus had. . . .

No. None of it made any sense. There was no way on God's green earth that Marcus would've hurt a fly, much less held up a store. He was the most mild-mannered soul she had ever known. And he would've no more threatened a cop than he would've tried to set the moon on fire. Why were people telling such crazy lies about her boy? He'd never done anything to anybody. He was . . . he was . . .

Fresh sobs tore through her raw throat. Was. That was how she had to talk about her baby from now on. All the things she wanted for him that would never be. She believed he'd be the first of her children to go to college. She'd even pictured him going on to become a doctor or lawyer. Despite his grades being so bad last year, he continued to score in the top percentage on aptitude tests. He'd been a brilliant child. He'd been her hope.

With a dull awareness, she realized the squad car had stopped. She looked out the window. "Oh, Jesus," she moaned at the sight of her home. The driveway was jammed with cars and people were streaming into the house and milling about the yard. There was even a TV crew from Channel Four News.

The thought of having to get out of the cruiser was too much. *I'm not strong enough for this,* she thought, clutching her purse and soggy bandanna.

"Momma!" Ed hollered from the front porch. He elbowed his way through the crowd and ran to her. With tears running down his face, he jerked open the car door and grabbed her. She held onto him, sobbing onto one of his broad shoulders.

She kept her face buried against him as he guided her toward the house. Her legs buckled and despite his strong hold, she sunk toward the ground. Her other son, Otis Lee, appeared through the knot of people that had formed around her and helped to lift her. He kissed her and pressed her tear-stained cheek against his. "It's gonna be okay, Momma. We gonna get through this."

How? Emma wanted to ask but couldn't get the word out. She allowed him to grip her from one side and Ed from the other as they half-carried her toward the house. *My boys,* she thought. *The only two I've got left now.*

The throng of people walked alongside and behind them to the house. In her anguish, Emma didn't look to see who they were but bits and pieces of what they said penetrated her consciousness—"in cold blood"... "that's his mother"... "a shame that"...

She forced her legs to work as she and her sons mounted the steps onto the porch. The TV crew reached them before they made it to the front door. The same reporter she'd seen on TV covering the NAACP rally at City Hall that morning thrust a microphone at her. "Mrs. Jennings," he said, "I'm Leon Franklin with Channel 4 News. You must be devastated at hearing this shocking news about your son."

Emma buried her face again into the curve of Ed's neck. When would this end?

She and her sons pushed their way past the reporter and into the crowded house. She found her two daughters in the den and locked with them in a mournful embrace. Over muffled sobs, Stephanie wailed, "Oh, Lord! Why? Why my baby brother?"

So many questions, Emma thought, but no answers. How were they going to live without any answers? She gripped her four surviving children tighter, wishing there were some way she could return them to her womb. She could protect them there. Her love could keep them safe.

Through the jumble of voices in the house, Emma heard Otis's. "Where's y'all's daddy?" she asked her kids.

The oldest one, Brenda, pressed a wad of toilet paper to her reddened eyes. "In the kitchen."

Emma started for the kitchen but was stopped at nearly every step by someone who wanted to say how bad they felt for her, how the Lord gaveth and tooketh away, how He must've needed another angel in heaven for Marcus to have died so young, how trying times came to make people stronger. A bunch of empty, stupid words, Emma thought as she limply accepted their embraces. She regretted the many times she said such meaningless things to other people after tragic deaths. She had meant well, just as the people saying such words now meant well. She knew that, but their words left her grief untouched and unbearable.

She spotted Dottie on the couch wedged between a neighbor and one of Otis's cousins. Dottie managed to reach her and they held each other tightly for several moments.

"As soon as you left with that policeman I called everyone I could think of and told them what happened," Dottie said.

That explained why so many people were there. As much as Emma wished she'd had some time alone to pull herself together before having to face others, she was grateful for her friend breaking the news to everyone. There was no way she would've been up to doing it.

She gave Dottie's wrinkled hand a soft squeeze. "Thank you."

Dottie let out a heavy sigh. "Ah, girl, you going through hell and you got a lot more to go through before it gets better; it will get better though. I know it's hard to believe that, but it will by and by."

By and by. How long was that? A year? A decade? A lifetime?

"I've got to find Otis," Emma said.

She found him slumped in a chair at the kitchen table with a bunch of his kinfolk, including one of his aunts who patted his shoulder rhythmically while speaking softly to him. He had one hand over his eyes and the other clenched into a tight fist.

"I'm back from the hospital, honey," Emma said, kissing his forehead.

He dropped his hand from his face, revealing only the second time she'd ever seen him cry. The other time was at his mother's funeral.

"You saw him?" he asked.

Nodding, she started to weep again. "They had him laid out on a table in the—oh, God—" Her voice broke off as she collapsed again into wrenching sobs.

He stood and took her in his arms. It was so good to be within them again, to feel protected from the day's madness. She rested her head against his shoulder and cried.

He held her tighter. "They ain't going to get away with this, baby. If it's the last goddamned thing I do, I'm going to see that those motherfucking cops pay for killing our boy."

Despite her grief, Emma drew back in shock. She'd never heard him use such ugly language before. "Otis!"

He continued to rage. "Them crackers think because he was black they could shoot him down like a fucking dog. Well, they're going to learn different real quick."

His brother Willis jumped up. "That's right!" he hollered. "They think just 'cause they got away with killing all them other black fellas that they can get away with killing Marcus. They think 'cause we living here in Waverton they can do us any kind of way, but they done messed with the wrong goddamned family. We gonna give them something they ain't never dealt with before!"

Before Emma could tell him to hush with such hateful talk, one of Otis's sisters screamed, "Marcus! Marcus!" She threw herself onto the floor in a fit of frenzied anguish, not unlike she'd often done during other family tragedies.

"For God's sake," Emma groaned. She couldn't cope with her sister-in-law's theatrics on top of everything else. She wished everyone would get out of her home and leave her, her husband, and their children alone to absorb what had happened. Instead, more people rushed in to see what the commotion was about.

As if she'd caught her aunt's hysteria, Stephanie shrieked, "This ain't right! The police murdered my brother!"

Otis said to her, "Don't you worry none, sugar. By the time I get finished with them, them fucking cops are going to wish they never laid eyes on Marcus."

"Otis, please," Emma cautioned.

"Mr. Jennings! Mr. Jennings!" the reporter from Channel 4 News shouted while forcing his way into the kitchen with the cameraman trailing behind, filming as he went along. "Do you believe your son was the victim of racially-motivated police brutality?"

Emma glared at him.

"Of course," Otis snapped. "As far as them cops were concerned, he was only another dumb nigger to gun down like all the others they've been making a sport of murdering this summer. If that ain't bad enough, now they're trying to drag my boy's name through the mud to cover themselves. They're trying to say they had to shoot him because he was holding up a store and threatening a cop. That's the most ridiculous lie I've ever heard in all my life. My boy wouldn't hurt a fly. He's an—"

His voice caught as he fought back tears. Emma put her arm around him.

He drew in a deep breath then continued. "My boy was an honor roll student. He was involved in church. He was a good kid, the best son a man could ask for. He never gave us a moment's trouble. Ain't no way in hell he'd hold up a store or try to hurt nobody. That's a damned lie the police are telling, like they've been lying about the other people they've shot down in cold blood."

"What do you intend to do about it?" the reporter asked.

"Well, for starters I got a good mind to go to the police department and tell them to their faces that they ain't getting away with murdering Marcus," Otis said.

Shouts of agreement filled the room.

"We ought to go over there right now, Daddy," Stephanie declared, "before they kill somebody else's child!"

This is getting crazy, Emma thought. She sensed a dangerous cycle forming with the anger of her family and that of the crowd feeding off of each other. She had to do something, but what?

"Yeah," Otis yelled, "c'mon on everybody – we going to the police station!"

Another chorus of agreement rose up and people surged outside.

Emma grabbed Otis. "Honey, no!" she whispered to him. "Won't nothing good come from going down there. We need to leave this in the hands of the Lord."

"The Lord?" Otis sneered. "He wasn't the one who killed our boy, the police did, and they're going to pay." He pulled her toward the back door. "I'm gonna make sure of it."

As she got into the car with Otis, Otis Lee, and Willis, Emma thought back to another hot summer afternoon when she was a girl and had gone to the rocky banks of nearby Cherokee River with her uncle and his kids for relief from the miserable heat. While her uncle fished and her cousins cannonballed into the water with loud whoops, she sat on a slab of granite jutting out over the river's edge and splashed her feet. The river scared her – she'd never been in more water than what she needed to take a bath in. After a while, however, the temptation to play with her cousins and have as much fun as they were obviously having overcame her fear. Sliding into the water, she bobbed up and down, amazed at her sudden weightlessness. She started playing with her cousins and was enjoying herself so much that by the time she realized the river's current had grown vicious, it was too late. Her uncle, her cousins, the rocky shore, the trees, the sky—everything disappeared. She screamed into the swirling blue-greenness that sucked her downward. She clawed to reach its surface, yet the more she struggled, the stronger the current grew.

Looks like the same thing's happening all over again, she thought as Otis drove away from the house and a long line of vehicles fell in behind, including the van from Channel 4 News. Where would the strong hands come from to snatch her and her family out of this nightmare the way her uncle rescued her from the river?

"This don't make no sense," she announced. "Even if we go down to the police station every day for the rest of our lives, it ain't going to bring Marcus back."

"We can't let them get away with this, Momma," Otis Lee said. "You heard what Stephanie said—if we don't do something, them cops are going to keep on killing innocent people. Do you want another family to have to go through what we are?"

Just thinking of that made her wince. "Of course not," she said. "But I don't see how raising a bunch of sand at the police station is going to stop them. What we need to do is to call somebody in Washington and get an investigation going."

"That ain't going to do any good," her brother-in-law said from the back seat. "Them crackers don't do nothing but cover for each other."

"Yeah," Otis added. "Look at them cops out in Los Angeles. They beat and kill black folks left and right. They even put it on tape—show it all on TV—but what happens to them? Not a damned thing. Them investigations ain't nothing but for show. They always end up only patting them dirty cops on the back and letting them keep gunning down people."

There was enough truth in Otis' words to silence Emma. She folded her arms, stared out the window, and tried not to listen as he, his brother, and Otis Lee kept on and on about how rotten cops were. She saw people gathering on a Waverton street corner. They saw her, too. A number of them waved while others raised their fists in a defiant show of solidarity. They know, she thought. Nothing spreads faster in this neighborhood than bad news.

Another group had formed further down the street in front of a Laundromat. They were all boys who looked to be in their early to mid-teens. They moved about as if they had more energy than they knew what to do with, and she heard agitation in their loud, angry voices. One of them snatched a trash can from the sidewalk and flung it through the Laundromat's plate glass window.

"Oh, my God!" Emma yelled and asked the others in the car, "Did y'all see that?"

"Crazy niggers," Otis complained. "They ain't got the good sense to go over to where the crackers live to tear something up. They got to smash stuff in their own neighborhood."

The boys broke into loud cheering and kicked out the lower section of the window still clinging in place.

Emma watched the teenagers grow smaller in the rearview mirror. *The whole world's gone crazy.*

Otis parked near the front of police headquarters and for the second time that day, Emma dreaded having to get out of a car. She wanted to go home, to be among her flowers, to have peace.

"I can't do this," she said to Otis. "Please, let's go back home."

"That's what they want us to do," he said, pointing at the two-story brick and glass building facing them. "They want us to turn tail and run like a bunch of scared field hands. We got to go in there and stand up for what's right. We got to stand up for Marcus. He had just as much right to live as any of their kids. We got to tell them that. Now are you coming with us or not?"

It was a clear line. She couldn't be on one side of it with her family on the other. "Lord, help us," she said softly as she climbed out of the car.

She felt like a vise gripped her chest as she, her family, friends, neighbors, the Channel 4 News crew, and dozens of other people crammed into the lobby of police headquarters. *Breathe, girl, breathe,* she told herself. She was sure she looked as nervous as the receptionist and two uniformed cops sitting behind a glassed, enclosed counter.

When Otis marched up to the counter, the receptionist, a young black woman, slid open its glass panel. "May I help you, sir?" she asked him in a shaky voice.

Emma guessed she was about Stephanie's age, too young to have to face a mass of people who viewed her as being within the enemy's ranks despite the color of her skin.

"My name is Otis Jennings," Otis announced loudly, "and I just got word that one of the cops here killed my boy, Marcus Jennings. I want to see the chief."

"I'm sorry, sir, but he's in a meeting."

Emma heard someone from behind her shout, "Tell him to come out of it!"

"I betcha' he ain't in no meeting," someone else hollered. "He's probably up in his office hiding!"

"I want to see the chief," Otis repeated to the receptionist, "and I want to see him right now."

"Perhaps I can have someone else help you?" the young woman said, her voice even shakier.

Leave her alone, Emma wished she had the guts to tell her husband. She ain't to blame for what happened.

"No," Otis said. "I don't want to talk to no flunky. Get McDonald out here now."

Emma noticed the news cameraman moving in closer while the reporter glanced back and forth between Otis and the receptionist as if they were opponents on a tennis court.

"Like I said, sir," the receptionist replied, "he's in a

meeting. I can take your name and number and have him to contact you later, if you'd like to do that."

"I ain't leaving here till I talk to him," Otis said.

"You tell her, Daddy!" Stephanie said.

Emma shot her daughter a stern look, but Stephanie didn't seem to notice.

"Tell that McDonald to come out here and face me like a man!" Otis demanded.

"Justice for Marcus! Justice for Marcus!" someone chanted. The crowd took up the chant, clapping to its rhythm.

The angry chanting, the press of so many people, the heat and odor from their sweat-soaked bodies—it was too much for Emma. A wave of dizziness hit her, forcing her to grab the edge of the counter to steady herself. A side door flew open and about a dozen cops rushed into the lobby. "What the heck are y'all carrying on about?" one of them asked.

"We want justice for my baby brother!" Stephanie yelled at him. "Marcus Jennings! Y'all shot him down today like a dog. He was an innocent child!"

Closing her eyes for a moment, Emma saw the coroner lift the sheet from Marcus's lifeless body. She was again struck by the unreality of it. It didn't make any sense. If something as crazy as the police killing Marcus could happen, anything could. What was to keep the sun from falling to earth and burning it to ashes? How was she supposed to go on when everything she'd believed to be sure and steady wasn't?

"Murderers!" a woman screamed at the police.

"Cold blooded killers!" someone else added.

"Justice for Marcus!" another cried and the crowd started chanting again, "Justice for Marcus!"

More cops poured into the lobby. Emma didn't see a black one among them. They clustered together for a few seconds to talk, then spread out to form a wall of dark blue uniforms. One of them put a hand on the butt of his holstered gun while using the other to point to the entrance doors. "Y'all have to exit this building immediately," he shouted to be heard above the chanting. "We'll arrest anyone who doesn't obey this order."

He was close enough for Emma to read his name stenciled above his left breast pocket—"Capt. J. Nelson."

"This is America!" someone in the crowd shouted back. "We got the right to protest if we want to!"

"Not in here, you don't," the captain snapped. "I repeat—exit this building immediately. You've got thirty seconds to obey. Anyone remaining in this lobby after that will be arrested."

"On what charge?" a young man demanded to know.

"Disorderly conduct, for starters," Capt. Nelson answered. He glanced at his wristwatch. "Twenty-eight seconds."

Trying not to be overheard, Emma said to Otis. "We've got to get out of here."

Otis shouted, "Justice for Marcus!"

"Justice for Marcus!" the crowd picked up the chant again. "Justice for Marcus!"

Emma grabbed her husband, forcing him to face her. "Do you hear me? We've got to get everybody out of here before somebody gets hurt! There's women and children in this place."

"Look at 'em, baby," he said, gesturing toward the police. "They try to act like they're all big and bad, but just look at 'em. They're the ones who're scared." Turning away from her, he joined in the chanting.

The police advanced.

"Justice for Marcus!" the crowd roared louder. Emma watched in horror as the two sides collided. The lobby exploded into chaos as protesters shoved, kicked, punched, cursed, and yelled at the cops who closed in on them with handcuffs, steel batons, Taser guns, and pepper spray. With the ear-splitting screams, shrieks, and shouts, Emma could barely hear herself crying out the names of her loved ones as she searched for them amidst the jumbled mass of people.

She had to dash behind a pillar to avoid getting trampled by a cop chasing two teenage boys. From there, she scanned the frenzy. The thought of two of her grandchildren being trapped somewhere in it made her legs go weak. Spotting a guy from her block dashing for the exit doors, she grabbed him. "Have you seen my two grandbabies, any of my kids, or Otis?"

"I don't know who I seen or ain't seen, Miz Jennings," he said, panting hard. "All I know is I'm getting the hell outta here!" He broke from her grip and escaped outside along with a blur of other protesters.

Emma saw another neighbor, but before she could reach her, a cop tried to handcuff the woman, and the woman fought back by swinging her large purse at him and trying to stomp his toes with her high-heeled pumps.

Feeling hands clamp down on her shoulders, Emma screamed, but when she was whirled around, she found herself facing one of her daughters. "Momma!" Brenda hollered as tears streamed down her face.

"Thank God you're okay," Emma said, throwing her arms around her with relief. "Where are Courtney and Sean?" she asked of Brenda's nine-year-old daughter and eleven-year-old son.

"I got Stephanie to take Courtney out to the car, but I can't find Sean anywhere!" Brenda wailed.

"He could get killed around here!" Emma looked around, her heart thundering. She caught sight of her husband and two sons helping a family friend off the floor and yelled for them.

They ran over. "Y'all need to get outta here!" Otis ordered. "Stephanie and the grandkids too!"

"Stephanie and Courtney are in the car but we can't find Sean!" Brenda said.

Otis steered Emma and Brenda toward the front doors. "We'll find him."

"I ain't leaving here without my baby!" Brenda cried.

"They'll find him, honey," Emma promised. She could only pray that her words proved to be true. As she tried to get her daughter outside, she took another glance around the lobby and caught a glimpse of Sean cringing behind a pillar. "There he is!" Emma shouted and raced after the child. She barreled right into a cop running in the opposite direction with another cop. Their collision knocked her to the floor.

The cop grabbed Emma and helped her to stand. "I'm sorry, ma'am. I'm so sorry."

"No, it's my fault. I'm sorry—I didn't see you," she said.

The other cop pulled him away. "C'mon, man, we've got to get out of here." They disappeared from the lobby through a side door.

After weaving quickly through the crowd, Otis, Otis Lee, Ed, and Brenda surrounded Emma. "Are you all right?" Brenda asked.

Emma put her hand to her forehead. The room was spinning and pain thudded in her head and ripped down her spine. Sinking to the floor, she moaned, "Oh, Jesus."

Ed and Otis grabbed her. "Baby, what's the matter?" Otis asked.

"My head—it's killing me."

"Help!" Brenda yelled out. "Help! We need an ambulance!"

"No, no," Emma said. "Just let me rest here for a second and try to get my bearings." She fingered her scalp, wondering if it was bleeding anywhere, however her hand came away glistening only with sweat.

The captain who had warned the protesters that they would be arrested if they didn't leave the building rushed over.

Emma looked up at him. "I don't want no ambulance."

"Are you sure?" Capt. Nelson asked.

"Yes," she answered. From behind the captain, she saw a neighbor running over with Sean in tow. "Oh, thank the Lord," she sighed and tried to massage away the near-blinding pain from her head.

With Brenda sweeping her son in a fierce embrace, the neighbor crouched down beside Emma. "What happened, Miss Emma?"

"I bumped into somebody and fell and hit my head."

"You may have a concussion," the captain said. "It would probably be a good idea for you to go to the ER."

"The only place I want to go is home," she answered. Something inside her crumbled and she began to cry. "I just want to go home."

"That's where we're going to take you right now," Otis said, pulling her close and then glaring up at Capt. Nelson. "That is unless we're under arrest."

"No sir, you're free to take her home," the captain said. "Ma'am, are you sure you'll be okay?"

"No," Emma sobbed. "I ain't sure of nothing no more."

Otis helped her up and turned to Capt. Nelson. "I'm taking my wife home now, but y'all ain't seen the last of me, not by a long shot. Y'all ain't getting away with killing my boy."

"You're Marcus Jennings's father?"

"Yes, and this is his mother," Otis said, pointing to Emma. With her eyes filled with tears, the image of the captain wavered in front of her.

"I'm sorry for your loss," the captain said to her and Otis.

"Not half as sorry as you're going to be," Otis snapped.

Emma was too embarrassed by her husband's behavior to look at the captain. She kept her gaze fixed on the tiled floor while her family helped her outside.

"What in the world is going on now?" she said when they stepped out of police headquarters. Thick smoke hung in the air and sirens screamed.

Bolting from her car in the parking lot, Stephanie ran up to them. "Thank God y'all made it out of there! I was worried sick."

"What's burning?" Ed asked and pulled the edge of his T-shirt over his nose.

"Lowman's Drugstore," Stephanie answered. "Some kids set it on fire. That old warehouse beside it, too. Courtney and I have been in the car listening to news on the radio. There's fighting, burning, and looting all over. It's a race riot. The governor's called out the National Guard."

"Oh, my God!" Emma said. How could such a thing be happening? This wasn't Los Angeles, New York,

Detroit, Miami; it was a place where people still sat on front porches and chatted with their neighbors, where kids were raised to say "please, ma'am" and "thank you, sir" to their elders, where they could play outside without fear of drive-by shootings and kidnappings, where you couldn't go anywhere without running into someone you knew.

She'd lived there her entire life, had been born right over in the "colored" hospital on Magnolia Street before it was bulldozed to make room for a parking garage. Life in the city had always been harder for blacks than whites, yet where in America was that any different? Progress was slow in coming, but it was coming. She knew of too many blacks who were doing well to believe otherwise. But she also knew that didn't mean a thing to the young folk stuck in Waverton who felt they had nothing to lose.

From somewhere in the distance gunfire rang out.

"Move it, y'all!" Otis hollered. "We got to get out of here right now!"

Pain shot through Emma with each jarring step while running with her family across the parking lot to their cars. She'd barely climbed into the Skylark before Otis put it in gear.

More gunfire rang out. Sliding down the seat, she pressed her fingers against her ears and began humming "Precious Lord, Take My Hand."

Upon returning home from police headquarters, her hope of finding a quiet oasis from the day's madness amidst her flowers was shattered when she saw dozens of people still milling about the yard and streaming in and out of the house. Lord Jesus, she thought, when are these people going to leave us be?

Rubbing her throbbing head, she trudged behind her family as they went into the kitchen. It was crowded with people helping themselves to the platters of fried chicken, assorted fixings, cakes, pies, and jugs of tea that had already arrived. Despite the tragic reason for the gathering, she realized that for many it would also be a chance to share memories and the latest news with the distant relatives, old friends, former classmates, and ex-lovers they hadn't seen since the last sad occasion that had brought them together. It would be a reunion for them, the way it had been for her when she visited people who had lost loved ones. Now she realized how painful it must've been for them to see her and others lounging around with plates heaped high and chatting and laughing while their worlds fell apart. She would do as they did though—somehow force herself to smile and say things she didn't mean like how much she appreciated them coming over and staying for such a long time, and how it was so thoughtful of them to offer to return the next day as well. Somehow, she had to do that. Simply thinking about it made her head hurt worse.

Dottie hobbled over to her. "Thank the Lord y'all made it back here. All hell's done broke loose."

As if to punctuate her words, a siren shrieked in the distance.

"I know," Emma said. "We saw enough of it at the police station and more on the way home." In truth, she hadn't seen the destruction while returning home because instead of looking out the window, she stared at the folds of her denim shorts as if she would need to draw them later from memory. Yet while she could refuse to look at the violence, even humming with her fingers pressed against her ears couldn't completely block out the noise of gunfire and sirens.

She put a hand to her head again. "Oh, mercy, I've got to sit down."

"C'mon." Dottie took her by her other hand. "Let's go in the den. Ain't as many people in there."

The TV was on, though, and showing police wrestling several young black men to the sidewalk in front of a department store with shattered plate glass windows.

"Turn that somewhere else," Emma said to her grandchildren who were huddled near the screen.

One of them protested, "But we wanna watch it."

"You heard Momma," Brenda said.

Sighing, Dottie said, "Satan's done turned his demons loose tonight."

"Yeah," Otis Lee said, "and they're wearing blue uniforms. You should've seen how they did us down at the police station, Miss Dottie. One minute Daddy was asking to talk to the chief and the next minute them police set on us, punching and kicking us and trying to arrest as many of us as they could. You would've thought we'd gone down there pointing Glocks and sawed-off shotguns at them."

"I betcha' they said y'all was a threat just like they said Marcus was a threat," a church member reasoned.

"God only knows what they're going to do to Tyrell, Jo Jo, Sam, Bunny, and all the others they locked up," Brenda said.

"We need to go back down there tonight and make them police let 'em go," Willis said.

Emma gave her brother-in-law another harsh glare. She'd had enough of his mouth. Had it not been for him egging Otis on, they might not have gone down to police headquarters in the first place.

"We ain't going back down there until we got a team of lawyers with us," Otis said. "See if them police start laying their hands on us then."

"What we need to do is call some big-time news shows," Stephanie said. "If we had reporters from shows like *60 Minutes*, we'd see some changes in how black folks get treated around here."

"Sure enough," her father said.

"Something's got to be done and soon," a cousin added. "Because as it is, all of us are walking around with a bull's eye on our backs. It was Marcus today, but who will it be tomorrow?"

"With this rioting going on, it might be somebody tonight," Ed said.

That same thought plagued Emma, and it made her head hurt even more. "Sweetheart," she said to Brenda, "go and get me some Tylenol."

Brenda reached for her purse. "I've got some right here."

Emma gratefully accepted the small bottle of pain relievers, shook out five of them and gulped them down with iced tea.

Stephanie stood. "I'm going to start calling those TV shows right now. Daddy, pass me the phone."

Handing it to her, Otis said, "Be sure to tell them to hurry and send reporters down here before someone else gets gunned down in cold blood."

"I will," Stephanie said as she took the cordless phone into another room.

"It won't make no difference who y'all call," Willis said. "Hot lead's the only thing them cops respect and that's exactly what we ought to go back down there and give 'em tonight. I betcha I could light some of 'em up with my .22."

Emma knew if she sat there another minute, she was going to say something she'd regret. There was no escaping to the sanctuary of her yard, not with so many people in it, sirens blaring, and smoke poisoning the air. That only left her bedroom. She excused herself, saying she needed to be alone for awhile to rest.

After slowly trudging up the stairs, she reached the landing. With relief, she saw she had the upstairs to herself, but straight ahead was the door to Marcus's room. Soon she'd have to summon the strength to open it and go inside. A suit hung in the room's closet. It was a handsome, dark gray one from J.C. Penney for Marcus to wear on dressy occasions. He preferred Oxford shirts and khaki pants to it, but that suit made him look like the doctor or lawyer she always hoped he'd become. She'd bury him in that suit.

She also needed to go through the rest of his clothes to see what might fit other boys in the family and what would be left to donate to Goodwill. His CD's, video game DVD's, books—she'd need to do the same with them, too. Others would offer to do the task, but she wanted the hands that sorted through his belongings to be hers.

Fresh, warm tears streamed down her cheeks. It wasn't fair. Marcus was supposed to bury her, not the other way around. He was supposed to be over at a friend's house, not lying in a morgue. And although he'd never even so much as jaywalked, the police had branded him a dangerous criminal. It was wrong—all of it.

She started toward her bedroom, however the door

to Marcus's room pulled her back. She remembered the arguments she had with him about the room. No matter how much she pleaded, badgered, and threatened, he wouldn't make up his bed and he left his clothes, shoes, video game DVD's, books, magazines and other stuff strewn across the floor. It drove her crazy. She figured that it must've been part of some sort of teenage rebellion because he used to keep the room fairly neat until he started high school last year. Despite how much his sloppiness had irritated her, she wouldn't care anymore if it took a bulldozer to clear a path through the room if she could only have him back. There was nothing she or anyone else could do to make that happen though. She'd have to learn to accept that.

She put a hand on the doorknob. As much as it would hurt, she wanted to pick up some of his clothes off the floor and hold them while she lay in his rumpled bed, breathing in his scent. She swallowed hard, opened the door, and stepped inside.

She stood there open-mouthed. The room was spotless. The bed was neatly made, the carpet recently vacuumed, the oak chest of drawers gleamed and reflected the sunlight coming through the freshly cleaned window. The smell of glass cleaner, carpet deodorizer, and lemon furniture polish scented the air.

Adding to the room's bizarreness was a white envelope taped to the center of the mirror above the chest of drawers. She recognized Marcus's handwriting on it, but it was not in his usual hasty scribble. In careful print, he had written "Mom."

CHAPTER 4

Jammed into a small conference room with the chief of police and several of the chief's underlings, the police department's head of legal affairs, and three members of the Internal Affairs team, Rusty tried to calm his churning stomach. Despite the sweat that kept dampening his face, his mouth was parched from answering the zillions of questions that the people in the room kept firing at him like rounds from a M-16.

"What did Jennings say when you told him to drop his weapon?" one of the IA guys asked as he leaned so close to Rusty that Rusty had to fight the urge to back away. The guy was only trying to get him to crack, just like the others there who kept asking the same questions over and over again to see if his story changed with any variation of how they phrased the questions.

"Like I told you before, he never said one word to me," Rusty said. Wiping away sweat, he figured that interrogating him in the cramped, overheated room when there were plenty of larger, more comfortable conference spaces in the building was also part of their plan to break him down.

"Not one word during the whole time?" asked another IA team member.

"No, not one," Rusty said over the eruptions in his stomach. It felt like it was on fire.

"What exactly did you say to him when you saw his weapon?" asked Chief McDonald.

Two thousand and one—that had to be the number of times he'd been asked that same question. He was sick to death of it and them. How much longer did they plan to keep this up? Despite his resolve, he didn't know how much more he could take. If his stomach kept up like it was, he was liable to spew vomit all over them. Would serve them right, the damned bastards.

"I told him to drop his weapon and put his hands up. I must've told him to do that at least twice, but he kept aiming at me."

For a moment, the room turned silent. Chief McDonald exchanged a look with the lead IA guy, but Rusty couldn't decode what it meant.

"Any other questions for Officer Carter, gentlemen?" McDonald asked.

"I don't have any," the lead IA guy said before ominously adding, "for now."

No one else did either, to Rusty's relief.

"Remember what I told you about the media," McDonald said to Rusty.

"Right, don't talk to them." Rusty ran a hand through his strawberry blond hair that was sticking up in short, sweat-dampened spikes. "Tell them to contact PIO," he said, referring to the department's Public Information Office.

"Correct," the chief said as if Rusty were a dog who had fetched a ball just right. Not that Rusty cared. He only wanted to get the hell out of there.

Once released from the conference room, he found his friend Scott waiting for him in a hallway. Scott's face clouded with concern as Rusty came closer. "Damn," he said, "you look like shit."

Loosening his collar, Rusty replied, "I feel like it, too."

He bent over the water fountain next to Scott and was thankful for each gulp of the icy cold water that helped quell his stomach. Before straightening, he splashed his face and ran a hand through his hair again. "Oh, man," he muttered, still feeling like crap.

Scott glanced past him toward Rusty's interrogators who lingered near the doorway of the conference room. Though they weren't within earshot, he lowered his voice, "Let's get outta here."

"Best idea I've heard all day."

But it turned out it wasn't. As soon as they stepped out of the building, the screeching of sirens, the distant crackle of gunfire, and the stench of smoke immediately assaulted them. "What's going on?" Rusty asked, blinking against the gray haze of smoke that stung his eyes and throat and turned what had been a bright clear sky into a dark, threatening one.

"A race riot," Scott answered. "It broke out once word spread about Marcus Jennings."

"A race riot?" Rusty said numbly. How could such a thing happen in his home town—his po-dunk, slow-as-molasses hometown where hardly anything interesting ever happened? "That's crazy."

"Totally," Scott agreed. "It's true, though. The governor's called in the National Guard and reporters are pouring in from all over creation."

"Aw, man," Rusty groaned as a wave of nausea suddenly hit him. With a hand clamped over his mouth, he dashed toward a grassy area beyond the paved parking lot and barely made it there before collapsing onto all fours and splattering vomit onto the parched sod. It added to the stench created by smoke from the widespread arson.

Scott knelt beside him and draped an arm over his shoulder. "You're not to blame for any of this."

His words hit Rusty harder than the nausea had. "What would make me think that?"

"Well, uh . . . ." Scott pulled away and shifted his gaze toward the glow from smoldering buildings. "It would be easy to make the mistake of believing that if you hadn't had to shoot Jennings, none of this would be going on." He turned to Rusty and with more sureness in his voice, he added, "The fuse to this bomb was lit months ago when Tyquan Green got killed," referring to another young black man from Waverton who had been killed by a white officer three months earlier. "Thanks to that most fair and accurate of coverage by our local press, all the folks in Waverton heard was that he'd been shot in the back by a white cop. Never mind that Green had fired first and was spun around after he took a bullet to the chest. I guess fine points like that don't rate headlines. So even though he'd taken his ex-girlfriend hostage and was threatening to blow her brains out in front of her kids, the press makes him out to be some kind of goddamned martyr.

"And it got worse every time any of us white guys on the force did anything against any black person around here, no matter how justified it was," Scott continued. "They've been itching for an excuse to do this, and I guess they figure that Marcus Jennings's death is about as good as any."

Rusty blurted out the first thing that came to his mind. "I need a drink." He had no intention of using alcohol as a crutch like his dad did; it was only that he needed something to rinse the disgusting taste of vomit from his mouth.

"Wanna go to the Silver Spur?"

The idea of going to a honky tonk filled with loud-mouthed drunks, dueling TVs, blaring music, and jarring lights made Rusty cringe. "Let's just get some beer and hang out for a while at Medford's Landing."

"Sounds good. Ride with me, though. You're way too shaky to drive."

"I'm okay," Rusty said, though his head spun a little as he got to his feet.

"Like hell you are. You ain't getting behind the wheel of your truck and that's all there is to it."

Something suddenly dawned on Rusty. "Hey, why ain't you on patrol along with everybody else?"

"I promised the chief I'd get you home safely."

"I'm okay, man, really. You don't have to babysit me

while this town is going up in smoke."

"With the National Guard helping to enforce the curfew, the worst is already over with." He gave Rusty's shoulder a quick squeeze. "Trust, me, buddy, this whole thing will be over with before you know it, and everything will be back to normal."

For a moment, Rusty didn't say anything, but then he murmured, "That's the same thing Dad thought after he shot Hugh Jefferson."

"Your situation's totally different from your father's," Scott said, appearing to choose his words carefully. "There are three eyewitnesses from the store backing up everything you said and then some, and all three of them are black. They've already given statements that you had no choice but to shoot Marcus Jennings. Everything's going to be okay."

Raking his fingers through his hair, Rusty said, "I just want this to be over."

"It will be soon."

Scott waited until they were on the far outskirts of town before stopping at a convenience store to buy a six pack. Despite the remoteness of the place, Rusty still felt edgy as he sat in the truck. He kept scanning around, searching for anything out of the ordinary, but nothing was. It was only a small run-down cinder block building plastered with brightly colored ads amidst which someone had spray painted on the wall: "No Drinking! No Loud Talking! No Hanging Around!"

There was only one other vehicle in the parking lot, a Toyota Camry that—like the building it was parked in front of—had seen better days a very long time ago. No doubt it belonged to the clerk inside who was probably from India and whose last name was Patel. Seemed like they had taken over all the convenience stores and cheap motels in the state. Pretty soon they'd be running the whole fucking country.

Scott emerged from the store with a six pack dangling from his hand. He handed one of the cans to Rusty.

"Thanks, man," Rusty said, popping the top.

"No problem."

The beer was deliciously cold as Rusty chugged it down, and it was good to be rid of the taste of vomit. He drained the can with only a few swallows, then popped open another can. Scott glanced at him, but didn't say anything. Carrie Underwood serenaded them with an upbeat tune until they reached Medford's Landing.

The area was even more deserted than the convenience store had been. They had the lightly forested place all to themselves. Scott parked the pickup in a dirt clearing between two live oaks whose thick, twisting branches spanned over the river's edge and skimmed its dark surface. Despite that the only light came from the milky half-moon above, Rusty could make out white caps cresting on the water as it roared past them over granite boulders.

"The river's mighty rough tonight," Scott said, settling on a boulder that was speckled with greenish-gray lichen.

"I've never seen it churned up like this, and I've been coming here since I was knee high to a rooster," Rusty said, gazing at river. "Considering how bad the drought's been, you'd think it would be almost dried up." And yet the river was at full strength and seemed as angry as the blacks who had set fire to the buildings downtown. "Hope nobody's fool enough to try swimming or tubing in it tonight."

"They'd get more than they bargained for."

Rusty peered across the river to its other side where General Sherman's troops had stood about one hundred and fifty years ago before crossing the river and marching into town. They reduced the town's center to ashes before heading further south. Rusty wondered if the descendants of the slaves the Union troops helped free were the same ones who had set fire to the buildings that were smoldering now.

He braced one foot against a piece of granite jutting from the dry ground and felt something small and hard press against his upper right thigh. His cell phone. He'd turned it off right before the meeting with Chief McDonald and the other brass, but then forgot to turn it back on.

With a press of a button, the device lit up and

displayed that he had thirty-six messages. Scrolling down the screen revealed that nearly all of them were from his parents. They had learned what happened and were probably beside themselves by now. "Damn," Rusty muttered.

"What?"

Rusty showed him the phone's screen. "My folks have been trying to get hold of me. I'd better get home before they worry themselves to death."

"You can just call 'em back if you don't feel like leaving."

Rusty considered the option for a moment. "Naw, I don't feel like getting into this with them over the phone. I should talk to them about it face-to-face."

"Okay." Scott picked up a pebble and sent it skipping across the water's surface before standing. "Let's go."

He followed Rusty to the front door which flew open before Rusty could turn the door knob. Rusty's mom yanked him against her bony chest. "Oh, thank God you're finally home! Are you okay? Where you been? Me and your daddy's been calling you almost every five minutes! Why didn't you answer? We've been worried sick!"

"How did you find out what happened?" Rusty asked.

His dad appeared from around the corner. "Jimmy called me," he said, referring to one of his former coworkers who was still on the force and remained a friend. "Some of the other guys I used to work with too."

Doris Carter steered her son to the sofa. "Sit down, honey. You're as white as a sheet."

Rusty slumped onto the faded sofa that his mother had decorated with crocheted doilies. "Jeesh," he sighed with weariness.

"The brass grilled you pretty good, didn't they?" his dad asked, taking a seat in his recliner.

"Like a rack of baby back ribs," Rusty said. "They went on and on. I didn't think they were ever going to stop."

"Assholes," Russell Carter, Sr. grumbled and cracked open a can of Budweiser. Rusty noticed that the waste basket beside the recliner was nearly overflowing with crushed beer cans.

His dad continued. "That's the same way they did me when I shot Hugh Jefferson. What did they tell you would happen after the investigation was over?"

"Not much, not that I can remember anyway."

Scott said, "You'll be back on duty in no time flat. With those three black eyewitnesses backing up everything you said and then some, it'll be an open and shut case. Jennings scared the bejesus out of those poor people waving around that gun that looked as real as real could be. It would've served him right for one of them to have shot him before you got there."

"Yeah, but they didn't," Russ, Sr. said. He leaned toward his son. "You had to do it. You had to do your job just like I did, and you'll have to pay for it just like I did."

Rusty swallowed over the hard lump in his throat.

"No disrespect, Mr. Carter," Scott spoke up, "but Rusty's situation is completely different from the one you were in. Sure, the chief and the rest of that crew worked him over real good today, but that's SOP. It doesn't change the fact that what he told them exactly matched what those three witnesses inside that store said and even put in writing. I'm not saying that it probably won't be rough until IA and SBLE finish their investigations," referring to the department's Internal Affairs unit and the State Bureau of Law Enforcement, "but it usually doesn't take them more than a few weeks to wrap up these kinds of investigations. They'll formally clear Rusty, he'll return to duty, and things will get back to normal."

A few weeks? Rusty thought. It almost sounded like a lifetime, especially since Scott admitted the possibility of it dragging on longer. What was he supposed to do in the meanwhile?

"Oh, Lord," his mother moaned, burying her face in her hands. "I can't believe this is happening to us again. Any minute now reporters are going to start harassing us, we'll get threatening calls, and people will look at us like we've got horns. I can't go through this again. My nerves been bad enough as it is."

"Everything's going to be okay, Mrs. Carter," Scott said.

"I don't mean no harm, but that's easy for you to say, darlin'." She wiped her eyes with trembling hands. "You're not the one that's got to go through it."

"No, ma'am, you're right, and this guy," he patted Rusty on the shoulder, "is going to get the worst of it before it all blows over. He's going to need all of our support."

"That's for sure," Doris said and clasped Rusty's hand.

"You okay, man?" Scott asked Rusty. "Want to head back to Medford's Landing. Ain't no law that says we can't fish at night and it might help get your mind off this crap for a while."

"Maybe tomorrow, I'm pretty beat now."

"And I'll bet you haven't had a thing to eat since breakfast," his mother said.

"I didn't even have that," Rusty said, realizing the only thing he'd eaten all day was a pack of peanuts he'd gotten from a vending machine before starting his shift.

"C'mon in the kitchen and let me heat you up some spaghetti," Doris said.

It sounded tempting, but only a little. "I'm not all that hungry," he told her.

"You've got to keep your strength up, honey."

He sighed. "All right."

"Take it easy, man," Scott said, heading for the door. "I'll talk to you tomorrow."

"Okay," Rusty said. "And thanks for everything."

"No problem."

After Scott left, Rusty followed his mother into the kitchen and sat at the same Formica dinette table that they'd had his entire life. Along with the rest of the furniture, it added to the sense that the house was still trapped in the 1970's.

Though he saw his mom place his dinner in the microwave, the sound of beeping when the microwave's timer went off still startled him. Good thing his mother had her back to him so she couldn't notice.

She slid the steaming plate of spaghetti in front of him. "Here you go."

He stared at it.

"What's the matter, honey?"

He stared harder. Was his mind playing tricks on him or were strands of the spaghetti slithering?

"Honey, are you okay?" his mother asked.

With his heart thudding so loud that he was afraid she'd hear it, he looked up at her. Her face seemed strangely elastic, as if it could be stretched like a wad of silly putty.

He put a hand to his throat. He couldn't breathe.

"Rusty! What's wrong?"

"I don't know," he gasped and bolted out the back door.

He was no more aware of her calling after him than he was of the boxwoods at the edge of their yard tearing at his clothes and scraping his skin when he dashed through them. Neighbors' homes and yards formed a hazy blur while he ran down the street and then onto another and another. The asphalt beneath his feet gave way to a dirt road, then to a narrow trail through the woods.

He emerged on the other side of the woods into an open field. Panting, he bent over with his hands braced against his thighs. His lungs filled with the humid evening air that was still acrid with smoke.

When he was finally able to take in deep, even breaths, he straightened and wiped away the sweat streaming down his face and neck. He glanced around. Where the hell am I? He figured he had to be somewhere close to his neighborhood but exactly where, he couldn't tell. The dense trees ringing the field of tall grass blocked the view of any familiar landmarks and the night's darkness made his surroundings all the more unrecognizable. The direction he came from through the woods was just as much a mystery. He hadn't paid attention to where he was going and now one spot in the woods looked the same as any other.

He put his hands on his hips. Somehow he had to figure out how to get through the ordeal of Marcus Jennings's death without losing his mind, but first, he had to find his way back home.

CHAPTER 5

Dear Mom,

By the time you read this letter, I will be gone. Please do not cry for me. There is no need for tears. I am in a better place. No more suffering. Remember that.

I know it may be hard to understand what I have done, but believe me, this is for the best. Say goodbye to everyone for me and if I have done anything to hurt anybody, I am sorry.

I love you,

Marcus

Emma read the letter again as she sat on the edge of Marcus's bed. She touched her cheek where he kissed her earlier that day, remembering his surprising words of love and the sorrow in his eyes. He'd been saying goodbye—for the last time. She should've known that. She should've realized the changes she'd seen in him over the past months hadn't been just some passing teenage phase but clear warnings that he was drowning in pain. If there was anyone who should've been his lifeline, it was her. She was the one he'd been closest to. Yes, Otis loved him, but it was clear as day that Marcus never had that rough and tumble quality Otis enjoyed in Otis Lee and Ed. And with Marcus having been so much younger than his brothers and sisters, he hadn't had that much in common with them, and their adult lives and responsibilities allowed little room for him anyway. He had no friends. That left her. Only her.

Yet what had she done when he needed her most? Fussed at him about stupid, meaningless things like book reports turned in late and towels left on the bathroom floor. It was a policeman's gun that killed him, but it might as well have been her finger on the trigger.

She was still sitting motionless on the bed when Otis appeared in the doorway. He looked years older than he had that morning. She didn't know how to tell him about the letter she held. It was the only thing she could think of that would make Marcus's death even more unbearable for him.

"So this is where you've been for the past two hours," he said to her. "You should've been resting instead of in here cleaning."

"No, Marcus left it this way."

Otis leaned against the door frame. Climbing the stairs seemed to have taken the last of his strength. He let out a weary sigh. "Of all the days for him to finally clean up this room after we'd been on him for months."

It took Emma a moment to respond. She said softly, "It's no coincidence, honey."

"What are you talking about?"

She looked down at the letter. He had a right to know about it, no matter how much it hurt. "Come in and close the door," she said to him. "I have to show you something."

Hanging back, he gestured to the folded letter. "Is that more bad news?"

"I'm afraid so," she said, her eyes burning again with tears. She felt like she was killing him just as she had Marcus.

"I've had about all the bad news I can take for one day."

"I know," she said, crying. "And it's all my fault."

He rushed to her and pulled her close. "What in the world are you talking about? You ain't to blame for none of this."

"Yes, I am. If only I'd—"

"Baby, stop it," he said, cutting her off. "Keep at it and you'll 'if only' your way right into a straightjacket. All of us could look back from now until Kingdom come wondering what we could've done to change things, but all the wishing in the world ain't going to change the fact that the police killed our boy."

"No, they didn't."

His face clouded with worry. "Good Lord, you've done hurt your head worse than I thought." Getting to his feet, he gestured for her to do the same. "C'mon. We're going to the hospital, and this time I ain't putting up with none of your fussing about it."

She pulled him back to where he'd been sitting. "I didn't mean that the police didn't shoot Marcus, what I meant was—" The next words caught in her throat. Speaking them would make their son's suicide a reality, one that she didn't feel any more prepared to deal with than she knew Otis would be. Yet having opened the door to the truth, she didn't know how to close it.

"What? What are you saying?"

With the letter trembling in her hand, she held it out to him. "This will explain everything. Marcus left it on the dresser mirror."

Otis took it slowly. As he read it aloud, each of Marcus's words hit Emma like body blows. His moodiness, all the problems he had in school, his wanting to stay shut up in his room for days on end—he'd been dying right in front of her. How could she have been so blind?

Otis frowned. "This letter don't explain nothing except that Marcus had run off, but hell, kids do that all the time. Get mad at their parents for one thing or the other and run off, but then they miss one meal and decide home ain't so bad after all. He'd have been back here before sundown if it hadn't been for that cop killing him."

Emma didn't know what to say. Otis held the truth in front of him, yet he refused to see it. But was it her place to make him?

Obviously sensing her hesitation, he said, "Speak your mind."

She couldn't remember the last time he used such a sharp tone of voice with her.

"You don't think Marcus had run off?" he asked.

"No," she whispered.

"Then what do you think this is all about?" He held up the letter.

Drawing in a deep breath, she said, "Do you really want to know? Because if you do, I'll tell you."

"Quit talking in circles. I asked you a question. I want an answer, and I want it now—what do you think Marcus's saying in this letter?"

"That he committed suicide, that he made that policeman shoot him." The words had tumbled out before she could stop them, and they kept tumbling. "I should've realized how bad off he was. It was as plain as day. If only I'd paid more attention and gotten him some help. Now it's too late. Oh, God, my baby!" Her guilt was so searing that it took her a moment to notice Otis staring at her like she'd announced that she was the real queen of England.

"Now you talking crazy," he said. He read the letter aloud again. "There ain't one word in this about Marcus wanting to kill himself. He says he's going to a better place. He could've meant catching the Greyhound to the beach for all we know."

"But how he's been acting lately, this room—"

Otis took her by the shoulders. In a gentler tone, he said, "Listen to me, Emma, I know this day has come straight from hell, but you got to get hold of yourself. Marcus didn't commit no suicide. The police killed him because he was a black kid, and that's all the reason they think they need." He tightened his grip on her. "You're not the only one suffering, sugar. We all are—me, the kids, everybody. The last thing we need is for you to help the police drag Marcus's name through the mud."

Tears sprung to her eyes. She wanted to defend herself—to say that she wasn't siding with the police, but with the truth. All she could do, though, was weep.

"Give me your word that you ain't going to bring up this foolishness with nobody else," Otis said.

Knowing what she said was true couldn't blind her to what she saw at the heart of that truth—that whenever Marcus had been troubled, she was the one he turned to, yet when he'd needed her most, she only added to his pain. She'd been too busy with her own life to save his. Only his memory was left. She couldn't destroy that, too.

"Give me your word," Otis repeated.

"I. . ." She swallowed hard. "I promise."

She let him hold her close and murmur that everything would be okay, but after a few moments she was desperate to escape his embrace, the room, and all the memories it held. Pulling away from him, she said, "I need to go outside, to get some fresh air."

"Ain't too much of that. They got them fires out, but it's still so smoky that you're liable to catch a coughing fit."

"I won't stay long."

She went downstairs and quickly slipped out the back door with the hope of no one seeing her. As Otis warned, the humid, early evening air was pungent with smoke. The smoky haze and waning sunlight added a dreamy quality to the deserted backyard, making her lantana, hollyhocks, roses, butterfly bushes, and dogwood and crape myrtle trees appear like softer versions of themselves.

While making her way to the weather-beaten picnic table that doubled as her potting bench, she paused at one of the rose bushes and studied its blossoms that were a delicate pink at their centers, but then turned a deep shade of coral at their outer petals. Even the smoke couldn't mask their fragrance. They were among her favorite roses. She remembered when she'd planted them—Marcus had just made the honor roll for the first time in the sixth grade.

Lowering her head, she breathed in more of the roses' scent. There he was—her boy—flying into the kitchen with a grin as big as Texas to show her his honor roll certificate.

Dark, rigid thorns jutted out from the blossom's long stem. At first touch, she couldn't feel their sharpness through her callused skin. She pressed harder on one of them until her body jolted with pain and a stream of bright red blood trickled down her hand.

She snatched back her hand and wiped it on her shorts, smearing them. *What's wrong with me?* she thought as she sat at the picnic table, massaged her thumb, and stared out into the hazy nightfall.

In the moments between the backdoor opening and closing, light from the kitchen outlined a small figure in the doorway. Even without being able to see the person through the dimness, Emma could tell by the rhythmic tap-tap-tapping of metal upon ground who it was.

"How you doing, sugar?" Dottie asked, nearing her.

Emma glanced down at her thumb. The blood was gone, but the pain wasn't. "Not too good."

Dottie sat beside her and put an arm around her. "It's going to take time. Ain't nothing worse than losing a child."

Yes, there is, Emma wanted to say. *There is when you know it's your fault he's dead.* She rested her head on Dottie's shoulder. She'd never kept anything from her before. Dottie was the only person on earth who knew what her mother's step-father had done to her when she was seven years old and how thoughts of that used to come back to her when Otis climbed into bed beside her.

Considering how she and Dottie had laid their souls bare to each other throughout the years, not telling her the truth of Marcus's death felt the same as telling her a horrible lie. "I'm sorry," she murmured.

"For what?"

Instead of answering, Emma pulled back and straightened. "Have you ever done something so awful that there was no forgiving it?"

"What you getting at?" Dottie asked, studying her closely.

"Nothing," Emma said and looked away. Dottie could see the lie on her face, she was certain of it. "Don't pay me no mind. I ain't myself tonight. I'm not making a bit of sense."

"You can tell me anything. You know that, don't you?"

"Of course," Emma said, however she still couldn't look Dottie in the eye. She focused her gaze into the distance. Darkness had overtaken all but a thin edge of the horizon. Only a few moments were needed for darkness's conquering of the horizon to be complete.

"We probably ought to go back inside before the mosquitoes haul us off," she said to Dottie. "Better yet, let me walk you home. It's getting late, and you've done too much already. I won't have you wearing yourself out on my account."

"I'm tougher than you think. So are you. You going to get through this, girl. I promise."

Emma took one of her friend's hands into both of hers. "I love you, Dottie, more than a sister, but you shouldn't make promises you can't keep."

"I don't," Dottie said, giving Emma's hands a firm squeeze.

Emma helped her up from the picnic table and while they walked to Dottie's house, fireflies circled them in crazy patterns, punctuating the darkness with tiny flashes of light. The fireflies sparked more memories of Marcus. When he was a little boy, he thought they were magical. She could still hear his squeals as he dashed this way and that through the yard trying to catch them in her Mason jars.

"You want some of my nerve pills?"

"Huh?" Emma said, shaken from her memories. She realized she and Dottie had arrived at the foot of Dottie's porch steps.

"Them nerve pills the doctor gave me when he operated on my heart," Dottie explained. "I've almost got a whole bottle of them left. You're welcome to them. They'll help you rest."

"No, but thanks anyway."

"If you change your mind, holler," Dottie said. Grasping the railing with one hand and leaning on her cane with the other, she groaned a little when she climbed the sloping porch steps that creaked beneath her weight. She turned again to Emma. "And if you need me tonight, call me. I don't care if it's at three in the morning. If we can't think of nothing else to do, we can sit up and watch them dirty movies on HBO. See, I got a smile out of you. It ain't much of one, but it still is one."

"It is," Emma admitted, continuing to smile weakly.

"Ah, girl, I know it's hard. Remember, I buried my momma and daddy, my brothers, and all but one of my sisters. All that wasn't nothing, though, compared to losing Stony," Dottie said of her husband who died ten years ago. "That laid me low. You know how bad I got. It was all I could do to keep putting one foot in front of the other. Didn't think I'd ever be happy about nothing ever again. And what's worse, I hated seeing other people happy. Watching them carry on like they didn't have a care in the world worked on my nerves something fierce.

"But little by little, things got better. Before I knew it, I had something to smile about again, something to laugh about, and before long, I was back to myself. When you get to be as old as I am, you see that no matter how bad things get, it can all work out in the end."

Emma nodded but didn't say anything. She knew there was truth to what Dottie said, for she'd seen a number of people who endured terrible tragedies and yet came out the better for it. They were fortunate that way, the same way that others seemed to have been born under lucky stars like one of her co-workers who won six thousand dollars playing bingo and then won a Jeep Grand Cherokee a few years later in a radio station promotion contest. That hadn't changed the fact, however, that Emma had never won anything in her life worth keeping.

"You got to keep in mind, too," Dottie went on, "that this ain't the end. You'll see Marcus again. You'll meet him on the streets of Glory. I can see him up there right now." Indeed, she beamed as if she could. "He's there with all the saints, and they at the right hand of Jesus having a good ol' time. Praise the Lord!"

"Yes," Emma said, but instead of Dottie's words comforting her, they filled her with worry. Where was

Marcus's soul? Lots of people said committing suicide was an unforgivable sin. Had her boy doomed his soul to hell for all eternity? The very thought of it was enough to force her to grab the porch railing to steady herself.

"What's wrong?"

"I, uh. . . ." Emma struggled to come up with a believable explanation for her near collapse. "It's . . . it's that there's so much to do. I don't know where to begin. We haven't even started making arrangements for Marcus's . . ." her voice trailed off. Funeral. It was odd how a little word could suddenly become so hard to say.

"You won't be going through none of this alone. You'll have plenty of folk, including this ol' bag of bones, to help you. We'll get everything done when it needs to be done. Don't you trouble yourself about that."

"I appreciate everything you're doing for me."

"You'd do the same for me."

"I would," Emma agreed. She sighed again. "Well, I guess we'd both better turn in. Tomorrow's going to be one hard, long day."

Thoughts of Marcus slowed her steps back to her house. When she reached a magnolia tree in her front yard, she stopped beneath it and looked beyond its massive boughs into the night sky. *Lord,* she prayed silently, *please have mercy on my baby. He was sick. He didn't know what he was doing. If you want to put the blame on anybody, put it on me. I'm the one who deserves it. I'll take it all.*

Fresh tears spilled down her cheeks. She could only hope her prayer would be answered.

She went inside and was relieved to find no visitors in the front of the house. Only the voices of her husband and children came from the den and kitchen.

Her grandchildren had taken temporary refuge from the day's tragedy by clustering together in the living room and playing video games. While watching them erupt into excited shouts whenever one of them scored, Emma could imagine that it was an ordinary day and Marcus was upstairs reading. What she realized Otis and the children were talking about in the den, however, was more unmistakable proof that her life had become a nightmare.

She rushed into where they were. "What's this about somebody calling Creighton Jones?"

"I just left a message for him," Stephanie announced with pride.

Stunned, Emma sank to the couch and tried to make sense of that. She'd watched Rev. Creighton Jones dozens of times on the national news, had walked by book racks in Walmart that featured his bestseller about why African-Americans should receive reparations, and had seen him on the cover of the latest *Time* magazine. The accompanying article proclaimed him the new voice of "Black America," although some who he supposedly spoke for despised him and accused him of having stopped at nothing to steal the spotlight from Jesse Jackson, Al Sharpton, and other well-known black activists.

Emma wasn't certain if the accusation was true, but that didn't stop her from disliking the man. It wasn't so much the aggressive way he demanded economic, social, and political justice for blacks, it was how he made it seem like the only way for them to get it was to make whites feel guilty enough to give it to them. "Playing the victim card"—that was how she heard one of his critics put it. Marcus hadn't been a victim of racial injustice, and they didn't need Rev. Creighton Jones around trying to make him into one. But with Otis eyeing her carefully and Stephanie and her brothers and sister obviously expecting her to be pleased by the news, Emma couldn't think of a single thing to say except, "How in the world did you manage that? None of us has connections with anyone who knows him, and it's not like you can look up famous people like him in the phone book."

"I called the reference desk at the library, and they found the phone number to his office in Los Angeles," Stephanie explained. "I got through to his assistant's voice mail."

That blunted the edges of Emma's worry. Stephanie's message would probably have to clear several high hurdles before reaching a man as busy as Creighton Jones. Lord willing, it would get buried beneath all the other demands for his attention, especially since he was expanding his focus to include the problems not only of blacks in America, but those around the world. From what she saw on the news the other night, he was in Africa holding a series of marches to shame American drug manufacturers into donating medicine to help African countries fight the AIDS epidemic. No doubt he already had a place picked out in his home to showcase his future Nobel Peace Prize.

"That's kind of like leaving a message for Oprah though," Emma said of Stephanie's favorite celebrity. "Don't be surprised if you never hear back from him."

"Yeah, well even if I don't, there's plenty of other people who are interested in what happened to Marcus," Stephanie said. "I've talked to folks at CNN, MSNBC, CBS, ABC—you name them; I called them. They asked me all kinds of questions. One of them even gave me his fax number and told me to fax him a signed statement of everything I told him."

The edges of Emma's worry sharpened again. "I can't handle any more reporters," she said. "Those people from Channel 4 News were bad enough with how they barged in here and shoved microphones into our faces before we'd even had time to pull ourselves together. They're nothing but maggots who feed off of other people's misery. The only thing they care about is ratings."

"They can help us make someone pay for killing Marcus," Otis said. "That's all that matters."

"You're right, Daddy," Brenda said. "If there's one thing that'll get the police shaking in their boots it's having reporters from New York swarming all over them. They won't try running them out of the building like they did us."

"Yeah," Ed said, "I'll bet you those reporters will get some answers out of the police for sure."

Emma crossed her arms tightly against her chest,

unsure of what else she could say that wouldn't draw questions from her children about why she was so set against what they wanted to do. Their plan was like a train gaining speed and she didn't know how to stop it or explain to them why she wanted to. If she had time to regain her footing without getting rocked by something else, perhaps she could come up with a way to convince them that the last thing they wanted to do was to bring Marcus's death to national attention. The only way she could think of to do that, however, was to reveal the truth of what he'd done.

She remained silent as they went on and on about who else should be called. A dull ache began near the base of her neck, signaling that the painkillers Brenda gave her were wearing off. She tried to massage the pain away but listening to her husband and children only intensified it. Had it been less than eight hours ago that it seemed the worst of what was beyond her control was the iron weed that kept popping up between her rose beds and azaleas?

The doorbell rang and she heard one of her grandchildren answer it. She groaned. The night would never end. Friends and neighbors would find no time too late or inconvenient to keep a steady supply of finger sandwiches, fried chicken, fixings, desserts, and jugs of sweet tea coming. They'd expect their efforts to console to be met with endless thanks and offers to sit and visit a while and still a while longer. She considered asking Brenda for more pain pills.

Her grandson burst into the room. "Grandma, there're two detectives at the door. They said they need to talk to you and Granddaddy."

Emma shared surprised looks with Otis. What in the world could the police want this late in the evening? She wondered if it had anything to do with the fighting that broke out at police headquarters. That captain had said they were free to leave, hadn't he? Had he changed his mind?

"Did they say what it's about?" she asked her grandson.

"No, ma'am."

"They got a lot of nerve showing up here," Otis grumbled and headed for the front door.

Emma followed him.

Two men stood waiting for them outside on the porch. One was tall and black. Emma guessed he was in his late forties or early fifties. Despite the heat lingering in the summer night, he wore a smartly tailored dark suit with his police badge prominently displayed on a breast pocket. The other man was white. He was about a half-foot shorter than his partner and he was younger, stockier, and wore his badge clipped to a pair of rumpled khakis.

The black man spoke first. "I'm Detective Larry Entzminger with the State Bureau of Law Enforcement." He pointed to the man beside him. "And this is Andy Jamison who's also with SBLE. We're sorry to bother you this late in the evening, especially after what you've been through today, but it's urgent that we speak with you."

"About what?" Otis demanded to know. "What's so urgent that it can't wait till we've at least had time to bury our son?"

"Because it's about your son," Det. Entzminger said. "May we come in?"

The throbbing at the back of Emma's head grew more intense. Nothing good could come of a visit with these two men. They'd probably come to bring more troubling news about Marcus. "It's really not a good time," she said to them. "Are you sure it can't wait at least until tomorrow morning?"

"I'm sorry, ma'am, but it can't," Det. Entzminger said, taking a step closer as if in preparation to keep the door from being closed in his face.

Emma drew in a deep breath. There was nothing to do but brace for more pain. "All right then." She heard the defeat in her voice.

Otis glared at the men when they stepped inside the small foyer. She touched his arm, hoping that he read the message in her touch—*Let them say whatever they've come to say so they can leave us be.*

"Do you need to talk with us alone?" she asked the detectives.

The young white man took this as his cue to speak.

"If your other children and any other significant family members who were close to Marcus are here, we'd like to talk to y'all together."

"The children are down the hall in the den," Emma told him. "Our grandkids are around here somewhere, but I don't think they'd be of much help."

"Well, if you wouldn't mind leading us to the den, we'd appreciate it," Det. Jamison said.

She nodded and they followed her and Otis down the hallway.

Upon their arrival to the den, Otis motioned in the direction of the officers and said to his children, "These guys are with SBLE. They said they need to talk to us about Marcus."

Emma was embarrassed that her children greeted the men with the same cold stares their father had. She wished she could tell her kids that it wasn't the SBLE agents who deserved their anger. They were simply doing their job. Had it not been for her, they'd have no reason to be there in the first place. She could only offer the detectives refreshments and seats on uncomfortable, mismatched metal folding chairs someone hauled over earlier that afternoon from Waverton Baptist as a way of apologizing to the detectives.

Both of them declined refreshments but accepted the invitation to sit. While sitting, Det. Entzminger unbuttoned his jacket and smoothed his silky tie. He said to them, "Det. Jamison and I appreciate your willingness to meet with us given the tragedy you've experienced today." He spoke like he was unaware, or simply didn't care, about the hostility in the room that was as solid as the metal chair beneath him. "I should start by explaining that whenever a law enforcement officer in this state injures or kills anyone in the line of duty, it's the State Bureau of Law Enforcement's responsibility to do an investigation to help a grand jury determine whether there was just cause. Our purpose isn't to defend the officer or whoever the officer injured or killed—our purpose is to find out exactly what happened and why."

Emma felt something like an electrical shock strike her. *Lord, no.*

"I can save y'all the trouble," Otis said. "What happened is that the police shot down my son, and why it happened is that they think they can kill black fellas around here for any reason or none at all. They ain't never been all that good, but they've really been off the chain ever since spring. They started with the guy who lived a few streets over and got to fussing and fighting with his ex-girlfriend and then took her hostage. He had a gun. True. But how does that explain the police shooting him in the back?"

Without waiting for the detectives to answer, he went on. "Then there was that fella who the police said shot at them when they came to arrest him for not paying parking tickets. I don't believe for a skinny minute that anybody would risk the electric chair over a few measly parking tickets. And what they did to Maceo Wilson was a God-awful shame. I don't care if he did go crazy and take a swing at his nephew with a piece of pipe, if a dozen cops can't get a doggone short pipe away from one man without blowing him to bits in front of his family, they got no business being cops."

"Don't forget about LaQuise Rogers, Daddy," Stephanie prompted. "Remember, he was the one who died in a wreck on Hwy. 331. You might as well say they killed him, too, because if they hadn't been chasing him, he wouldn't have lost control of that car."

"Now tell me how that was necessary," Otis challenged the detectives. "It wasn't like he'd murdered anybody. All he did was steal a car, and the cops admitted they knew who he was and where he lived when they took off after him. They could've arrested him later at his house instead of chasing him down a busy highway at over a hundred miles an hour. The cops around here ain't nothing but thugs in uniforms."

If she hadn't found Marcus's note and spotless room, Emma suspected she would've said the same. Only a fool would believe the justifications the police offered after each of the deaths, she would've declared, especially the one about Tyquan Green getting shot in the back after supposedly getting killed and spun halfway around by a bullet to the chest. And only a fool would believe that her baby tried to hold up a store and threaten a cop.

Det. Entzminger said, "We're here this evening to discuss Marcus, not unrelated cases."

"SBLE investigated them, too, though didn't they?" Ed asked.

"Yes, but—" Det. Entzminger said.

Cutting him off, Ed said, "All those black guys killed and not one cop served a day behind bars for it."

Det. Jamison spoke up. "Whether or not an officer is prosecuted is out of our hands. That's the grand jury's call."

While Brenda muttered something under her breath about cover-ups, Emma shifted nervously on the couch. She felt awful for the two detectives. They faced an impossible task in trying to convince her family that their agency didn't automatically side with the police. No matter what they said, she knew there was no getting around the fact that none of the white police officers on the city's police force had ever been punished for killing a black person in the line of duty, or at least none that she could remember. Even when that cop shot a black house painter to death about eight years ago, he'd been allowed to finish out his career despite his story about the shooting being shakier than a one-legged stool. He claimed to have caught the painter trying to rape the wife of state Senator Wilson McKenna in a car out on an abandoned logging road. The black man had supposedly drawn a gun on the cop, but everyone in Waverton knew the real story was one which had been repeated too many times throughout generations in the Deep South: A white woman hollers "rape" after being discovered in a sexual dalliance with a black man, and he's killed by a white man who believes it is his duty to defend the woman's honor and protect the purity of the white race. Only the differences in names, locations, and dates added any variations to the story.

And what happened after one of the city's white cops killed a black suspect was as predictable. There wouldn't be enough evidence to convict the officer of anything, yet there also wouldn't be enough to convince blacks that another of their own hadn't been unjustly killed. Emma supposed she should wish the same end for the investigation into Marcus's death. Both sides could claim victory. The cop who shot Marcus could continue on with his career and life and her family's memory of Marcus would remain untarnished. She and her secret would remain trapped between them.

"I understand your concerns," Det. Entzminger said. "I'd probably feel the same if I were in your place. I can assure you, however, that this investigation will be comprehensive, accurate, and totally unbiased. We want the same thing you do—to learn the truth."

Lord, no, Emma thought again.

"I'm glad to hear that," Stephanie told him, "and I'm sure the reporters I called in New York with all the major television networks will be as well. They're very interested in what happened to my brother. One of them even gave me his fax number and asked me to send him more details. I also spoke with an assistant to Rev. Creighton Jones today, so I wouldn't be surprised if he'll want to follow this closely, too."

If any of that intimidated Det. Entzminger, he hid it well, although Emma noticed the same couldn't be said for Det. Jamison. He reminded her of how that poor receptionist at police headquarters looked when the lobby filled with demonstrators.

Det. Entzminger said, "Part of our work on this case will involve examining the scene of the shooting, interviewing eye witnesses, analyzing ballistic evidence, and going over reports from the medical examiner's office, but that can only tell us so much. To do a good, thorough investigation, we need to know as much about Marcus as possible. We need to know who he was, what he was like, how he behaved. That kind of information has to come from people who knew him well, people like you."

Emma clasped her hands together tightly. She didn't know if she could lie—or at least not be completely honest—without stumbling somehow. Maybe if she let

Otis and the children do the talking, the detectives would ignore her.

"What about the cop who killed Marcus?" Otis asked.

"Believe me, sir," Det. Jamison said, "we'll be going over details of his life with a fine tooth comb, but like Det. Entzminger said, since Marcus's not here to speak for himself, we need y'all to help fill us in about him."

Det. Entzminger took a small memo pad and pen from an inside pocket of his jacket. "Let's start out with some general things. What grade was he in?"

An uncomfortable silence filled the room. Emma realized her family was waiting for her to answer. Why had she thought one of them could? She was the one who'd been involved with Marcus's schooling, not any of them. The only reason they even knew which school he went to was because they'd attended Waverton High too. "Ninth," she answered softly. "He was to start the tenth in a few weeks."

Det. Entzminger jotted in his note pad and then asked, "How were his grades?"

"Average," she said. That wasn't far from the truth, she told herself. Most of the boys in his school had failing grades, too. Waverton High had a far better reputation for its basketball team and marching band than for its students' test scores. They usually ranked among the lowest in the state no matter what school administrators tried.

"No, baby," Otis said with obvious concern. "Marcus was an honor roll student. Remember?"

"That was when he was in middle school," she said.

"So his grades had gone down?" Det. Jamison asked.

"Well, uh..." Emma looked from one family member to the next, wishing they could rescue her, but of course, they couldn't. "Most kids' grades drop some when they start high school. I mean, the tests get harder and they have to write bunches and bunches of term papers, book reports, and stuff." And though worried that she had begun to babble, she couldn't help but add, "There's all those projects they have to do, too, like science projects. I couldn't help him with a bit of it either. I never was any good with anything having to do with science or math."

"Did he like going to school?" Det. Entzminger asked.

She tried to muster a laugh, but it came out more like a weird croak. "About as much as any kid does."

For whatever reason, that earned a jot in the detective's notepad. Emma wished she could see what he was writing. Was it just shorthanded recordings of her answers or was he writing things like, "Mom holding back info – what and why???" She also didn't know whether to be concerned or relieved that Det. Jamison wasn't taking notes.

"Had he ever been suspended or anything like that?"

"No," Emma said. That was true as well. The punishment for refusing to do schoolwork was limited to receiving failing grades and threats of being held back.

"Marcus was a good boy," Otis volunteered. "He never gave us a moment's trouble."

He could say that without a hint of dishonesty, Emma thought angrily. He wasn't the one who had met endlessly with Marcus's teachers. He wasn't the one who had talked himself dry-mouthed trying to get Marcus to pay attention in class, to study, to do his homework and turn it in, to bathe and do something with his hair so he didn't look like he lived under a bridge. He wasn't the one who had done any of that. What did he know about their son?

But if he wasn't as involved with Marcus as much as he should've been, she was partly at fault. From early on in their marriage, she and Otis staked out their territories – he was the main breadwinner, she tended to the kids. Although there was some overlap, they generally had given each other wide leeway in what they felt they were best at. She enjoyed raising the kids without a lot of interference and second-guessing, and she'd taken guilty pleasure in knowing that when they needed someone to confide in, seek advice from, or share exciting news with, they came to her first. It was only when there was heartache to shoulder that she wished Otis was more involved with them, and she realized how unfair that was.

She looked over at him. He was a good man. He'd been the best father he knew how to be and that she'd allowed him to be.

"Did Marcus participate in any extracurricular activities at school like any clubs or sports teams?" Det. Entzminger asked.

"No," Emma answered.

"How about a part-time job? Did he work anywhere?"

"No," she said.

"Did he have a girlfriend?"

"No." Something made her add, "Um. . .he hadn't started dating yet."

Det. Entzminger flipped to another page. "Who did he hang out with?"

"He stayed to himself," she said quietly. "He was like me—real shy."

"Hmmm. . ." Det. Entzminger said.

What? Emma wanted to yell at him. What does that mean?

"He just went to school, came home, and read or did his homework," Otis said. "He was so quiet you wouldn't hardly know he was in the house. Any father would give his eye teeth for a boy like him."

"And he was the best brother anyone could ask for," Stephanie said with a voice heavy with sorrow.

"But being a parent myself," Det. Jamison said, "I know there's no such thing as a perfect child. What were the things y'all butted heads with him about?"

Otis shrugged. "Nothing much except cleaning his bedroom. We had to stay on him all the time about that."

Emma thought about how it looked now. What had been going through Marcus's mind while he put fresh linen on his bed, picked up his dirty clothes, neatly stacked his books and magazines, vacuumed the carpet, straightened his closet, and polished his chest of drawers and mirror until they gleamed? He probably thought that they'd be better off without him. She remembered the words from his note—*I know it may be hard to understand what I have done, but believe me, this is for the best.* Her poor child.

"How was his health?" Det. Entzminger asked.

"Fine," Otis said, obviously surprised by the question. It seemed to have come from out of the blue to Emma as well. She wondered what had prompted the detective to ask it.

"Did he have a regular doctor?"

She nodded. "Dr. Jim McLaurin with Midtown Pediatrics."

Probing deeper, Det. Entzminger said, "Did Marcus have any health problems at all?"

"Nothing other than a cold every now and again," she said.

"Did he take any kind of medicine, either prescribed or over the counter?"

"No," she said. Where was he going with this?

"How about alcohol or street drugs?" Det. Entzminger asked. "Had he experimented with any of that?"

"No," Emma said and "no's" from Otis and several of their children echoed hers.

"He knew better than to mess with that crap," Otis said.

"He was L-7," Ed added, "a total square. He didn't even smoke cigarettes."

Det. Entzminger jotted in his notepad and zeroed in on Emma once more. "Had there been any changes in his mood or state of mind?"

She had to force herself to take a slow, measured breath. She knew what she had to do. She had to do it for Otis, for her children gathered around her, for Marcus. Especially for Marcus. She had failed him before, she wouldn't again. *Lord forgive me.* "No," she answered.

"Had he seemed depressed or troubled about anything lately?" Det. Entzminger asked. He studied her as if she were something to be deciphered.

"No," she said. She felt sweat trickle down her back. Calm, stay calm.

Finally releasing her from his nerve-wracking gaze, Det. Entzminger directed it to the others in the room. "Had Marcus seemed depressed or troubled recently to any of you?"

"He wasn't crazy, if that's what you're getting at," Otis said sharply. Too sharply, Emma thought. The detective had hit a nerve, and he knew it. She could tell by the deepening intensity on his face.

"It's not unusual for kids Marcus's age to get depressed, Mr. Jennings," Det. Jamison said. "That doesn't mean that they're. . ." he paused to make invisible quotation marks in the air with his fingers, "'crazy'. It just means that they've got a medical condition, like how other kids have asthma or juvenile diabetes."

"Wasn't nothing wrong with Marcus," Otis said, although he kept his tone even. Emma suspected he also realized how his reaction to the last question was a mistake.

Scanning over Brenda, Otis Lee, Ed, and Stephanie, Det. Entzminger made another attempt at drawing information from them. "Had any of you noticed any changes recently in your brother?"

"He seemed the same to me as he'd always been," Stephanie said.

Was she purposely lying about Marcus? Emma doubted it. The odds were that Stephanie simply hadn't been aware of how troubled her brother was, and Emma was certain the same could be said for the rest of her children. And why should they have been aware when she and Otis hadn't despite having lived under the same roof as Marcus?

"He kept his nose stuck in a book," Otis Lee said. "I remember one time I came over here and found him reading one of the encyclopedias Momma bought at a yard sale when I was a kid. Those books were older than dirt and about as dusty, but he was reading them from cover to cover like they were the latest hip-hop magazines. He was—" Otis Lee's voice cracked. He lowered his head for a moment and when he raised it, tears glistened in his eyes and threatened to overflow and spill down his cheeks. "He was so smart."

"Oh, Lord," Brenda moaned and sagged against her father who put an arm around her.

Emma felt the familiar sting of tears. She wondered when she and her family would be able to get past simple memories of Marcus without dissolving into tears. He was everywhere. They couldn't look at the couch there in the den without thinking of how he used to sprawl on it to read. They couldn't walk past the porcelain harlequin figurine in a curio cabinet near the room's doorway without remembering how he'd given it to her for Mother's Day last year. Even the faded carpet spoke of him. It bore a blotchy pink stain where he spilled some fruit punch. Marcus was the center of their attention, something he'd rarely been while he was alive.

"I'm sorry," Det. Entzminger said. He sounded like he truly was. It made the first time Emma sensed any emotion in him. "I know this isn't easy for any of you."

"It's torture," Stephanie said. She buried her face in her hands and broke down into heaving sobs.

Emma rushed to her and took her in her arms. She longed for the days when it took little more than one of her kisses and a dab of Mercurochrome to heal her children's hurts.

Det. Jamison shook his head sadly. "I wouldn't wish what y'all are going through on my worst enemy. There's nothing worse than losing someone you love, especially someone so young."

Emma noticed that he shared a look with Det. Entzminger that seemed to telegraph a mutual agreement that their visit should draw to an end.

"We appreciate your time," Det. Entzminger said to everyone. He and Det. Jamison got to their feet. "Depending on how things go, we may need to get back in touch with you. In the meanwhile, if you think of any other information that may be of help or if you have any questions or concerns about this investigation, please don't hesitate to contact us."

Business cards materialized on the coffee table in front of Emma. She turned away from them. She never wanted to see the detectives again.

CHAPTER 6

Tuning out the conversations of his parents, great-aunt, sister, niece, and nephew, Rusty crouched near a window in his home and peeked between two slats of the closed mini-blinds. He scanned the front yard and the houses across the street. He didn't see any signs of them, but he couldn't go by that. They might be hiding anywhere, just waiting for him to come out. For all he knew, they could be in that van parked in the driveway of a nearby house. Mid-State Electric & Gas's logo was emblazoned across the side of the van, but those reporters weren't above disguising a vehicle to make it appear like it belonged to the utility company. They might've even stolen the van from MSE&G. He didn't put anything past them.

"Rusty," his mother whined, "your pacing back and forth to that window is driving me crazy!"

He shot her an angry glare. Who was she to complain about somebody driving her crazy? If she nagged at him one more time to relax, he was going to snap.

"I've got to see if they're out there anywhere," he said sharply, ignoring her wounded expression. He peeked through the blinds again. Across the street, a neighbor watered plants on her porch. Two girls rode by on bikes. A monarch butterfly appeared, hovered for a moment, then vanished. It was all too normal. No matter what his father had done, it was hard to believe he had frightened off the reporters for good, especially given a story as sensational as this one. They'd return. The only question was when.

His seven-year-old nephew, Blake, ran over and hunkered down beside him. "You see 'em, Uncle Rusty? You think they're behind them pecan trees?"

Rusty peeked through the blinds again. "Not that I can tell."

"Want me to go outside to see if I can find 'em?" Blake asked.

"No," Rusty told him. "Go back in Grandma and Granddaddy's bedroom and watch cartoons."

"Nuh-uh, I'm staying out here with you!"

"Jesus Christ," Rusty muttered. He loved his nephew, but the boy was grating on his last damned nerve. Blake's younger sister Abby was just as aggravating. Rusty's father and sister were fussing at the girl in the kitchen about something or the other. He wished his sister would take her children home. He wished his dad's aunt would go home, too, however, she'd announced that as the matriarch of the Carter clan, it was her duty to rally around them during their "hour of need." Like they weren't able to put one foot in front of the other without her.

She snapped at Rusty, "I know you're under a lot of pressure right now, but that's no excuse to take the Lord's name in vain."

"I didn't mean to," Rusty said between gritted teeth.

"It's trials and tribulations like this when we need to turn to God, not toss his name about," Aunt Edna went on.

"That's what I've been trying to tell him," Doris Carter said, sighing her martyr's sigh. "He never listens to anything I've got to say, though."

Straining against the temptation to cuss them out, Rusty rubbed his bloodshot eyes. He was exhausted. It had been nearly fifty hours since he last slept, yet when he lay in bed, he kept seeing Marcus Jennings' body on the asphalt with pieces of his toy gun scattered nearby.

The sound of a car rumbling down the street caught his nephew's imagination. Blake yanked apart two slats of the mini-blinds. "Is that one of 'em, Uncle Rusty?" he asked, full of excitement.

Rusty scrutinized the passing car. "I don't think so."

His father came in from the kitchen with another Budweiser. It was his fourth of the day although it was still early in the afternoon. He normally didn't start on his fourth beer until the evening. "You caught sight of any of them yet?" he asked Rusty and Blake.

Before Rusty could answer, Blake said, "No, Granddaddy, but we keepin' a real good lookout!"

Russ laughed. "That's my boy." He settled into his recliner and popped open the beer tab.

"I don't reckon they'll come back here, not after the what-for you gave them yesterday," Aunt Edna said to Russ, Sr.

A part of Rusty was angry about his father's outburst when nearly a dozen reporters descended upon the house with cameras rolling. What had his father been thinking while blocking the front entrance of his home and ranting at them like a freaking maniac? Or had he been so caught up in his rage that he hadn't been thinking at all?

God only knew how much damage his father rashly caused yesterday. Scott and others on the police force told him not to worry about it. They tried to convince him that the video clip of his father being televised from there to Timbuktu was only a few seconds long and besides, Rusty's innocence or guilt would be determined by his own actions, not his father's, but Rusty was sure they were only saying that because they were his friends.

His niece dashed into the room towards the TV, her blond ringlets bouncing with her every step. With all the force her four-year-old body could muster, she hollered, "I wanna watch the Granddaddy Show! I wanna watch the Granddaddy Show!"

Laughing, Aunt Edna said to Russ, Sr, "See there, you've got the child thinking you got your own TV show."

Rusty didn't find anything funny about it.

His sister Charlene came to the doorway holding a half-eaten sandwich. She said to Abby, "Come back in the kitchen right this minute, young lady, and finish this ham sandwich you had me make for you."

"I wanna watch the Granddaddy Show," Abby repeated.

Charlene glanced at the wall clock. "It's not coming on again until the big hand is on the twelve and the little hand is on the two."

Rusty flinched at the thought of having to watch the clip of his father on CNN *Headline News* again. Every thirty minutes, CNN included it as part of its follow-up coverage of the riot that resulted in nearly four million dollars in property damage, one hundred and fifteen arrests, twenty-nine people—including four cops—needing medical treatment for injuries, and the entire city being put under a curfew and patrolled by the National Guard. Every thirty minutes, anyone on the planet with cable or a satellite dish was able to see his father making a goddamned spectacle of himself. Rusty pictured peasants in remote Chinese villages, Aborigines in forgotten backwaters of Australia, and tribesmen on grassy African plains gathered in front of small TV's and deciding that if the son of the man they were watching acted anything like his father, he must be guilty of what he'd been accused of.

"I wanna see the Granddaddy Show now!" Abby demanded.

"You're not watching anything until you finish your lunch!" Charlene said, but her daughter didn't budge.

"Leave her be, Charlene," Doris said, flopping back against the couch like a rag doll. "I can't take any more commotion. My nerves are shot through as it is. Look a here—" She held up a hand. Even from across the room, Rusty could see it trembling.

"You're putting it into her head that it's okay to waste food," Charlene complained. "That may be fine here with you and Daddy, but it's not a luxury I can afford, especially since it's been a month of Sundays since I've gotten any child support."

"If you need us to help you out, all you've got to do is say so," Russ, Sr, grumbled.

"That's not the point—" Charlene said, her voice rising.

"You sorry sons of bitches!" Abby hollered, pointing a stubby finger at make-believe reporters and repeating what she'd heard her grandfather yell at real reporters yesterday before slamming the door in their faces. "You get the hell off my property now, dammit, 'fore I pump your asses full of buckshot!"

"Yeah!" Blake whooped. Jumping in front of his sister, he aimed an imaginary shotgun. "Pow! Pow! Pow!"

Rusty froze as bullets tore into Marcus Jennings and knocked him backward onto the carpeted floor. "Shut up!" Rusty screamed at the kids. "Shut the fuck up!"

His mother gasped in shock and his father bolted out of his recliner and yelled at him. "Who the hell you think you are?"

"You don't talk to my kids like that!" Charlene shrieked as Blake and Abby ran to her, wailing at the top of their lungs.

"Get hold of yourself, boy!" Aunt Edna commanded.

Their voices were unnaturally shrill and reverberated with a strange static. It was like they were being amplified by an overcharged sound system that turned intelligible speech into high-pitched buzzing. Rusty could barely make out who was saying what.

He backed away from them, his throat suddenly dry and his heart pounding like it could hammer its way out of his chest. *What's going on?* He looked from one person to the other. Their mouths contorted as they emitted more static. More terrifying was how everyone in the room was turning into grotesque magnifications of themselves, as if they were blow-up dolls being pumped with too much air. His father drew closer, gesturing wildly, and opening and closing his rubberized mouth like a grotesque phantom.

"Stay away from me!" Rusty yelled, backing into the front door. He was shocked that he could hear his own voice over the thudding of his heart. Reaching behind, he fumbled for the doorknob.

His father loomed closer, his face blood red. He

roared more static as the others in the room watched with horrified expressions.

The doorknob was slippery as a wet bar of soap in Rusty's sweaty hands. He gripped it harder. Oh, God. Oh, God. If allowed to come any closer, his father would kill him, not through any physical action, but through his very presence. Somehow, Russell Carter, Sr. had been infused with the power to kill simply by radiating fury.

Terror forced tears to Rusty's eyes. Turning, he grabbed the doorknob with all his might. The door flew open so suddenly that he almost stumbled backward. In an instant, the hot summer air wrapped around him like a heavy shroud. He glanced over his shoulder. His father had turned completely blood red, from his hair that had been blondish-gray only moments ago to his worn, once-brown house slippers. Rusty bolted outside and ran for his life.

He finally came to a stop in the middle of a backyard. It wasn't his. He didn't know whose it was. For that matter, he didn't even know where he was. He felt like a character from a Star Trek re-run who kept being haphazardly beamed to strange surroundings.

Panting hard, he fought to catch his breath and wondered what the hell was wrong with him. *I'm fucking crazy,* he thought glumly. He was losing his mind. Worse yet, he was probably scaring the daylights out of his family. No telling what they thought of him now. He didn't know how he could ever face them again. For the second time within two days, he'd raced from the house like a ghost was chasing him. Then again, one was—Marcus Jennings's—and he couldn't outrun it, no matter how hard he tried.

A growing sense of hopelessness slowed his breathing. Maybe he should just put an end to his and his family's misery by . . .

"Stop it, Carter," he muttered. Suicide was crazy. Really crazy. It would be taking the easy way out and confirm people's worst suspicions about him. He had to find a way to clear his name and rebuild his life, not just for himself, but for his family, too. He was putting them through hell. He wouldn't be surprised if they were at the county mental health office arranging for him to be committed. Maybe getting committed would be a blessing in disguise. There had to be some kind of treatment for his condition, whatever it was called. He supposed it was something akin to panic attacks, only a million times worse. It made things like slithering spaghetti and supernaturally evil fathers mind-numbing realities, not ridiculous notions.

If it took being put in a rubber room to rid himself of such an affliction, so be it. Like suicide, insanity was something he couldn't allow himself to escape into. He needed all his wits about him to get the nightmare of Marcus Jennings' death behind him. The pity party had to stop. He wasn't the first cop who'd had to kill someone and he wouldn't be the last. It went with the territory. He knew that going in, and Marcus Jennings had given him no choice. Why though? What had been going through that kid's mind?

Using the frayed edge of his T-shirt to wipe away sweat, Rusty tried to remember every detail about Jennings. The main thing that kept coming back to him was the deep sorrow in the boy's brown eyes. Rusty couldn't remember ever seeing such sadness in anyone. Had the kid wanted to die? Why? From everything Rusty had heard, Jennings shouldn't have had a care in the world. No issues with his family had turned up nor any talk of a romance having gone bad; he hadn't had any scrapes with the law or any history of running with the wrong crowd or having problems with drugs or alcohol. According to those who knew him, Marcus Jennings had been a straight arrow who never troubled anyone. What made him turn Jesse James all of the sudden, and a sorrowful one at that? Marcus Jennings was a puzzle with missing pieces; Rusty could only hope that they'd be discovered soon.

Wiping away sweat, he studied his surroundings and tried to remember which way he came. The unfenced backyard and those bordering it offered few clues. However, the houses appeared to be the same ones Titan Textiles built for its workers about ninety years ago so he knew he was somewhere in his neighborhood. He cut through the yard to a crossroads and read the street signs: Yancy and Williston Roads. He was about a mile from home. He started walking.

He slowed as he approached his house. There were so many vehicles parked in the yard that it looked like a used car lot. Even from two blocks away, he recognized a cousin's Civic, an uncle's battered S-10 pickup loaded with a lawn mower, and the Lincoln Town Car an aunt had driven since the beginning of time. His parents obviously had sounded the alarm after he left. "Rusty's gone fool," he imagined them explaining to family over the phone. "Get over here quick!"

Who else had they called? He saw no squad cars, no ambulances. Of course not. His parents would want to keep this secret. It was embarrassing enough to have to tell kinfolk.

He raked a hand through his hair that was slick with sweat. Remaining outside in the punishing heat was accomplishing nothing. It was only making the band of nervousness around his chest tighter and was most likely ratcheting up his family's anxiety as well. They had no idea where he'd run off to or what crazy thing he might've done. For all they knew, he had thrown himself in the river that he and Scott had been at the night before.

He needed to face them. He owed them that as well as an apology and a pledge to get help. Better to do it now and get it over with.

If only there weren't so many of them at the house. He believed he could deal with his parents and his sister along with her children, but having aunts, uncles, cousins, and other relatives gathered around too made it hard to take another step toward the house. The stares. He couldn't stand the idea of them all staring at him like he was an exhibit in a freak show. They'd try not to, of course, but their curiosity of how the fates had conspired to produce such a weakling from a lineage of men meaner and tougher than junkyard dogs would get the better of them.

They were probably clustered near the windows, gaping at him, and wondering why the hell he had come to a standstill in front of the house. He imagined some suggesting he must be so out of it that he'd forgotten where he lived. He looked ridiculous. He knew that. He couldn't stay there forever, if for no reason other than that he would pass out from the heat.

Aunt Edna was right—he had to get hold of himself. While accounting for his bizarre behavior wouldn't be pleasant, he knew others had it worse than he did. There were people fighting for their lives in hospitals, doctors having to tell patients to get their affairs in order, and Army chaplains having to tell women they weren't wives anymore, but young widows. He could face his family.

The sun burned the back of his neck as he walked toward his home. It must be at least a hundred degrees. The heat wave had stretched on for so long that it was hard to imagine ever feeling the crisp chill of winter again. But winter would come—eventually. Would he be back in uniform by then or behind bars?

Take it one day at a time. That was what Scott kept saying, but he wasn't the one having to wait helplessly while others determined his fate.

Rusty wondered what was going on with the investigation. The two SBLE agents leading the investigation showed up at the house yesterday afternoon. Finding the tall, reserved Det. Larry Entzminger and the slightly rumpled Det. Andy Jamison at his door only a few hours after his nerves were frayed by his dad's confrontation with the reporters was the last thing he needed. When the detectives said they wanted to talk to him though, he didn't have a choice but to let them in.

"I've already told you everything I know about what happened," he said to them as they stepped inside. "I can't think of anything else I can say that would be of use."

"We just want to clarify a few things," Det. Entzminger said. With one sweeping glance, he seemed to take measure of Rusty, his home, and his parents who looked on with clear animosity. *White trash.* That was what was probably going through the African-American's mind. He wore an air of superiority as elegantly as his stylish dove-gray suit which Rusty guessed was made in Italy and would eat up a month's salary for a rookie cop like him. He couldn't remember a black person ever entering the house before. It was ironic that a man like Det. Entzminger was the first.

Rusty was anxious to usher him and Det. Jamison to another room before his father said something that made a bad situation far worse. As the lead investigators of the case, the two detectives held his future in their hands. He couldn't afford for them to have more of a negative impression of him than he feared they already had. "We can talk in the kitchen," he said to them.

"That's fine," Det. Entzminger said.

The problem was that they had to go through the living room to reach the kitchen. While Det. Jamison gave a quick smile and nod of his head in greeting to Rusty's parents while walking by them, Det. Entzminger said, "Good afternoon."

Russ and Doris Carter only stared back in reply. Rusty felt his face flush. Damn, this couldn't get over with soon enough. He gestured for the two men to have a seat in the kitchen and said, "Would you like something to drink? We've got soda, tea, juice."

"Actually, a cold glass of water would hit the spot," Det. Jamison said, settling into a chair.

Rusty opened a cabinet door and searched for drinking glasses that hadn't originally been jelly jars. "Det. Entzminger, would you like one, too?"

"No, I'm good, but thanks anyway," he answered.

While Rusty filled two mismatched glasses with ice water for himself and Det. Jamison, he wondered how the black SBLE agent could seem so immune to the heat. Then again, from what he'd heard, few things affected Det. Larry Entzminger. He had a reputation for attacking each assignment with an unyielding, laser-like focus. Rusty wasn't sure if that would help him or not.

He brought the glasses of ice water to the table, handed one to Det. Jamison, and sat down.

"Thanks," Det. Jamison said. "How you holding up?"

Rusty was surprised by the question that hinted at genuine concern. "I'm managing." *Barely.*

"I'm sure this has been a rough time for you," Det. Jamison said.

An uneasy feeling stirred within Rusty. Where was Jamison going with this? Maybe it was a tactic to get him to break down. "I'll be glad to get it behind me," he said.

"That's perfectly understandable," Det. Entzminger said. He pulled out a small memo pad. "Like I mentioned, we'd like to go over a few details of the case with you, just to double-check some things. I'd like to start with when you were first alerted of the hold-up. You said you'd been near the scene, right?"

"Less than a block away. I was there in no time."

"Could you see inside the store?" Det. Jamison asked.

The question pulled Rusty back to the moment his cruiser skidded to a stop in front of the Seven-Eleven. He shook his head. "The doors and plate glass windows were plastered with ads for all kinds of crap."

"How long was it after you got there before you spotted Jennings?"

"Couldn't have been more than a few seconds. I'd hardly had time to call for backup and get out of my cruiser before he came out. He looked like—" His voice faltered for a moment as he remembered Marcus Jennings stepping out of the convenience store. "Sorrow, pure sorrow."

Why? The question was eating him alive. If there was a chance that the two men on either side of him had already discovered the answer, he wanted to know. He pushed on. "I realize you've just started the investigation, but have you found out anything to explain why he was like that?"

"I'm afraid at this point, we can only ask questions, not answer them," Det. Entzminger said.

"But he's turned my whole life upside down, and I don't know a damned thing about him."

"There's not much we can tell you until the investigation's completed," Det. Entzminger said like he was talking to a slow learner. "Now, you said he came out of the store right when you drove up."

The unfairness of the situation jabbed Rusty like shards of glass. Marcus Jennings could remain a complete mystery to him while he was probed, dissected, and studied like a lab rat. These detectives felt they had the absolute right to show up at his house unannounced and lob one question at him after another, and he just had to take it.

Det. Jamison tried a different angle. "How did he come out of the store? Was it fast, like he was trying to make a run for it?"

"No," Rusty said, "it was more like he was. . .surrendering, but not to me, to something else. Damn, I know this isn't making any sense." He raked his fingers through his hair again. He was probably talking his way straight to a state prison.

"It is a little," Det. Jamison said, sharing an enigmatic look with the older detective. "Keep going."

The scene started replaying again in Rusty's mind. "I saw the gun in his right hand. That's what it looked like anyway—a real gun. He was holding it at his side."

"Then what?"

Rusty closed his eyes against the memory, however nothing could block it. "I pulled mine out and ordered him to drop his. I yelled at him to do it at least twice, but he didn't. He aimed it at me—as deliberate as could be." Opening his eyes, he said softly, "I thought he was going to kill me so I shot him."

He fell silent and the jumble of voices from the TV in the living room filled the kitchen.

Det. Entzminger scribbled something in his memo pad and tucked it inside his jacket pocket. Det. Jamison seemed like he was about to say something but then thought better of it.

Partly to end the awkward silence and partly because he wanted to know, Rusty asked what he figured was a safe question, "How long do these kind of investigations normally take?"

"Depends," Det. Entzminger said.

Hard ass, Rusty fumed.

"We hope to wrap things up as soon as possible," Det. Jamison said as if he were offering more specific information. "Thanks for talking to us. It's been helpful."

Both he and the other agent got to their feet. "Yes, we appreciate your cooperation," Det. Entzminger said. "We'll be in touch if we have more questions."

"Of course you will," Rusty was tempted to say, but no good would come from becoming sarcastic. "All right," he said in what he hoped was a casual tone. He escorted the detectives to the front door under the stony watch of his parents.

He remained at the door until the detectives climbed into a silver Crown Vic and pulled away. Who else had they spoken to so far? Somewhere, there had to be someone who could solve the riddle of Marcus Jennings.

What would happen if that person wasn't found in time?

That question weighed on Rusty as he trudged toward his home packed with kinfolk. He tried to force thoughts of the teen and the investigation from his mind. His family was enough to deal with.

To cut down his nervousness, he jammed his hands in his pockets and was surprised to feel his truck keys. He thought he'd left them hanging from the key rack in the kitchen like he normally did. He hadn't planned to go anywhere so it was annoyingly puzzling why he'd stuffed the keys in his pocket.

Crossing into his yard, he wove through the parked vehicles that spilled over from the driveway onto the parched grass. Although the front door was only a few yards away, he headed for the back door, figuring he'd probably run into fewer people that way. But no sooner had he started for it than he saw his twelve-year old cousin Courtney Marie wobbling on rollerblades in the carport. Her pale blue eyes widened at the sight of him. He recognized that look. It was the same one he and his sister used to get whenever they were forced to be around their great-uncle Willis who kept his head covered with aluminum foil because he claimed it made him invisible to the space aliens that were hunting him.

"Uh . . . hey, Rusty," Courtney Marie said. She cast an anxious glance toward the back door as if needing assurance that help was within hollering distance.

He'd become the family's Uncle Willis. The kids would avoid him, and the adults would try to as well. He couldn't stand it.

Clearing his throat, he found his voice through his bitterness. "Hi, sweetie. Do me a favor, will ya? Go inside and let Mom and Daddy know that I'm needing to run an errand. Tell 'em I'll be back later on this afternoon."

"Sure," she said in a brighter tone, leaving little doubt she was relieved he was leaving.

"Thanks," he said and returned to his truck. He had no idea where to go, but still, the idea of driving anywhere held appeal. He set the air conditioning on full blast, turned the volume up on the radio, and took off.

It felt good to go beyond the confines of his neighborhood for the first time since the shooting. Only two days had passed, yet they felt like an eternity. Nighttime was proving to be the hardest. Chased from his bedroom by images of Marcus Jennings, he struggled through the seemingly endless dark hours in his father's recliner, channel surfing amidst the wasteland of infomercials, B-grade movies, and re-runs of re-runs.

He couldn't survive much more of that. Surely by nightfall his exhaustion would be so overpowering that it could defeat even the ghost of Marcus Jennings, and he could get some sleep. Maybe he should drop by a drugstore for some over-the-counter sleeping pills—just in case.

His surroundings appeared reassuringly normal while driving to the nearest drugstore which was located in a mall clustered by chain restaurants and hotels. The riot hadn't spread this far out. Being amidst such bland suburban sprawl made it almost possible to forget that sections of downtown resembled a war zone.

He found a parking space near the mall entrance and went inside. His previous trips there had been brief—he quickly bought whatever he came for and left with little veering from his planned route, but he wasn't in any hurry to reach his destination today. It felt so good to be in a place left unscarred by the chaos that had erupted a few miles away. Shoppers ambled around as if completely unaware their city had exploded with racial tension and attracted worldwide scrutiny. It was just another lazy summer afternoon to hang out at the mall.

Rusty stopped a store that had a rack of CDs and DVDs near its entrance, and as he scanned the rack for the latest country music CDs, his stomach rumbled. Although he knew that feeling hungry for the first time since the shooting wasn't as monumental as Noah seeing a dove descending from the heavens after the flood, he still took it as a hopeful sign. Perhaps it was only a matter of time before the rest of his life fell back into a natural order as well.

He went to the mall's sunlit food court that had a small carousel in its center. There wasn't much of a selection as far as the food went—it didn't matter. He was hungry enough to dig through trash cans for scraps. He bought a mound of chicken nuggets and devoured them in minutes, washing them down with lemonade. With his hunger satiated, sleepiness swept over him and made him wish he could stretch out on the floor without drawing attention. He watched a lone little girl on the carousel through hooded eyelids. A young woman who appeared to be her mother stood close and kept watch while the girl rode around and around . . . .

"Rusty?"

"Huh?" Startled, Rusty looked up at fellow cop Josh Tomlinson who was standing beside him. Josh's street clothes and the bulging Macy's shopping bag he held made it clear he was off-duty.

Josh slid into a chair on the opposite side of the table. "You okay, man?"

"Yeah." Rusty straightened. The thought of getting caught sleeping in public like some homeless bum made his face hot. "I must've dozed off. I've been running on empty for so long that I guess it finally caught up with me."

"You gotta be going through hell."

"You don't know the half of it."

"I've got a pretty good idea. Taking somebody out is hard enough to handle without having a bunch of assholes who don't know what they're talking about playing Monday morning quarterback with you."

How would you know? Rusty wanted to ask. Instead he gave a half-hearted shrug and said, "Guess it goes with the job." Rusty liked Josh, but he wished Josh had left him the hell alone. Obviously finding a sanctuary from his misery had been too much to hope for. Josh's mere presence brought back bad memories—he'd been the first cop to arrive at the Seven-Eleven after the shooting and he appeared all too eager to rehash what happened. Maybe only being on the fringe of a case that was grabbing headlines wasn't enough for him—maybe he wanted to vicariously experience the shooting by getting Rusty to open up about it.

"Well, it still sucks," Josh said. "And it makes me sick to my stomach to watch how those fucking reporters keep twisting everything around. They're cherry-picking information about the black guys who've gotten killed over the last few months to make all of us on the force look like a bunch of damned skinheads. To hear them tell it, Tyquan Green, Antonio Cavanagh, Maceo Wilson, LaQuise Rogers, and Marcus Jennings were saints, especially Jennings since he didn't have a record and because he was so young."

Rusty hadn't needed another reminder of Marcus's age. Fifteen—the age for suddenly noticeable Adam's apples, peach fuzz-like stubble and first-time romances. Not for dying. A heavy sigh escaped Rusty as he swished around the watery remains of his soft drink.

"Sorry, man," Josh mumbled.

"It's okay." Rusty said. "What's really getting next to me is that Marcus Jennings has turned into the most important person in my life, but I know next to nothing about him."

"He threatened you. He gave you no choice but to take him down. That's all you need to know."

"No, it's not. I need to know a lot more, but I don't know how to find it out."

"You'll know everything you need to once SBLE finishes their investigation and clears you."

Rusty could only run his fingers through his hair in response.

"C'mon," Josh said, "let me buy you a beer. The Silver Spur's right around the corner."

"Thanks, but I'm too bushed to be good company."

"Then you ought to head home and get some rest."

"Yeah, I think you're right," Rusty said, standing.

"See you around, man. Take care of yourself."

"You, too, Josh."

As they began walking away from each other, Rusty turned back. "Hey, Josh, one more thing—what was Jennings' address?"

"1246 Edgemont. Why?"

"Just curious," Rusty lied.

Josh studied him for a moment. "Well, holler whenever you want me to make good on that rain check to the Silver Spur."

"You bet."

1246 Edgemont Road. Rusty mentally repeated the address while buying a pack of sleeping pills at the mall drugstore and returning to his truck. What would he find there? An angry crowd of blacks? A horde of reporters? What if someone recognized him?

He started the truck and listened to Allison Krause sing "The Lucky One". Ha. That description sure as hell didn't fit him or the boy whose home he had to see, no matter what waited for him there.

He turned onto Edgemont, paying attention to the addresses painted on mailboxes or posted near front doors. The even numbered homes were on the right. 204 Edgemont. 206 Edgemont. One run-down house after another with yards that looked like they'd been given up on years ago.

388 Edgemont. 390 Edgemont. The twelve hundredth block was probably about another half-mile or so down the road. With relief, he noted that the hot weather had driven most people indoors. There were a few brave souls venturing out, but only a few. Still, he angled the truck's sun visor to block full view of his face and he readjusted his sunglasses.

He rehearsed what he'd do if he were recognized. He'd take the quickest route to the interstate and try to lose his pursuers in traffic that was normally heavy this time of day. Simply thinking about being chased made him glance into the rearview mirror. Nothing trailed him, though, except the brutal heat.

944 Edgemont. 946 Edgemont. Only another three blocks to go. Not too late to turn around and go home. What, after all, could he really learn about Marcus Jennings simply from seeing where he had lived? But if there was a chance he could find out anything—anything at all—he had to take it. He took a deep breath and held the steering wheel steady with sweaty hands.

1202 Edgemont. 1204 Edgemont. His mouth was as dry as chalk dust and he could hear the galloping of his heart. *Get hold of yourself, boy.*

1246 Edgemont. It stood in complete contrast to the rest of Waverton. The house was a well-maintained, two-story clapboard painted in a robin's egg shade of blue. Although simply constructed, it radiated class. It was the yard, however, that stunned him. It was a lush kaleidoscope of beauty. Finding it in the midst of Waverton was like discovering a stunning jewel in a pile of garbage. Someone was clearly devoted to it. Who? It certainly hadn't been Marcus Jennings. The creation of such perfection was far beyond the interest or skill of any fifteen-year-old boy. It had to be one of his parents, or perhaps both of them given the endless amount of work obviously involved. But perhaps Marcus had helped. Yes, Rusty could see him being roused from bed on early summer mornings to help mow, prune, weed, and fertilize. Had he grumbled and whined or had he enjoyed taking part in turning plain earth into something so magical?

Marcus's family—they could answer that question and many more. Judging by the number of cars in the carport and driveway, some of them were home. What were they doing? Were they on the phone with lawyers? Gazing at baby pictures of Marcus? Making his funeral plans?

The front door opened, and Rusty recognized the heavy-set, middle-age black man from having seen him on the news the day before. He was Marcus Jennings' father. Glaring in Rusty's direction, he yelled, "Who are you and what are you doing here?"

"Shit," Rusty said, breaking out in a cold sweat. He stomped on the accelerator and sped off.

CHAPTER 7

Sandwiched between her husband and oldest daughter on a crowded front church pew, Emma half-listened to Rev. Creighton Jones while he delivered her boy's eulogy. It was wrong, all of it. Creighton Jones had never laid eyes on Marcus until only an hour before. It made about as much sense for him to do the eulogy as it was for Marcus to be dead at fifteen.

And if Marcus had to have a funeral anywhere, it should've been at Waverton Baptist where he attended his entire life along with most everyone else in the family, but their church was too small to hold the huge mass of people wanting to attend his funeral. So against her wishes, it was moved to this large, black Methodist church downtown. It wasn't even big enough, though, to accommodate everyone. Hundreds had to be ushered into the fellowship hall to watch the service on large screen TV monitors. Still countless more were standing outside in the merciless heat.

She folded her arms tightly against her chest and stared ahead at the gleaming white casket blanketed by a thick cascade of white and golden yellow roses. Her only request that had been followed was that the casket be closed by the time she entered the sanctuary. Seeing her baby lying in it was more than she could've handled, especially knowing the medical examiner's office had mutilated his body. She tried to keep them from doing the autopsy, but they told her she had no say-so in the matter. It didn't seem she had much say-so in anything anymore.

"... We will not stumble. We will not grow faint. We will not stop. We will stay the course until this innocent boy's murderer is punished to the fullest extent of the law," Creighton Jones said to thundering amens. "Rest assured that Marcus Abraham Jennings has not died in vain. His spirit is leading us on to demand justice . . . ."

Emma was glad Jones stood behind a pulpit yards away from her instead of within reach for she feared what she might do if she were able to lay hands on him. It troubled her that she could despise another human being with such fierceness. God had created him as he had her, yet ever since Creighton Jones showed up at her home two days ago in a stretch limousine with a bunch of flunkies in tow and reporters in pursuit, she couldn't look at him without all manner of hateful thoughts filling her mind.

Like the winds from an approaching hurricane, the force of his arrival hit her before she actually saw him. She'd been upstairs ironing Marcus's burial suit when a commotion erupted downstairs. "Lord, what now?" she murmured as dread flooded her. She turned off the iron and started out of the room, but she didn't have time to reach the stairs before Stephanie came running up to her and whirled her around. "He's here, Momma!" she said breathlessly. "He's here! Rev. Creighton Jones is here!"

"What?"

"You can see him with your own eyes! He just pulled up in his limo! He got my message, and he came! Oh, my God, Momma, I can't believe it!"

"Me, either," Emma said in a flat tone.

Stephanie's joy dimmed. "What's wrong?"

For an instant, Emma was tempted to tell her everything. The secrecy was eating her alive. Even taking one of Dottie's tranquilizers hadn't kept her from waking up throughout the night in torment about whether she was doing the right thing. She'd gotten down on her knees and prayed, but her mind was as troubled when she finished as when she began.

"Momma, what's the matter with you? You're acting like you don't want him here."

"I don't," Emma blurted.

Stephanie drew back in shock. "Why not?"

The flash of temptation passed as had the right moment to reveal the truth. If there was ever a time for that, it was when she told it to Otis. How different would things be if she'd showed Marcus's note to everyone close to her instead of only him? Too late for second-guessing. She'd made her pledge. There was no going back on it now. However heavy the burden of bearing this secret, she had to do it.

"I wish we could bury Marcus in peace, that's all," she offered to Stephanie as a weak explanation. "This hullabaloo is working on my nerves and having Creighton Jones around is only going to make things worse."

"But he can help us—"

Ed burst into the room. "What are y'all yakking about? Didn't you hear us hollering that Rev. Creighton Jones is here? He's getting out of his limo right now."

"I know," Stephanie said. "That's what I came up here to tell Momma, but she's acting real funny about it."

"I don't like the man," Emma said. "He's nothing but a vulture, getting free publicity off of other people's heartaches. You never should've called him in the first place."

"Now you tell me!" Stephanie said, putting her hands on her hips.

"If you'd asked me before you called him, I would've."

Ed cut in. "You're going to have to fuss about this later, Momma. He's here now with a heap of reporters. He cut his trip short to Africa to see us, and it wouldn't look right for you to stay up here after all the trouble he's gone to."

"That's right," Stephanie seconded.

Feeling defeated, Emma sighed. "I'll be glad when this whole thing is over with," she said.

Her son hugged her. "You won't be the only one."

* * *

She followed Ed and Stephanie out into the front yard where everyone who'd been downstairs went to welcome Creighton Jones and his entourage. Between cameramen, photographers, and their equipment, Emma glimpsed Otis greeting Jones while Brenda, Otis Lee, and Dottie, and other friends and neighbors gaped at the civil rights leader like he'd walked across the Atlantic Ocean to be with them.

"C'mon," Ed said, motioning Emma forward. She reluctantly followed him. Too soon, she was standing next to Otis and Creighton Jones.

"Rev. Jones," Otis said, "this is my wife, Emma."

Jones took her hands in his and from the feel of his skin, she doubted he had ever handled anything coarser than the expertly knotted, cranberry-colored silk tie he wore. She was certain her hands—callused from decades of work in her yard—must've felt like those of a longshoreman to him. However, that didn't embarrass her as much as how casually she and her loved ones were dressed in comparison to him. His stylish suit made their worn and faded T-shirts, jeans, shorts, sneakers, and flip-flops appear that much shabbier. He could've called ahead to give them time to make themselves more presentable, but she supposed that would've ruined the effect.

"Mrs. Jennings, it's so good to meet you though I'm sorry it's under such tragic circumstances," he said while camera shutters clicked away rhythmically.

"Yessir," she mumbled.

"I promise you and your family that I won't rest until your son's murderer is brought to justice. The days of this city's police department getting away with killing and maiming our young brothers because of their race are over."

"Glory hallelujah!" Dottie said, clapping.

"Amen!" Brenda yelled.

Emma cringed inwardly as Creighton Jones put his arms around her and Otis. Had she the power to vanish, the arm that Jones draped over her shoulders would suddenly fall to his side.

He went on. "I'm sure the police think they can whitewash Marcus's murder the same way they've done with the other brothers they've cut down here like blades of grass, but I won't let them get away with it, believe you me. You have my pledge that I'll do whatever it takes to stop this racially-motivated carnage."

Oh, Lord, Emma thought as more whoops of agreement rose from her family, neighbors, and friends. The photographers and cameramen moved in for better shots and one of the reporters called out, "Rev. Jones, what prompted you to get involved in this?"

"I received such an urgent plea for help from the Jennings family that I was absolutely compelled to get here as soon as possible," he answered. "Wherever there's a fight to be waged against racism, you'll find me leading the charge, and this is one of the most heinous examples of government-led racism I've seen in a long, long time."

A young woman from the local Fox affiliate said, "Sir, how can you say that when three blacks inside the Seven-Eleven say Marcus Jennings aimed what appeared to be a gun at Ofc. Rusty Carter?"

Emma felt the ground beneath her feet shift unsteadily. The last thing she'd expected to hear was that three eyewitnesses—black ones at that—had stepped forward to confirm Marcus caused his own death. They answered the question of what happened. What they couldn't answer was why it happened. Why would a kid who'd never been in trouble with the law suddenly rob a store and aim an apparent weapon at a policeman? Only she could answer that. Or could Otis now, too? Maybe, just maybe, after hearing that three blacks inside the store backed up what the police said was enough to force him to finally accept the truth.

"Them people are damned liars," Otis snapped at the reporter, dashing Emma's hopes. "My boy wouldn't no more threaten a cop than the pope would."

The woman with Fox News said, "But those witnesses said—"

Otis cut her off. "I don't care what they said. The cops probably put them up to it. I know my son. I know him through and through, and he wouldn't do no such thing."

Jesus, Emma thought. What would it take to make him recognize what was as obvious as the sun above? And why wasn't he challenging Jones's apparent acknowledgment that Marcus tried to rob the store? If he was willing to accept Marcus doing something that out of character, why couldn't he accept that Marcus had also pointed a fake gun at a cop? Surely he could see Creighton Jones was making Marcus out to be just another young thug gunned down by the cops, not a troubled child escaping from his hell. Was that the price he was willing to pay to keep from having to admit his son committed suicide?

Yes, it was. She could tell from looking at him. He was willing to make the tradeoff because it allowed him to still paint Marcus as a victim, maybe not the saintly victim he wanted him portrayed as, but a victim nonetheless. He'd be able to direct his anger at the police, not at Marcus for killing himself and not at her for having missed all the warning signs.

"That may be what those three people are claiming," Creighton Jones said, "but we've had contact with others who saw what happened and they've given statements to the agents with the State Bureau of Law Enforcement that Marcus Jennings was surrendering peacefully when Ofc. Rusty Carter opened fire on him."

Emma gasped along with others around her. Marcus was surrendering? Had he changed his mind and decided he wanted to live?

"The police murdered my son for no good reason!" Otis announced loudly over the rising rumble of voices.

Dazed with the possibility that Marcus hadn't committed suicide after all, Emma kept silent.

"What are the names of the witnesses you're referring to?" a reporter asked Jones while another simultaneously shouted, "Were they inside the store too, and if so, why do they give a different account than the other three people?"

"Sorry, no more questions this afternoon," Jones said. "Right now my first priority is comforting this grieving family."

Otis said, "And we sure appreciate it. There're a thousand other places where people need you, but you came to see about us. We ain't going to make you keep standing in this heat, though. Come on in the house. It ain't nothing fancy, but it's a heck of a lot cooler than out here, and we can offer you and your folk some refreshments."

"Thank you, sir," Creighton Jones said, dabbing his glistening forehead with a silk handkerchief. "That's mighty kind of you."

With others rushing forward to accompany the two men into the house, Emma hung back and tried to make sense of the bombshells dropped by Jones and the Fox News reporter. For them to say there were people who supposedly saw the same incident and yet came up with completely different accounts about what happened troubled her. Was the difference in the accounts because of where the people were during the shooting? Certainly a person who was only a few feet away could come to a different conclusion than another person watching from across the street. Then again, some of the people might simply be lying and if any were, it was probably those who backed up Creighton Jones' accusations. What if they were telling the truth though? Even if it only eased away a little of the guilt weighing on her like a slab of concrete, it was worth knowing, and it was worth knowing now, not when Creighton Jones felt like talking about it.

She briefly considered trying to pry more details from him once the reporters weren't within earshot but then decided she'd be able to get much more information about all the witnesses by contacting the person who was most likely to know which of them was telling the truth. The irony didn't escape her that she'd have to call a man she'd hoped to never speak to again: SBLE Det. Larry Entzminger.

Dottie broke into her thoughts by tottering over to her. "Oooh, girl!" she gushed, "I know you ain't too hepped up on having a bunch of reporters hanging around, but this is exciting! I wouldn't have dreamed in a million years I'd ever meet Rev. Creighton Jones in real life. I figured Stephanie was talking pie-in-the-sky when she left that message for him. She proved me wrong, and am I ever glad she did."

At the mention of her name, Stephanie broke away from her brothers, sister, and the others trailing Otis and Jones. She was full of joy again, and Emma didn't have it in her to douse that joy with any doubts about the witnesses Jones mentioned until she spoke with Det. Entzminger.

"You're glad I did what, Miss Dottie?" Stephanie asked.

"Why, calling Rev. Jones!" Dottie said. "I never would've thought to do such a thing. Wish I had your boldness, sugar. You sure enough know how to make things happen."

Stephanie giggled. "Well, that's the only way to get what you want. Nothing happens just because you sit around wishing for it." She turned to Emma and her expression grew more serious. "What have you got to say about Rev. Jones now, Momma?"

"He's a powerful man," Emma said, mindful not only of her daughter's feelings but also of the media being within earshot. "The Lord can use him for a lot of good."

Despite the answer being vague, it seemed to satisfy Stephanie. "God's already using him for good," she said. "Rev. Jones coming today is doing wonders for us. And to think—he dropped everything to fly here."

"He'll help us a heap more, too," Dottie said. She glanced at Emma and added, "I really believe that."

Emma didn't say anything. No matter how things turned out, Jones was still a spotlight-chasing weasel as far as she was concerned, and the sooner he got gone, the better. She didn't understand why the people she loved most in the world were so blind about him. He even had Dottie bamboozled. She gazed at him like some goofy, star-struck teenager. Yet then again, everyone was acting kind of strange lately, Otis worse of all. The aftermath of Marcus's death revealed a side to him she'd never seen before, and it was mean and bitter. He was obsessed with figuring out how to strike back, to wound as deeply as he'd been wounded. She didn't know what to do about it, and she hated to think how much worse he'd get if it were proven that Marcus was surrendering when the cop killed him.

She followed Dottie, Stephanie, and the others into the crowded house. Creighton Jones being the center of attention made it easy for her to slip upstairs to her bedroom without drawing much notice. Since she'd thrown away the business cards Entzminger and his partner left, she had to look up SBLE's phone number and then ask the agency's switchboard operator to connect her to the black detective's extension. While his phone rang, she looked outside. Her yard was a faded version of itself. Little wonder. She'd forgotten to run the sprinkler on it for the past few days, and the heat had taken its toll. A few more days without water in such blistering weather and all her plants and flowers would be dead.

"Entzminger," a baritone voice said over the phone, startling her. She realized she hadn't prepared what to say.

"Hello? Hello?" he said.

Resisting the temptation to hang up, she said, "Uh—yes, hello, Det. Entzminger. This is Emma Jennings, Marcus Jennings' mother. How are you?"

"Fine. And you?"

"Oh, about as well as can be expected," she said, struggling to think of what to say next.

After a long, uncomfortable pause, he said, "Is there something I can help you with today, Mrs. Jennings?"

"Yes," she said, determined to go on. "Rev. Creighton Jones is here at my house along with a bunch of reporters. He says some witnesses have told you that my boy was surrendering when he got shot, but a reporter claims three black folk who were inside the Seven-Eleven say Marcus forced the cop to kill him in self-defense. Do you know which of them is telling the truth?"

"I'm sorry, I'm not at liberty to make any comments about the case until the investigation is completed."

"I'm not asking you to make comments about the case, I'm only asking you to answer a simple question."

"Mrs. Jennings, I'm not trying to be difficult," he said

in a tone that signaled his patience was wearing thin. "But I cannot discuss this with you."

What little pride she had crumbled. "Please, sir, I'm begging you. I've got to know. I swear to you and the Good Master above I won't tell anyone."

"I'm sorry, Mrs. Jennings. You'll simply have to wait until the investigation is completed. Goodbye."

She heard a click and then the hum of a dial tone. Slowly, she hung up the phone. She felt like a pawn in a cruel game where people dangled what she most needed in front of her and then snatched it away right before she grabbed it. *I'm not at liberty to discuss* . . . . No one should have the right to hide behind such flimsy words. That white SBLE agent who had come with Entzminger would probably spout the same garbage so there was no use in calling him.

Stretching out on the bed, she buried her face in a pillow and tried not to cry. The tears came anyway. They'd been her constant companions lately, ones she'd grown weary of but couldn't keep away. After a few minutes of silent weeping, she turned over, wiped her eyes and replayed the events of the afternoon in her mind. She suddenly realized that while she still knew little about any of the witnesses, the fact that three of them claimed to have been inside the Seven-Eleven offered hope that they were either employees or regular customers. If that was the case, they might be there now and be willing to talk to her. There was only one way to find out.

With hands that were damp with sweat, she maneuvered her ten-year-old Buick Skylark into a parking space in front of the Seven-Eleven. For a few moments, she couldn't move, couldn't even breathe. This was where her baby's life, and in a way her own, had come to an end. She stared ahead at a poster of Dale Earnhardt, Jr. advertising a motor oil for fear that if her focus wandered, she'd discover Marcus's bloodstains splattered nearby on the asphalt. Had she parked over the exact spot where he'd drawn his last breath? The thought of it made her slump forward and rest her head against the steering wheel.

"You all right, ma'am?"

Emma looked up to see a thin young black man with long dreadlocks. His narrow face was marked by acne and obvious worry.

She tried to smile, but couldn't quite do it. "Yes, thank you. I . . . I was just thinking about something, that's all."

"Okay," the young man said, sounding unconvinced. He walked toward a souped-up Mustang parked next to one of the gas pumps, but she noticed he kept glancing over his shoulder in her direction. Fretting that he'd return with more questions if she kept sitting there in such blazing heat like an idiot, she went inside the store.

Its refreshing coolness did nothing to relax the tangle of knots inside her. While she stood rooted near the entranceway, she realized that just like she'd called Det. Entzminger before working out what to say to him, she'd also come to the store without the slightest idea of how to approach anyone.

Feeling stupid, she considered going home, but then a delivery man wheeling in a hand truck piled high with cases of soft drinks forced her to move close to a rack of chips. She pretended to study the chips while surveying her surroundings. Two clerks stood behind the counter—both of them were black women. One was on the phone while another one rang up the purchases of a man who fished a thick wallet from his back pocket. Were they two of the witnesses?

Emma moved down the aisle to racks of assorted cookies and crackers. A few feet away, a young white woman with a toddler on her hip reached for a bottle of juice inside a refrigerated display case while another child whose curls were the same color as the woman's bright red ones begged for a candy bar. They couldn't have been among the three witnesses—that was for sure.

Dawdling about the store, Emma waited for a moment when the place was free of customers so she could talk to the clerks in private, however, no sooner did one customer leave than one or two more stream in. She grimmaced.

The situation was hopeless, and if they hadn't already, her family would soon notice her absence and wonder where she'd taken off to without telling anyone.

As if Emma had radiated her despair, the younger of the two clerks came over and asked, "Ma 'am, you needing help with anything?"

"Well . . . um . . . uh," Emma stammered while scanning the store to see how many people were within hearing range. Some teenage girls were bunched together at a magazine stand a few yards away, but Emma hoped they were too absorbed in a magazine that had a rapper with chiseled stomach muscles on its cover to pay her any mind.

"What's the matter?" the clerk asked. She eyed Emma with a mixture of curiosity and concern. And maybe with a little suspicion, too.

Emma could hardly blame her. Had she seen someone loitering about the store for so long, she would've called the police, especially after what had recently happened there. She worried that if she didn't start saying something soon that made any sense, that was probably what the clerk would do. Nervously clasping her hands together, she said, "No, nothing's the matter, it's only that—if you don't mind—I'd like to ask you about something that happened here a few days ago."

"A few days ago? When exactly?"

"Saturday."

"I was off that day. You'll have to talk to Jessie Lee," she said, motioning toward the other clerk who was stocking packs of cigarettes in an overhead bin.

"Thank you," Emma said. She took a deep breath and walked up to the counter.

"Watcha' need, honey?" the older clerk asked. She kept loading the cigarette bin without a hitch in her rhythm.

"You were working here Saturday?"

The middle-age black woman froze, then looked at her intently. "Yes. Why you want to know?"

Emma couldn't think of anything to tell her except the truth. "That boy who got shot here—Marcus Jennings. He was my son."

The woman's hands flew to her mouth. "Oh, my God! I'm so sorry, honey! I'm so sorry!"

Before Emma knew it, the woman had raced from around the counter and gathered her in her arms. The unexpected outburst of kindness reduced Emma to tears. She knew she was making a spectacle of herself, but she could no more stop herself than she could control the blistering weather.

The woman made soft shushing noises as if soothing a wounded child. "C'mon back in the office where we can talk," she said, steering Emma around the counter and towards an office door.

They entered a room that was barely big enough to hold the small desk that was covered with forms and printouts, a swivel chair that looked like it had been dragged from out of a dumpster, a beat-up looking folding metal chair, and two file cabinets that were crammed with so much paper that some of it poked out from the drawers.

Jessie Lee positioned Emma in the swivel chair and she took a seat on the metal one. "I wish I had some tissue to give you, honey. That's just about the only thing that ain't in this shoe box of an office."

"Oh, I'm fine," Emma said, wiping her nose against the back of her hand.

"No, you ain't," Jessie Lee countered. "And you got no reason to be either. Lord, I feel so bad for you I don't know what to do."

The convenience store clerk's compassion went through Emma like warmth from the sun. She sensed an instant closeness forming between them. "Actually," she said, "there is something you can do that would mean a lot to me."

"What?"

Emma took in a deep breath and let it out slowly. "Tell me what happened when my boy came here Saturday."

Jessie Lee made it clear from her reaction that she would've rather Emma asked her to do anything than that. "If it's the truth you want, I'll give it to you, but I don't think you gonna like it."

The sliver of hope that Marcus hadn't committed suicide after all slipped from Emma's grasp. She hadn't realized how tightly she'd been gripping it and now that it was gone, she felt an aching emptiness take its place. The tenderhearted woman in front of her could only confirm what she'd known from the time she read Marcus's note. No, that wasn't altogether true because Jessie Lee was one of the few people on earth who could also tell her about the last moments of her son's life, and no matter how painful it would be, she needed to hear every detail about them. Taking Jessie Lee's hand in hers, she said, "Tell me anyway."

"All right then," Jessie Lee said with a resigned tone. "I didn't see him come in. I'd just stepped back here to add something to the inventory list when I heard Shameika scream—"

"Who's Shameika?"

"That's the girl who was working with me that day. She was at the cash register. Something told me to peep out from behind the door to see what was going on and when I did, your son had a gun aimed at Shameika that looked more real than the one my husband threatened to shoot me with before I left his evil ass for good. I eased the door closed and dialed the police. I was trying to whisper but your son must've heard me because the next thing I know, he bust in here and pressed that gun to my head. Lord, I was scared to death. I was barely able to walk as he marched me out and lined me up along with Shameika and some poor customer who'd come in to pay for gas."

The telling of what Marcus had done, especially to a woman who would've gladly given him the shirt off her back, brought more tears to Emma's eyes. He'd terrified three innocent people—her Marcus, her baby.

Jessie Lee went on like she was talking more to herself than to Emma, "I've been held up before in this store, but never by somebody like that. He had the strangest look on his face, like he felt really awful for us, but he had no choice. What really got me scared, though, was how he acted once he got us out from behind the counter. I figured he'd smash open the register, grab the cash, and run, especially since we could already hear sirens closing in, but instead he acted like he had all the time in the world. And when he aimed that gun at me again and asked me if I'd called the cops, my blood ran cold. I knew as sure as I'm sitting here that he was going to kill all three of us so he wouldn't leave no witnesses."

She paused and took a deep, steadying breath. "I was too scared to speak. I tried to work my mouth, but I couldn't say nary a word. He asked me again, talking to me real calm like, and that scared me even more. I figured that if I admitted I'd called the cops, I'd be signing our death warrants. I couldn't come up with a good lie off the top of my head though.

"'You did, didn't you?' That's what he said. He could tell I had. I reckon it showed on my face. I was about to start begging him to spare us when the cop drove up." Jessie Lee's lips began to tremble, and she looked at the ceiling as if pleading for strength from above.

"Please," Emma said, "I know it's hard, but please go on."

"I'll never forget it as long as I live," Jessie Lee continued in a strained voice. "He went outside like that cop wasn't nothing but a taxi driver who he'd called to take him somewhere. At first, he was holding that pistol like this—" She demonstrated by loosely curling her right hand and letting it dangle at her side. "But when the cop started hollering at him to drop it and put his hands in the air, your boy aimed at him just as calm as you please. That's when the cop shot him. I'm sorry, honey, but your boy left him no choice. That cop had no more way of knowing that gun wasn't real than I did. By the time we found out, it was too late." She wiped her eyes. "I'm sorry."

Emma squeezed her hand gently. "No, I'm the one who ought to apologize to you. If only I'd done so many things differently, none of this would've happened." Her failures were like stones carelessly tossed into a pond, causing ripples of tragedy to form and spread outward and harming everyone in their wake.

What had been her first failure? What was the first sign she'd missed that things were starting to go horribly wrong? Marcus's first day in high school. He'd been fine up until then, but he came home that day quieter than usual. She remembered him going straight to his room and not coming down until she called him for dinner. Though she served fried chicken, collards, and macaroni and cheese—one of his favorite meals—he picked at it like the thought of eating turned his stomach.

When she asked what was the matter, he said everyone at school was mean and stupid, he didn't fit in there, and he wanted to transfer. She brushed him off and told him he'd better get used to going to Waverton High because he wasn't transferring anywhere, and that was that. He was only being a moody teenager, she reasoned. He'd be back to himself by the next day. But he wasn't. He never was.

"I don't know you from Adam and Eve's house cat," Jessie Lee said, breaking into Emma's thoughts, "so I can't say for sure whether you're right or wrong about that, but I got a feeling you wrong. I can't think of nothing you could've done to give your son an excuse to scare the living daylights out of us and make like he was going to shoot that poor young cop."

But Emma could think of many things. If only she had another chance. If only. Those words tormented her.

"Thank you," she said to Jessie Lee. "I know it wasn't easy talking about this, especially to me. I can't tell you how much I appreciate it. I wish there was a way I could make up for what you've been through."

"Just ask the good Lord to keep his hand of protection over me."

"I will," Emma promised as warm tears spilled down her cheeks. "I surely will."

While stopped at a red light on the way home from the Seven-Eleven, Emma gazed at an interstate highway on the distant, hazy horizon. She was tempted to get on the highway and never turn back. Every mile marker could put her that much further from those who her love for had trapped her in a suffocating lie. She could also escape from Creighton Jones, all those awful reporters, and the swarms of other people who were searching for embers to re-ignite the city's smoldering racial tensions. She could start a new life where no one knew her. She could . . . She sighed. She couldn't do a damned thing except go home. Her car had less than a half tank of gas, and she had a grand total of eight dollars and twenty-five cents in her purse. Besides, her problems weren't the kind that she could run from, even if she fled to the ends of the earth.

A horn blared from behind, making her realize the light had turned green.

"Sorry," she murmured and drove home.

While parking her car beside Otis' truck, she felt like a jumble of raw nerves. Once inside the house, she either had to continue her sickening charade or tell everyone the truth. Both seemed impossible. She rubbed her throbbing temples. That Creighton Jones' limo and cars and vans from various news organizations were gone gave her little comfort. Jones and the reporters weren't the ones she most dreaded facing. She got out of the car and walked toward the front door. In her gloom, it took her a moment to realize that Dottie was calling out to her.

"Oh, hey," Emma replied, shielding her eyes from the sun's blinding glare to look across the yard at her best friend.

Dottie was stretched out in the recliner on her cluttered porch with her puffy feet—which swelled whenever she stood for a long time—propped up on the recliner's footrest. "Where'd you get off to?" she asked. "You missed being in the pictures we made with Rev. Jones before him and his people left for their hotel."

"Yeah, well, I had to . . . uh . . . I had to go somewhere."

Dottie put the recliner in its upright position. "You okay?"

Emma couldn't summon enough strength to lie. "No," she said miserably, "and I don't expect I ever will be either."

"What's the matter? I'm not talking about Marcus's dying. Something else has happened. I can see it on your face."

A wilted, straggly bed of impatiens, begonias, coleus, hostas, and Johnny-jump-ups started swimming in front of Emma. *Quit crying. Quit crying.* "All my plants are about dead," she said, breaking into sobs. She couldn't take the weight of her problems any more. She braced herself against a gnarly magnolia to keep from sinking to the parched ground.

With more speed than seemed possible for her, Dottie hobbled over. "Bless your heart," she murmured and pulled Emma close. "What happened?"

"It's all my fault," Emma managed to say between sobs.

"What is?"

"Everything."

Dottie drew back, gripping her with surprising strength. "You've been holding back something ever since Marcus got killed. Now tell me what's going on."

"I can't," Emma said in a choked voice.

"Yes, you can. After everything we've been through together, you can tell me anything."

"Not this."

"Ain't nothing you could do or say that could turn me against you. Don't you know that by now?"

"It's too late."

"Too late for what?"

"To do what I should've done."

"What are you talking about?"

Emma shook her head. She'd said too much already.

"We going inside my house," Dottie told her firmly, "and we're going to get to the bottom of this for once and for all."

"No, I—" Emma tried to pull away, but Dottie strengthened her grip on her and for the second time that afternoon, Emma found herself being led like a child who easily got lost.

* * *

"All right," Dottie said after sitting down beside her at the dinette table. "Tell me what's going on."

Emma buried her face in her hands. "I can't. I promised."

"Who?"

Dropping her hands from her wet face, Emma said, "Marcus."

"You think he'd hold you to a promise that's tearing you up so?"

"It's not him, it's me."

"Good God, you're talking in circles," Dottie said, revealing her growing frustration.

"I'm sorry. I should go." Emma started to rise from her chair, but Dottie forced her to sit back down.

"You believe Marcus getting killed is your fault—that much I've figured out." She looked at Emma with such intensity that Emma felt like her friend could see into the darkest layers of her soul.

"He wanted something that cost a lot of money that he didn't want you to tell nobody about," Dottie said slowly, obviously piecing together a theory, "and you wouldn't buy it for him and that's why he killed himself holding up that store. Don't blame yourself for that! You can't cave in and buy whatever fool thing he wanted!"

"He didn't want money, he wanted to die!" The words had escaped from Emma's mouth before she could stop them.

Dottie fell back in her chair. "What?"

Guilt, grief, despair, and the entire story of what happened from the time Emma found the note to what she learned from talking to Jessie Lee burst from her like a torrent breaking its way through a levy.

"Lord have mercy," Dottie said with a heavy sigh when Emma finished. "I knew you been going through hell, but I had no idea it was anything like this."

Emma wiped her eyes that had become swollen and sore from weeping. "If only I had chance to do things over."

"You got to stop blaming yourself," Dottie said gently. "Short of getting hold of a crystal ball, ain't no way you could've seen this coming. Nobody else had, including me, and I saw Marcus nearly every day of his life."

"Not the way I did. I should've known. He gave one warning sign after another, but I just kept turning a blind eye to them."

"Couldn't have been too many of them if none of the rest of us saw them either. For heaven's sakes, Emma, if every kid who's acted like Marcus got put in an asylum, there wouldn't be a child walking the streets. They're all kind of crazy at that age. So were we. When I was fourteen, this boy quit me for another girl and I didn't want to live anymore. Had my plan to kill myself worked out, I wouldn't have either. But it didn't, and before long, I realized how foolish the whole thing was. The same would've happened to Marcus too, if everything he planned hadn't gone so goddamned right."

Emma didn't know whether Dottie was blaming Marcus for devising such an effective scheme or God for allowing it to work. It didn't matter. Neither was at fault—she was.

For a few moments, the only sound in the kitchen was the ticking of a wall clock until Dottie spoke again. "You going to tell Otis what that clerk told you?"

"What good would it do?" Emma said, rubbing her temples that throbbed at a steady rhythm. "You heard what he said to that reporter. He'd only say she's in cahoots with the police. There's no talking sense to him when it comes to Marcus. He's made up his mind—he wants to make somebody pay, it doesn't matter who they are or whether they had anything to do with what happened to Marcus. It's like he's got hate pumping through his veins."

Pausing, she gazed aimlessly at a blue jay perching itself outside on the sill of Dottie's kitchen window. One of the things that had first attracted her to Otis had been his easy-going nature and ability to find the best in even the worst situations. But that was the Otis before Marcus's death. A stranger had taken his place.

She was not only in mourning for her son, but for how her husband used to be—how she and he used to be together. The change was as unexpected and merciless as Marcus dying. They weren't two people who were so close as to almost be one anymore, what he made her swear never to discuss again had created a distance between them wider than a country mile.

Turning back to Dottie, she said, "He acts like I never showed him that note, like we never talked in Marcus's room. I've gotten to where sometimes I wonder if it all really happened or if I only imagined it, then I think about how mad he is all the time, and I know it happened."

"He's taking this hard for sure," Dottie said in glum agreement. "Maybe it's best not to bring it up with him, at least not now."

"There may never be a right time. In the meanwhile, him and the kids are digging themselves deeper and deeper into this story about that policeman killing Marcus because he was black, and by not saying nothing, I'm helping them ruin an innocent man when he wasn't doing nothing but protecting himself. I can't live with that, but I also can't live with what would happen if I told everyone the truth." She paused again, this time to try to steady herself. "You know the kinds of things they say about people who kill themselves. They'd say Marcus was crazy, that he was a nut case. They'd turn everything about him into a pitiful joke. I can't let them do that to him. Don't you see?" She burst into tears again.

"'Course, I do," Dottie said, rising from her seat and pulling Emma close.

"It would kill Otis, kill him dead. And the kids . . ." Emma sobbed harder.

Dottie held her tightly. "Shhhh . . . hush now. It's going to be all right."

No, it won't, Emma thought as she cried against Dottie's doughy bosom. Nothing was ever going to be all right again. The thought of her despair stretching into eternity made her wish she could stop existing, not die exactly, just not be.

"Listen to me," Dottie said and patted Emma. "The way I figure, you don't have to do nothing. That investigation is going to clear that cop no matter what Creighton Jones says because either he's telling stories or somebody's telling stories to him. So let him and whosoever else keep on about how Marcus was really surrendering. They won't be hurting nobody, and that may be the only way Otis and the kids can deal with what happened to Marcus."

"But they're accusing an innocent man!"

"I hate to say this, sugar, but the only folks who'll keep believing them are the ones who don't count. Everybody else will get tired of it and move on to the next big story. How many people you hear talking about Rodney King anymore?"

"Still, that poor young policeman. I feel horrible for him. He must be going through pure hell now."

"Don't be too sure about that. I'll bet you he ain't lost a minute's sleep over this."

"How in the world can you say that? You don't know him."

"No, but if I'm recollecting right, his daddy's the same Russell Carter who killed that black fellow who was going with Sen. McKenna's wife, and the apple don't fall far from the tree. I wouldn't be surprised if the two of them are sitting around laughing and joking about how they both killed themselves a nigger."

Emma felt like she'd been splashed with ice water. When she first heard the name Russell Carter, she thought it sounded vaguely familiar, yet she couldn't figure out why. Now she could. Too many years had passed for her to remember all the details from the sensational case, but there was one she'd never forget—Russell Carter, Sr. had gotten away with cold-blooded murder.

"Don't you fret over that fellow who shot Marcus," Dottie went on. "He was probably raised up to use black kids for target practice, so killing one won't mean nothing to him. You keep your mind set on your family. They who you need to be worrying about."

* * *

And as Emma sat with her family during Marcus's eulogy, she was worried about them. Getting revenge had become their shared obsession, one that they were almost drunk with. They didn't seem to really come alive unless they were talking about how to get back at the police for killing Marcus, and Creighton Jones' arrival was enough to make them think anything was possible. They went on and on about what should be their next move. She heard them carrying on until the early hours of that morning while she lay upstairs in bed, wide-awake and wishing she could tune out their excited voices as easily as they brushed aside her warnings that anger was more corrosive to its bearer than battery acid. They had no use for her talk about letting the Lord sort things out. That was for them to do.

It was strange not to be part of what had become the most important thing to them. While they united behind their single purpose, she stood alone, feeling like an outsider within her own family. To be honest, she suffered with more than a few flashes of jealousy to see Otis taking such a central role in the kids' lives after all the years he yielded nearly everything having to do with them to her. Marcus's death had thrown everything in her world out of order. It was a wonder the laws of gravity still held. What sense did it make for a mother to have to bury her fifteen-year-old child?

There he was though, in front of her, in that gleaming white casket topped with roses that were as beautiful as they were scentless. Soon, his body would be beneath the dark earth. She'd never see him again, hear his voice or feel his touch. Ever.

His high school yearbook photo had been blown up to poster-size, placed in a heavy, fancy gold frame, and mounted on a tripod set next to his casket. He'd hated that picture, complained that it made him look cross-eyed and to make matters worse, he hadn't known until it was too late that he had a piece of lint on his sweatshirt. She agreed with him that it wasn't his best photo, but she bought it anyway. It was the last time he was photographed. He'd be forever frozen in a picture he hated.

CHAPTER 8

Lying in his bed, Rusty watched the first rays of dawn give his bedroom window a faint golden glow. He heard someone stirring around in his parents' bedroom. He guessed it was his mother. Apparently sleep had deserted her early as well.

He turned his back on the dawn while it made its presence known. Another day to endure. The thought of getting through it without completely going nuts seemed like having to scale a cliff wall. He wondered if he ought to see a shrink. But what if the SBLE agents somehow found out about it and used it against him? They'd say he was unstable, couldn't be trusted, shouldn't ever be allowed to return to the force. No, he couldn't take the chance. He had to tough it out. He had to believe it would be over with soon. Reporters would quit hounding him. The death threats would stop. Life would get back to normal. Hadn't Scott and Josh come by yesterday to say that Creighton Jones was blowing smoke with his talk of there being people claiming that Jennings was surrendering? Hadn't they said that the area around the 7-Eleven had been thoroughly canvassed and the only new witnesses who had been found—two men across the street at a car title loan office—said the exact same thing as the three people inside the Seven-Eleven? Hadn't Scott and Josh reassured him once again that he'd be cleared?

But watching the heart-wrenching scenes of Marcus Jennings' funeral and burial on the TV news yesterday overpowered those reassuring words. The worst part of it was seeing the close-ups of Jennings' parents. The father was attempting to be stoic, but it was obvious that he was barely holding it together. The mother was grief personified. She collapsed during the burial and had it not been for two men on either side of her—they looked to be her older sons—she probably would've tumbled into the grave meant for her youngest child. It was a horrible thing to watch, yet Rusty couldn't tear himself away from it.

They'd be forever linked—he and the Jenningses—though they'd never really met and most likely never would. He wished he could go to them and tell them how badly he felt. What good would it do though? He was the last person they'd want to see, and he could apologize from now until Kingdom come and it wouldn't bring Marcus back to them. There was nothing to do but go forward, but he didn't know how. Just thinking about holstering his Sig Sauer was enough to break him out in a cold sweat. How good a cop would he be even if he were allowed back on the force? Would he freeze every time he had to respond to a call? Shit, maybe he shouldn't bother going back no matter how the investigation turned out. What could he do instead though? Do construction? Drive trucks? Wait tables? The only thing he had ever wanted to be was a cop.

What Scott said earlier came back to him—Take one day at a time. He had to find a way to make this one productive. Sitting around and dwelling on his problems sure wasn't doing any good and might even lead to him freaking out again.

The best plan of action seemed to be staying as busy as possible—to keep his mind off things. He'd do some work around the house. Yeah, that would be good. The mill house was nearly ninety years old, and despite the continuous maintenance his dad did on it, there still must be windows needing re-caulking, trim needing re-painting, or some such other work.

Maybe he could get his dad to help him. The man was

spending way too much time poring over the newspaper or glued to the TV to catch the latest about Jennings' death and the fallout from it. Every news story added another splash of fuel to his fury over what happened after he killed Hugh Jefferson. It was like the shooting happened yesterday, not eight years ago. He sat clutching a can of Bud grousing to anyone who'd listen about what a shitty deal he'd gotten, how niggers got everything handed to them on a silver platter, how whites had no rights anymore. He went on and on. He was making everybody crazy, Rusty especially. Yeah, getting him to lend a hand to do work around the house would help everyone.

He heard his mother's light footsteps go past his room. The poor woman was a nervous wreck. She'd gotten so frazzled while cooking dinner the other night that she glazed a ham with dish detergent instead of orange juice. Earlier that day she put a load of wet laundry in the stove instead of the dryer. When he found a remote control in the refrigerator, he knew she'd left it there, but he didn't say anything to her about it. It would only upset her more. As it was, saying "Hello" to her the wrong way was enough to make her burst into tears. She'd honed suffering almost to an art form, but even she had her limits and he worried that his problems, which had become hers, were pushing her over the edge.

The sound of running water came from the kitchen along with dull clinking. Moments later, he caught the aroma of freshly brewed coffee. It would take a lot more than that to wake his father from his beer-induced slumber. How many cans a day was he up to? Rusty had lost count.

He slowly sat up. The sleeping pills from the drug store left him groggy and dry-mouthed. He needed a shower and coffee. Lots and lots of coffee.

With the heart-of-pine floor cool beneath his bare feet, he walked to the bathroom across the hallway and glanced at the mirror. *Murderer.*

"Shut up," he ordered himself. He turned the shower on full blast and stepped into it. The hard spray felt like tiny needles pricking his flesh, but thankfully they drove away thoughts of Marcus Jennings. With focused concentration, he shampooed his hair and scrubbed his body under the relentless spray and when he emerged from the shower, he felt close to normal.

Returning to his room, he found it full of morning sunlight. He looked out the window—not a cloud in the sky. The day was bound to stretch the record for continuous days of the temperature hitting triple digits. Fall couldn't come soon enough.

He pulled on a pair of jeans and a T-shirt and was about to run a comb through his wet hair when he heard his mother shriek, "Oh my God!" A spark of dread flared inside him. *Damn, what's happened now?* He opened the door and called out, "What's the matter?"

She only answered in a low groan.

He rushed down the hallway and found her standing near the front door with a newspaper in her hands. She looked up from the paper with her thin, pinched face completely drained of color. "I'm sorry, honey," she said to him. "I'm so sorry."

The spark of dread in him burst into a raging fire. "For what?"

She clutched the newspaper against her chest for a moment before extending it toward him with a weary sigh. "No use trying to hide it from you. You'll see this sooner or later."

The first thing on the newspaper's front page that caught his attention was a photograph of his father in his police uniform next to grainy snapshots of two other men in 1950's-era clothing. His recognition of them buckled his knees. He sank to the couch and stared at the paper's headline and its subtitle in complete disbelief. He blinked in hopes that his eyes were playing tricks on him, but the words in bold print remained the same: OFFICER AT CENTER OF CONTROVERSY FROM FAMILY WITH NOTORIOUS PAST—Father remains under cloud of suspicion for killing black suspect eight years ago. Grandfather and great-grandfather were in the Klan.

"Goddamn," Rusty said in a voice barely above a whisper. There it was—the ugliest, most shameful parts of his family's history for everyone to see. And to judge him by. He had braced himself for the possibility that reporters would figure out that of the four Russell Carters in the city's phone directory, he was the son of the one who killed Hugh Jefferson. But how in the hell had they discovered that he was related to Halsey and Virgil Carter? Even at the height of the media feeding frenzy over the investigation into Hugh Jefferson's shooting death, nothing about the men ever surfaced. For that matter, no attention had been paid to any of Russ Carter's relatives.

Deep breaths – take deep breaths. Rusty slumped against the couch. The chance of anyone outside of family and close friends connecting him to his dad's father and grandfather was supposed to have been almost as remote as anyone knowing that the men had been in the Klan. According to what Rusty had been told, both were so secretive about their Klan activities that not even their wives knew many of the details.

He stared numbly at the newspaper. Obviously, his grandfather and great-grandfather hadn't been secretive enough.

His mother sat beside him. "I can't bear to read the rest of it. It's awful. They're twisting everything around to make it look like your daddy killed any colored men he caught with white women and that his daddy and granddaddy went around lynching coloreds right and left. It don't matter that none of it's true. All they care about is selling papers. They don't give a rat's rear end who they ruin in the process."

"How did they find out?" Rusty said while beginning to scan the article for the answer.

"No telling. Those people are so devious. There's nothing they won't stoop to. They're probably combing through files about all of us right now to find out who else in our family were in the Klan."

Rusty started pacing again. "Who else was? I can't remember."

"Most of the men on your daddy's side of the family joined from one generation to the next until about when your daddy came of age. You got to understand, honey, that the Klan wasn't all that bad until the mid-sixties when they let in a bunch of riffraff and things got out of hand. Up until then, it was a peaceful, God-fearing organization."

Rusty stopped pacing and stared through the front window. A peaceful, God-fearing organization. None of his kinsmen who had belonged to the Klan would lose a minute's sleep over killing Marcus Jennings, and it was getting forced from the police department that upset Rusty's father, not killing Hugh Jefferson. Not once had Rusty ever heard his dad utter anything close to regret for having taken the unarmed man's life. Coming from this lineage, Rusty felt like he ought to be able to shrug off killing Marcus Jennings, especially since the kid had forced him to do it. He had been forced, hadn't he? He hadn't had any way of knowing that Jennings's "gun" was only a plastic toy until it was too late, right?

The phone rang, causing him to flinch.

His mother appeared as undone by it as he was. "Who in the world could be calling at this time of the morning?"

It rang again.

"Let the answering machine get it," she advised.

The answering machine picked up on the fifth ring. "Hi," a voice that had been captured many times on the answering machine rang out. "Lynn Newbanks with Channel Four News again. Sorry for calling so early—"

"You're not sorry, you lying she-devil," Doris Carter yelled as if the reporter could hear her.

"But I'm still trying to connect with Officer Rusty Carter," the reporter went on breezily. "I need to talk to him about the Jennings case as well as to get his reaction to the story in today's paper about his family. Please have him call me here at the station as soon as possible." She rattled off her office number like she hadn't already left it at least a half-dozen times.

Rusty hit the "erase" button.

"For pity's sake," his mother said, "when will this be over?"

Will it ever be? Rusty was tempted to add, however, his mom couldn't handle that possibility. Neither could he.

As if in defiance of both of them, the phone rang once more until the answering machine picked up.

"You ain't gettin' away with this, Carter," a muffled baritone voice rumbled from the answering machine. "I gotta bullet with your name on it. . . ."

"Goddamn it!" Rusty said as he yanked the telephone cord from its receptacle. He was nearly as angry at his father as he was at the caller. If Russ Carter had let Rusty change their phone number to an unlisted one, they wouldn't be getting such nerve-rattling calls, but Russ firmly believed such a move amounted to caving in to their enemies. He also insisted that it wouldn't do any good; that people would eventually find out what the unlisted phone number was.

Maybe he was right. With how technology was, it seemed like anything was possible—except how to identify who was making the death threats. So far, tracing the calls had only led to dead ends.

A bleary-eyed Russ Carter appeared in the doorway. "What the hell are y'all yakking about? Between y'all and that phone, I can't get back to sleep."

"Sit down, honey," Doris said. "I got bad news to tell you."

Russ looked guardedly from her to Rusty then back to her. "Ain't we got enough as it is?"

"Yeah, but here's plenty more," Rusty said, handing the newspaper to him. At first, his father stared at the paper blankly, then his expression turned to shock, then to fury. He flung down the paper, grabbed a table lamp and smashed it against a wall. "Goddamn motherfuckers!"

"Russ!" Doris wailed just as the phone shrilled again.

With his heart pounding in his ears and the room shrinking in on him like melting plastic, Rusty snatched up the receiver and screamed into it, "Leave us alone!" He threw the receiver on the floor amidst the shards of the ginger jar lamp and bolted in the kitchen and yanked his truck keys from off the key rack.

His mother ran behind him. "Where are you going?"

Clawing at the neck of his T-shirt, Rusty gasped, "I can't breathe."

"What?" Doris Carter shrieked. "What's wrong with you?"

With what felt like his last breath, Rusty dashed for the front door.

"Come back here, boy!" his father yelled, but it was too late. Rusty had already fled outside.

He rode with his truck windows down, gulping in the morning air. Within the past week, the only times he'd left his home were in sheer terror. He had to stop it. He had to get a grip on himself. If only he could see the attacks coming—like twisters churning toward him—at least he could brace himself. Instead, only an instant separated the times he felt perfectly fine from the ones when it seemed he was snatched up by a power beyond his control.

Panic disorder—that was the name for what he had. He learned it by going onto the Internet and clicking on various websites. "A sudden surge of overwhelming fear that comes without warning and without any obvious reason," was how one website described what struck him. "Unexpected and repeated episodes of intense fear accompanied by physical symptoms that may include chest pain, heart palpitations, shortness of breath, dizziness . . ." said another website. Yeah, that fit him to a T. He was officially crazy.

According to what he read, between one to two percent of all Americans suffered with the disorder at some point in their lives. He supposed he should take comfort in knowing there were others in his same predicament, but why couldn't he have been in the other ninety-eight to ninety-nine percent?

Reading that many researchers believed there was a genetic component made him think about both sides of his family. He couldn't remember anyone on either side having panic attacks, but as that day's paper revealed, there was a lot about his family that he'd forgotten or never knew about.

How deeply had the newspaper dug into their history? He'd only skimmed over the beginning of the article and had been too rattled for any of the words to make sense. It had been like trying to read Greek.

He spotted a gas station with coin-operated newspaper stands and debated whether to stop and buy a paper. He felt calm enough now, but another twister could snatch him up within the blink of an eye depending on what was in that article. On the other hand, he needed to know how much reporters had discovered.

He pulled over, found some coins from the console bin, and got out of the truck, realizing for the first time that he'd fled from the house barefoot. It took a moment for him to gather enough courage to approach a battered stand with the headlines blaring at him from behind scuffed Plexiglass. He quickly bought the paper, folding it inward so its headlines wouldn't show, and returned to the truck.

While climbing in, an old Mercury Cougar slowed to a stop in the parking space beside him. Its windows were tinted so darkly that Rusty couldn't make out any of the features of the driver. Holy shit, what if it was the guy who called to say he had a bullet with Rusty's name on it? Had he followed Rusty from the house and was about to gun him down now?

The keys to Rusty's truck slipped from his sweat-slickened fingers. "Shit!" he said, ducking to pick them up. When he raised his head, he caught sight of a skinny young white girl getting out of the Cougar and pulling her greasy, strawberry blond hair into a pony tail before she headed for the convenience store.

Rusty collapsed with relief against his truck seat. For the zillionth time that morning, he told himself that he needed to get a grip. He had to start ignoring the calls coming to the house. The threats were empty ones from someone just trying to rattle his chain, and if he kept refusing to return any reporters' phone calls, they'd eventually give up.

"Hang tough, Carter," he muttered.

The folded newspaper lay in his lap. Damn, was he up to reading it? Maybe he ought to wait a while. No, might as well get it over with.

The article spilled from the front page to the fifth and sixth. It opened with an introduction of the three

Carters who were the focus of the in-depth exposé, then it portrayed Russ Carter as a racist cop from his first year on the force when he'd been heard using racial slurs with black suspects to when he killed Hugh Jefferson under suspicious circumstances. It insinuated from one paragraph to the next how the story he and Blair McKenna swore to didn't add up. How Jefferson had been a well-respected man who hadn't so much as received a parking ticket before Russ Carter shot and killed him. How a cook at the McKenna estate let it slip that she'd caught Blair McKenna coming on to Jefferson after he'd been hired to repaint the guest house. How he hadn't been the first black man rumored to have been trapped into trysts with the bored socialite.

It all added chilling effect to the inclusion of an interview with a black school principal who had vivid memories of the harassment he endured before Sgt. Russ Carter apparently realized the woman in the principal's car was a light-skinned black woman, not a white one.

After leaving little doubts about the intensity of Sgt. Carter's hatred of blacks, the article turned its focus to his father and grandfather. Archived SBLE files had been mined to reveal Halsey and Virgil Carter's transformation from hardscrabble mill workers by day to white-robed Klansmen at night. Clearly, neither man realized that at least one of the people they routinely gathered with inside a weather-beaten tobacco barn for Klan meetings was a SBLE informant who reported how the elder and younger Carter participated in terrorizing "uppity" blacks through cross burnings, vandalism, and anonymous death threats.

The article ended with a summary of two basic facts—the Carters had a family tradition steeped in racial hatred; Rusty was a Carter. No one needed to be a rocket scientist to understand what that meant.

Rusty buried his face in his hands. It was cold comfort that the newspaper obviously hadn't discovered that others in his family had been in the Klan. That would be the next shoe to drop.

A thought flashed through his mind of running away to where no one knew anything about him or his family.

Allowing the daydream to play out, he saw himself making a new start with a new identity. He had shed the name "Carter" like a dirty old shirt and traveled with nothing except what fit in his truck. Complete freedom.

He let out a heavy sigh. He couldn't go anywhere. He was trapped like a rat in a cage.

Another car pulled into the gas station and a garbage truck rumbled down the street. The city was waking. Rusty checked the time. Another hour or so and the morning traffic rush would be in full swing. It seemed a lifetime ago that he was among those who had to be somewhere at a specific time.

He threaded his fingers through his still damp hair. He didn't feel steady enough yet to return home and deal with his parents and the unrelenting phone calls. Driving around some more might help settle his nerves. Maybe over to the high school track field to watch the morning walkers. Maybe down by the river where he and Scott had been during the rioting. Anywhere but home.

He ended up where he least expected, yet somehow it felt right. The grounds stretched out ahead of him for acres. Except for occasional birdsong, it was quiet, so quiet it seemed impossible to still be within city limits.

A mild breeze stirred. It carried a faint though somewhat familiar fragrance. What was it? He took in a deep breath. Honeysuckle. Yes, it was growing somewhere nearby. He'd always loved the smell of the wild vine. It brought back memories of summer days when he was a kid and the world was a much simpler place.

Veering from the pathway, he stepped onto the grass that the heat wave had baked to a dull khaki tone. Unnaturally bright bouquets of flowers contrasted against the parched grass; then again, what the flowers were made of defied even the hottest temperatures. They decorated each of the graves in the sprawling cemetery.

It struck Rusty that the saying about death being the great equalizer was indeed true, for the graves were nearly identical to each other. Most of them were decorated only with the silk flowers and inscribed markers. There was no way to tell whether the person lying beneath them had been rich or poor, black or white.

The graves were a study of monotony. Only the newest one—with its small forest of elaborate flower arrangements partially covered by a canopy stenciled with the name of the city's most prominent black funeral home—stood out. Rusty was drawn toward it like a lost traveler to a road sign that pointed the way home.

Once he was close to the flower arrangements standing sentinel on metal tripods near the grave, Rusty saw the heat had ruined them. They were badly wilted, and their fragrance spoke of their decay. Florist foam and wiring held them in place, though, in shapes ranging from wreaths to oversized crosses. One was even shaped like a lyre. It had a white sash draped over it with gold lettering that said: Marcus—You'll Be Forever Remembered, Forever Loved.

A short distance away, sections of faded sod dusted with dirt outlined where the earth had been disturbed to receive Marcus Jennings' body. No headstone or marker had materialized yet. Only the white sash and the inscriptions on the cards attached to the pitiful floral arrangements identified who was buried there.

Rusty lowered himself onto the ground. He was no closer to knowing for sure why Marcus Jennings aimed a toy gun at him than when he'd killed the fifteen-year-old nearly a week ago. He had his theories—the one about Jennings deciding to die rather than be taken into custody made the most sense—they remained just theories, though, not solid answers.

While running a hand over the sod that was so dry that it crumbled beneath his touch, he wondered if he'd ever find out the truth. Perhaps the most he could hope for was to be cleared of any wrongdoing and to try to put his life back together.

Nothing would ever be the same. That much he

already knew. Not a day would go by that he wouldn't think about the teenager. Even if it were only for a moment, it would be enough to cast a shadow over him. And no matter what else he did, he'd always be remembered as the cop who killed Marcus Jennings. Any time someone wanted to dig up information about the killing to throw in his face, they could. What happened to his father was proof of that.

If he ever became a father, he'd do everything possible to steer his child away from becoming a cop. He didn't want talk about what he or his father did while on the force to cling to his son or daughter like a bad stench. Worse yet would be if they were forced to kill like he had.

Taking in a deep breath and absorbing the stillness surrounding him, he realized there was no sense tying himself in knots about a hypothetical situation that had only the remotest chances of becoming reality. He had enough real problems to deal with.

He propped his cheek against the palm of his hand and studied the freshly-laid rectangle of limp centipede. He supposed that if he were a character in a movie, this would be the time to launch into a dramatic soliloquy like Marcus could hear him. In the heart rendering scene, he'd tell Marcus how horrible he felt about what led both of them to the cemetery, then there would probably be a wide-angled, overhead shot of him amidst the sea of graves to highlight his sorry state. But it wasn't a movie, and there was nothing to do except sit in silence.

Hours later, he was still rooted to the same spot. He was thirsty, sunburned, and his clothes were damp with sweat, yet in a way that he didn't understand, there was something comforting about being near the person whose death was reshaping his life in so many ways. He wiped sweat from his forehead and noticed with dismay that he didn't have the grounds to himself anymore. Someone was walking up the pathway.

Rusty squinted into the distance to see the person

more clearly. It was a woman, a black woman. She stopped for a moment as if unsure whether to move forward before she resumed a slow but steady pace. Right in his direction.

Scrambling to his feet, he gaped as her features became more distinct. When he realized who she was, a fresh wave of guilt nearly knocked him back to the ground. He had no right to be there, to intrude on this sacred place after the agony he'd already caused her and her family. He wished the earth would open and swallow him whole, however, it remained firm beneath him, forcing him to consider through rising panic how he could get away before she recognized him, if she hadn't already.

He took off in the opposite direction with his heart racing. With each quick step, he silently cursed how big the cemetery was and how it had been clear-cut to make way for its eternal inhabitants. He was as exposed as a criminal caught in the beam of a searchlight. Over the thudding of his heart, he listened for her to come running up behind him so she could grab him, whirl him around and scream at him or hit him. He quickly weighed his options to reach his truck—he could either make a wide arc around her within the grounds or he could duck into a swath of forest bordering the cemetery and tromp through it to get to the frontage road leading to where he'd parked.

He headed for the forest with the desperate hope that its denseness would keep her from following him into it. Damned it, though, the forest seemed further away than the next state. He broke into a run, accepting that it was more evidence of his guilt.

By the time he reached the edge of the woods, his lungs burned and sweat poured from him. He dashed into the thick growth, tripped over a rotting log, and landed in a heap on the ground that filled his mouth and nostrils with dust. Wincing, he turned over and peered through the brush. Emma Jennings stood on the pathway not far from where he'd first spotted her, shielding her eyes from the sun and looking in his direction. She'd seen his every move—he was sure of it.

CHAPTER 9

Standing on the pathway that wound its way to where her son was buried, Emma searched for any sign of the young cop, but he'd disappeared into the woods like he'd been only a figment of her imagination. Before catching sight of him sitting cross-legged at the grave like he was keeping vigil over it, she'd almost convinced herself that what Dottie said about him was true. Emma had managed to create images of him joshing with his dad while they swapped stories of the fun they had while gunning down black men. Reading the paper that morning added more details to those images. It was hard to picture anyone from such a family giving a second thought to killing a black person, yet clearly, it troubled Russell "Rusty" Carter, Jr., and that weighed down her heart with more guilt.

If she had spent as much time tending to her son as she had her yard, neither she, Marcus, nor the young cop would have reason to be at the cemetery. There'd be nothing about either of their families to attract reporters' attention. The riot never would've happened. Dozens of people wouldn't have been injured. The city wouldn't be the national poster child for rotten race relations.. . . There was no end to the chain reaction of destruction her mistakes had sparked. Of course, its most tragic victims were Marcus and Ofc. Russell "Rusty" Carter. She'd blinded herself to Marcus's suffering, and what was she doing about the rookie cop's? Making it worse with her silence. She'd turned him into her sacrificial lamb to protect Marcus's memory and to shield those she loved from the devastating truth. But what else could she do? For all the days and mercilessly endless nights that the question tormented her, she still didn't have an answer. The only thing that kept coming to her was the certainty that Ofc. Carter would be cleared. She prayed it would be enough to make him understand he wasn't to blame for what had happened, and she prayed it would be enough to put the ghosts of his family's past back to where they had been hidden. He didn't deserve to be haunted by them. He was no more at fault for what his father, grandfather, and great-grandfather had done any more than Marcus had been at fault for what she'd done.

Marcus. When she awakened from an uneasy sleep that morning, it took her several minutes to remember why she didn't hear him scuffling about in his room. The realization that he was dead ebbed and flowed like an unpredictable tide, hitting her when she least expected it. She caught herself listening for his voice, setting a plate for him at the kitchen table, expecting to find his room in its usual chaos, and wondering why she didn't see him sprawled on the couch watching TV or playing video games. She wished she could stay suspended in those moments instead of reality shattering them to bits. In each instance, it felt too much like she was hearing about his death for the first time.

She started toward the grave again with no memory of ever having been there before. Had it been as indistinctive as the others in the cemetery, she'd have no idea where to begin looking for it. Everything that happened from the end of Creighton Jones' eulogy until the next morning was a blur. It added to the unreality of things although she supposed it was God's way of protecting her from what she wasn't ready to take in. *The Lord never puts more on us than we can bear.* She desperately wanted to believe that.

Fighting back the urge to flee and never return, she forced herself on. Her child was there, buried beneath the earth, and she needed to be with him, to try to make sense of everything that happened. Maybe in the peace and quiet of this place, she could.

Her legs grew unsteady when she reached where he was buried. She hadn't been prepared to find it decorated only with dead flowers, deflated Mylar balloons, and dried-up grass. It was like no one had given a damn about him either in life or in death.

Even once the pitiful flowers and balloons were cleared away, the centipede revived, and the burial marker placed, his grave would look like the hundreds of others there. They were lined up in perfect uniformity like spaces in a Walmart parking lot. And those fake flowers stuck in each of them looked worse than the drooping ones on Marcus's plot. They reminded her of those strings of wildly colored plastic pennants flapping in the breeze at used car dealerships. Why people thought it right to assault the dead with such loud, tacky things, she didn't know, but she wouldn't stand for them to do it to her boy. Only real flowers would do for him. She'd bring fresh ones every day. Better yet, she'd plant something on his grave that would be a steady source of them. The lavender rosebush growing near her front porch steps—it had began as a cutting from the rosebush that used to perfume part of her grandmother's yard, and it had been one of the first things Emma planted after she and Otis bought their home. It was rugged as it was beautiful, faithfully bursting with clusters of blossoms that looked like small pastel-colored pompoms. Their scent had floated over a newborn Marcus when she carried him into the house for the first time. It was only fitting that they cover him now.

When she returned home, she grimaced at the sight of an unfamiliar late model Escalade parked in the driveway along with Otis's old F-150 and Stephanie's Civic. She was sick and tired of visitors coming by, even longtime friends and neighbors were grating on her nerves with their assumption that there was nothing more she wanted to do than listen to them talk about how badly they felt for her and her family. She did all the expected things—invited them in, offered them refreshments, made pleasant chit-chat, thanked them for their show of concern—but she worried that if they kept streaming in, she'd eventually explode like a bottle rocket.

"Lord Jesus, help me," she muttered and climbed out of her car. The lavender roses interrupted her journey into the house. She leaned over, cupped a cluster of the velvety blossoms and inhaled their fragrance that was sweet enough to be in heaven. Yes, they were exactly what Marcus deserved.

She went inside and found Otis and Stephanie in the living room with two young women. Emma didn't need to be introduced to them. She detected from their phony smiles, chic hairdos, expensive-looking business suits and handsome briefcases that they worked for Creighton Jones, and Otis and Stephanie's excited expressions telegraphed that the women had come to stir up more trouble.

"Momma, you remember Rev. Jones' assistants Denise Hollingsworth and Serena McMillan, don't you?" Stephanie said, motioning to the two women.

"Uh . . . " Emma said. Despite having correctly guessed their connection to Jones, she didn't remember ever having met them.

"They attended Marcus's funeral with Rev. Jones," Stephanie said helpfully.

"I'm sorry," Emma said to the assistants. "I'm still kind of in a daze."

"No need to apologize," Serena McMillan said. "I'm sure you've met so many people during the past week that it's hard to keep track of everybody."

"Yes, it's been a tough time," Emma said. Glancing from Otis to Stephanie, she added, "For all of us."

"We know," Denise Hollingsworth said. "That's why we've been working with your husband and daughter on plans to make sure the officer who killed your son is held accountable for what he did."

"Plans?" Emma said. "What kind of plans?"

"There'll be a press conference Tuesday to announce that we're having a big rally at the city arena next Saturday," Otis said.

"What!" Emma nearly shouted. A press conference? A big rally at the arena? She almost asked Otis to repeat himself to check she'd heard him right. He and Stephanie understood full well how she'd react to such news and yet they had plunged ahead anyway. Clearly, her feelings didn't mean squat to them anymore and of the two, Emma was angriest at Otis—he was chaining their family to what he knew was a lie.

"Don't you get started," he warned her and in response to Denise and Serena's puzzled glances, he said to them, "As you can see, my wife isn't exactly thrilled about this. She's not one to rock the boat—she'd rather us let SBLE handle this."

"But Mrs. Jennings," Serena said, "SBLE has a vested interest in helping the police department in its cover up. Both of them are part of the government."

"I've explained that to Momma over and over," Stephanie said in a tone that revealed her growing frustration with her mother.

"And I still say that y'all ain't doing anything but making a bad situation worse," Emma countered. "I wish y'all would listen to me."

"So that cop can get off for murdering Marcus?" Otis said. "No dice. I ain't letting that happen. He's not getting away with what he did."

Once again, images of Ofc. Rusty Carter sitting sentinel at her son's grave and then running away at the sight of her filled Emma's mind, and the thought of what he was going through agonized her. *I'm sorry, Rusty. Please forgive me.*

"Don't you worry, Mr. Jennings," Denise said. "He'll be punished severely, and by the time we get finished shaking up this city's police department, there won't be a racist officer left on it."

"Yeah, they've met their match in us," Stephanie chimed in. "I want the whole world to know it, too." She paused and pursed her lips the way she did when she was thinking hard about something. "Oooh, I've got a great idea—we ought to have the press conference right here at the house to show folks Marcus wasn't some thug from the projects. He came from a good home and he had a family who loved him."

She seemed to purposely ignore the sharp look Emma gave her.

"I like it," Denise said. "It would also be a great counterweight to the police trying to focus attention on Marcus holding up the store."

"He wasn't holding up no store," Otis said. "He was probably playing a joke or something and them people took it wrong."

The fashionable women's tight, patronizing smiles and their nodding along with Otis's nonsense like it was gospel made Emma want to slap them. She wished she had the nerve to tell them her husband was no fool. It was his pain talking, not him.

Stephanie frowned. "That's one thing that keeps bothering me and even though I've turned it inside out and every which way a zillion times, I still don't have a clue why he did such a crazy thing."

"He wasn't crazy!" Otis snapped at her.

"She didn't say he was," Emma said coldly as she put an arm around Stephanie, who was stunned by her father's harshness. "She only said what he did was crazy." Pulling Stephanie closer, she hated how Otis was acting, how she was acting. They were giving two strangers ringside seats to their worsening warfare with each other. That their open hostility seemed to be making Jones's aides uncomfortable provided only a little satisfaction.

After a stretch of awkward silence, Stephanie said, "All I'm saying is that it doesn't add up. As meek as Marcus was, there's no way he would've tried to rob any place, but he was also smart enough to realize how people would react if he went in that Seven-Eleven with a toy gun to play some sort of joke."

"There's no figuring out teenagers," Denise said. "I

speak from experience. I've got two of them and I can't make sense of hardly anything they say or do. In any case, no matter why Marcus held up the store, he was surrendering peacefully when Ofc. Russell Carter, Jr., shot him. That's all that counts."

"Right," Serena said, regaining her confident air. She turned to Emma and Otis. "We've got to stay on message about that as well as how Marcus's death has devastated your family. I know it won't be easy, but I'd like for both of you to talk about that during the press conference."

"I can't come," Emma blurted.

"Why the hell not?" Otis said at the same time as Stephanie asked, "What're you talking about?"

Denise said, "What could possibly be more important than this?"

"My job at the hospital," Emma answered. "It may not pay much, but it helps keep a roof over our heads, and I promised my boss lady when she called yesterday that I'd work a twelve-hour shift on Tuesday since they're so short-handed there." That was true—mostly. Her supervisor, Carol Tyler, had called yesterday, however, it was to find out how Emma was doing, not to pressure her into returning to work. And though it was also true that the hospital was short-staffed, it hadn't stopped Mrs. Tyler from offering Emma the option of using more paid leave if she needed it. Emma was glad she hadn't taken her up on it, and she planned to use her job as an excuse to skip the rally too.

"Surely they'd let you have a little more time off," Denise insisted.

Before Emma could say anything, Stephanie said, "Of course they will. Momma's just being silly. She knows good and well she can get off from the hospital if she wants to. She's been working there since the dawn of creation and she's probably got more leave time than she could ever use. She doesn't like being around reporters is all. Like Daddy said, she doesn't like rocking the boat. Fortunately, we do."

Oozing charm, Serena said, "Mrs. Jennings, believe me, if I were in your place, I'd probably feel the same way.

I can't imagine how stressful this has been for you, to be suddenly thrust into the limelight like this, but we really need you to be here. People get numbed to reports of police brutality, however when they hear a mother talking about the police murdering her child, it makes them sit up and take notice. It makes it personal for them."

"I could talk from now until the end of time and it won't bring my boy back," Emma said, aggravated that she was being forced to justify herself. "In the meantime, they're so short-handed at work they're having to run double-shifts."

"That's their problem," Otis said.

"It'll be ours if I get fired," Emma shot back. "What'll we do then? You think we're going to get paid for doing doggone press conferences?" She could tell that she'd stung him. She was determined, though, to get through to him that they were only being used.

"It's not going to come to that," Stephanie said. "If need be, Momma, you can switch shifts with Miss Peggy or Miss Verta Mae. They'd be more than happy to help you any way they can. They said as much when they stopped by last night with that platter of fried chicken."

"We wouldn't ask if it wasn't important," Serena said to Emma. "The other thing is that it would raise a lot of red flags if people discovered you were working while the rest of your family was here."

"Don't worry. She'll be here," Otis said. He glared at Emma. "I'll make sure of it."

Emma said nothing. She realized Otis was probably taking her silence as a sign of surrender, but she'd set him straight once Jones's assistants were out of the house. Standing up against him wasn't going to be easy. She hadn't done it enough to get used to it, especially when it involved something he had strong opinions about. No matter what he said, though, she wasn't going to be part of the press conference or the rally and there was nothing he, Stephanie, or anyone else could do about it.

"Well . . . um . . . " Stephanie stammered. She cleared her throat and started again. "I'm glad that's settled. Serena, Denise, I'll see you to your car."

"Thank you," Denise said too brightly. She flipped the end of an oblong silk scarf over her shoulder. "Good to meet with you again, Mr. and Mrs. Jennings. Although we've got some challenges ahead of us, I've no doubt we'll be able to overcome them."

"You got that right," Otis said, "and we're going to give them police hell, that's for damn sure."

Speak for yourself, Emma thought while studying a worn spot in the carpet.

"Mrs. Jennings, I can appreciate how your being the center of media attention goes against your grain," Serena said, "remember, though, that you might help prevent another family from experiencing the same tragedy you're going through."

If you only knew what the real tragedy was, Emma wanted to say. Instead, she only nodded. Neither she nor Otis said anything as they watched Denise and Serena follow Stephanie outside, but Emma felt the tension rising between her and her husband like heat off hot asphalt.

When the front door closed, he grabbed her by the arm. "You need to make up your mind whether you're for us or against us. Because if you're for us, you better fucking well start acting like it."

For a moment, she was too shocked to speak. In their decades of marriage, he'd never put a hand on her in anger or used such hateful language with her. "You're hurting me," was all she could think of to say.

"I. . .I didn't mean to," he said, immediately releasing her. He acted like he was coming out of a dark trance. "I'm sorry," he said softly and massaged where he'd grabbed her. "I'm sorry," he repeated.

"What's happening to us?"

"Nothing, baby, we're just going through a bad time."

"We can't even talk anymore."

"'Course we can. We talking now, ain't we?" He took her into his arms. "I know that it's been rough, but it won't last forever. We'll get through this. I promise." He gave her an awkward kiss that landed halfway on her nose.

She gazed at him for a moment. Her Otis. He seemed

to have come back to her. "Please call this protesting stuff off, honey. It'll only make things worse."

He stiffened. "Yeah, for the police and that's exactly what I want."

"They're not to blame and you know that."

"Don't you get started with that stupid shit again!"

She could see she'd lost him once more. She was talking to a stranger. Maybe, just maybe if she kept trying, she'd get through. "We're living a lie."

"You gave me your word that you'd never bring up that foolishness again."

"But—"

"Ain't no 'buts' about it. You gave me your word and I expect you to keep it. This had better be the last time I have to tell you that."

She turned away from him, not wanting him to see her eyes filling with tears. He was a stranger, yes, but the most intimate one there was. He knew exactly where to stab to hurt her the most.

"Like I said, Emma, you're either for us or against us. It's that simple."

She fixed her watery gaze on a robin that lighted on the clothes line in the backyard. It hopped a little bit farther down the line, then took flight again. She envied it. If only she could fly away like that.

Later that evening, she picked at a plate of leftover fried chicken, turnip greens, and coleslaw while Dottie sat across from her.

"You're not eating enough to keep a gnat alive," Dottie fussed. "At least finish eating them greens. You got to keep your strength up, sugar."

Emma halfheartedly took several more bites of the greens. What little appetite she had was being ruined by overhearing Stephanie, Brenda, Otis Lee, Otis, and one of Otis's brothers in the den talking about the press conference and rally. She pushed her plate away. "That's it. I can't eat any more."

Shaking her head in disapproval, Dottie said, "Well, at least try to eat a piece of cake or something before you go to bed tonight. I can't have you wasting away to skin and bones."

"I'll try," Emma mumbled.

One of Dottie's great-grandsons suddenly appeared in the doorway. "Grandma, Aunt Marguerite's on the phone. She said she needs to talk to you right now."

A jolt of dread shot through Emma. Though Dottie's sister-in-law, who lived in upstate New York and occasionally came down to visit, could be calling for any number of reasons, something told her that it was to deliver bad news.

"Did she say what for?" Dottie asked the boy.

"No, ma'am."

Picking up her cane, Dottie said, "Tell her I'll be there in a minute."

"Yes, ma'am," he said and disappeared.

Emma helped Dottie to her feet. "I'm coming with you."

"You don't have to. I'll be fine."

"It's no trouble, and besides, it'd do me good to get out of this house for a little while."

"Well, all right then."

The sinking of the late afternoon sun did little to make it bearable outside. It was still so hot and sticky that Emma felt like she and Dottie were walking through steam to reach Dottie's house.

"Whew!" Dottie said, pausing after climbing her porch steps.

Emma wiped away sweat. "I can't take much more of this."

"Sure you can. All you got to do is hold on."

Emma silently repeated that to herself as she followed Dottie into the house.

Dottie shuffled over to her great-grandson and took the phone receiver that he held out for her and spoke into it, "Hey, Marguerite, what's going on up there?" Her expression immediately went from mild concern to shock. "What? Lord have mercy!"

Oh, no, Emma thought. Bad news—just as she suspected. She braced herself for whatever it was. She'd been leaning on Dottie for days now but the time had clearly come that she needed to be strong enough for Dottie to lean on her.

"Grandma, what happened?" Dottie's great-grandson said in a rough whisper.

Dottie shushed him and spoke into the receiver again, "What are the doctors saying?" she asked. Whatever her cousin said caused Dottie's face to crumple even more. "Lord have mercy."

Emma hated feeling so helpless. She didn't know what to do except sit stupidly.

Dottie wiped her eyes that were turning shiny. "I'm getting up there tomorrow one way or the other," she told her sister-in-law. "If one of the boys can't take me, I'll ride the train. I only hope to God that she can hang on till I get there."

So it was Sarah, Dottie's last surviving sibling. The notion occurred to Emma that she was spreading tragedy like a deadly virus. It was a ridiculous thought, yet she couldn't shake it.

"Sarah's had a bad stroke," Dottie said after getting off the phone. "They don't know if she's gonna make it."

Emma hugged her and was surprised at how small and frail her friend suddenly felt. "I'm so sorry, Dottie. I know how close y'all are."

"Used to be twelve head of us," Dottie said in a muffled voice. "Losing your brothers and sisters one after the other—Lord, it's a hurting thing."

"What can I do to help?" Emma asked.

"Pray. Pray as hard as you can."

Emma returned home to discover her family still jabbering away about plans for the press conference and rally. The sight of them doing that made her furious.

They should've been with her to comfort Dottie instead of scheming for that rotten, conniving Creighton Jones. If she didn't know better, she'd swear the man had cast an evil spell over them. With her hands on her hips, she stood stiffly in the doorway until she got their attention.

"What's the matter?" Otis asked.

"I'm just waiting to see if any of y'all will quit talking about that stupid stuff long enough to ask about Dottie."

After a quick swapping of confused expressions that made Emma even angrier, Stephanie said, "What about her? Isn't she in the kitchen?"

"No, she's at her house!" Emma erupted. "Didn't you see Terrell come over only a little while ago to get her?" Without waiting for a reply, she went on, "Well, of course you didn't! Y'all don't care about anybody but that damned Creighton Jones!"

Brenda got to her feet. "What in the world's gotten into you? What are you so riled up about?"

"I've had it up to here with that man!" Emma said, holding a hand high above her head. "He's no man of God. He's a low-down, rotten dog and I can't believe y'all can't see through him. I don't want him setting foot in this house again!"

Otis Lee said, "Momma, you don't understand—"

Emma cut him off. "I understand him a whole lot better than any of y'all do. He's playing y'all for fools and y'all are just going along with it!"

"You need to get a hold of yourself," Otis said in a tone that made Emma pause before saying anything else. There was more than anger that she heard in his voice; it was something much worse.

"Give him a chance, Momma," Brenda said. "He's sincere, and he and his people are doing everything they can to help us."

"No, they're not!" Emma said. She couldn't believe how her family had been taken in by such an obvious manipulator.

"You're not being reasonable," Stephanie said to Emma. "If you'd only calm down—"

"There's nothing wrong with me!" Emma screeched. "He's the one who's the problem, not me! Why can't y'all see that?" She burst into tears and ran blindly from the room. After stumbling through the kitchen, she escaped into the backyard, sank down at the sun-bleached picnic table, and buried her face in her hands. Had anyone told her before that the people she loved most in the world would side with someone as awful as Creighton Jones instead of her, she'd have said they were crazy, but nothing was making much sense anymore.

That her children only knew part of the story didn't excuse how they were acting and Otis had no excuse whatsoever. Even if none of them agreed with her, if she meant anything to them, they'd follow her wishes, not those of some outsider who'd brush them off like lint once he had no use for them anymore. She thought she knew them, even better than she knew herself, but she was wrong—dead wrong.

How had things gone so bad so quickly? Once again, she was reminded of how she'd been swept away in the river as a little girl. Then, as now, she had nothing to grab to save herself—nothing but the very thing she was drowning in. This time, though, she didn't have her uncle to come to her rescue. She didn't have anyone.

No sooner, however, had that thought come to her than she felt a gentle touch on her shoulder. She looked up at her firstborn.

"You okay?" Brenda asked hesitantly.

Emma shrugged and said with a sigh, "I've been better." It struck her as odd that Brenda came out by herself, then again, knowing Brenda, she'd probably suggested to everyone inside that she—and she alone—be with Emma for a while. She'd been Emma's rock through so many other times. It was like she'd come from the womb with a steadiness and maturity that others never reached no matter how long they lived. So how had Jones hoodooed her also?

"This mess has got all of us on edge," Brenda said as she straddled the wooden bench, put her arms around

Emma and held her close. "It's like a bad movie that I can't find a way to turn off."

For a few moments, Emma said nothing. She didn't want to do anything but feel her daughter's comforting embrace. It reminded her of how her mother used to hug her and make her feel loved and safe. Cicadas broke the silence by announcing the coming of dusk with a low rhythmic humming that soon turned into a crescendo of feverish, high-pitched chirping. Emma had always found their strange serenade to be soothing before, but now it got on her nerves. "I don't want to have nothing to do with that man," she said.

"We've heard you loud and clear on that," Brenda said with her arms still around Emma.

"Oh, so y'all just don't care."

Brenda drew back. "That's not true and you know it. We'd walk through fire for you, and believe it or not, the reason we're asking Rev. Jones for help is as much for you as for any of us."

"For me?" Emma asked, stunned almost to speechlessness. "The only thing I want him to do is to leave us the heck alone."

"And if he did, the police would just whitewash over this thing and sooner or later, you'd blame yourself for letting them get away with it. No, I know it goes against your nature to raise sand like this, but it's got to be done, and nobody does it better than Rev. Creighton Jones."

"Baby, we've got to let it go. All it's doing is keeping everybody stirred up, and it's not going to bring Marcus back."

"If we roll over on this, it'll make the police think they can keep killing black guys any time they feel like it, and they've been getting away with it for too long as it is. Maybe if somebody had stood up to them before now, Marcus would still be alive."

Choosing her words carefully, Emma said, "I'm not so sure about that. It's easy for us to say that policeman shouldn't have shot Marcus. We know Marcus wouldn't have hurt a fly, but Rusty Carter had no way of knowing that. As far as he knew, Marcus was an armed robber. So put yourself in his shoes—you're a cop coming up on someone who you've been told is armed and dangerous and they do something that makes you believe they're about to kill you. What would you do?"

"He didn't have to kill Marcus."

"You're not answering my question."

Brenda began to chew her bottom lip.

"C'mon," Emma said with a sharp snap of her fingers, "you've got a split-second to decide. It's either you or him. What're you going to do?"

"Maybe . . . um . . . ," Brenda sputtered, "maybe shoot in the air to try to scare him off?"

"Right, and while you're shooting into the air, he could be shooting you dead. I'm glad you're not a cop, honey, or else it'd probably be your funeral that we'd be going to next."

"I just can't imagine Marcus doing anything that someone would take as a real threat."

"It may not so much be a question of what Marcus was doing or what he wasn't doing, but what Rusty Carter believed he was doing." A phrase from a commercial came to Emma's mind. "It's like they say—perception's reality. Whatever you believe to be true is."

"But this is Marcus we're talking about—sweet, humble, mild Marcus. How could anyone truly believe he was dangerous?"

"Baby, two people can look at the same thing and yet see something completely different. Take Creighton Jones for instance. You believe he's a saint, I believe he's scum. Who's to say which one of us is right?"

"I don't know," Brenda said, shaking her head wearily. "I just don't know."

Long after Brenda and the others had left, Emma went into the den where Otis lay on the couch watching CNN. If he'd heard her approaching, he didn't act like he had. Instead, he stared straight ahead at the TV that re-played some foreign dignitary giving a speech at the UN.

"You coming to bed?" Emma asked him.

"In a little bit," he mumbled, still not looking at her.

"It's past midnight."

"Yeah, I know," he said, using the remote to change the channel to another twenty-four-hour news channel.

Emma remembered how their nights together used to be filled with gentle lovemaking and easy conversation. There'd been no need for her to have to decide what to say to him like she was picking her way through a minefield. She could tell him anything without fear of him exploding in anger. As much as she hated the fear gripping her now, she hated the silence between them even more. It left her without any idea of what was going through his mind. Was he as heartbroken as she was about how things were between them? Did he share her growing worry that their marriage was falling apart? Did he still love her? There was so much she wanted to ask him, yet she didn't know how to begin.

His face revealed nothing. He looked like he'd been carved from granite. She longed to touch him, to lay beside him and feel the warmth of his body, but she kept her distance.

"Well," she said, "I'm calling it a night."

"Okay," he said and switched the TV back to CNN.

Muffled voices from the TV followed her upstairs. Pausing at the top of the landing, she felt drawn toward the closed door that still bore the clumsy lettering of the boy who'd used a Phillips screwdriver to scratch his name onto one of its panels to let everyone know whose bedroom it was. How old had Marcus been when he did that? Seven? Eight?

She remembered fussing at him about it. She'd told him that she and his daddy worked too hard to have him ruin what few things they were able to afford. Things—stupid things like a door Otis could've gotten at a lumber scrap yard for next to nothing—that's what she'd focused on.

Resting her forehead against where Marcus etched his name, she wondered if there would ever be a time she could walk by it without being flooded with painful memories. Though it was hard for her, she sensed it was even harder for Otis because while she was able to go up and down the stairs as often as before Marcus's death, she noticed Otis had started avoiding the upstairs whenever possible. About the only times she saw him there anymore was when he had to shower or change clothes. If there was a full bathroom downstairs and enough closet space for his clothes, he'd probably never set foot again in the upper half of his own home. Whenever he did pass the closed bedroom door, his steps always quickened like he couldn't get by it fast enough.

Maybe . . . maybe they should sell the house and make a fresh start somewhere else in town where they didn't have to go by doors that hurt them so much. Maybe they shouldn't even wait until the house sold – maybe they ought to simply pack up and go. They could find a cheap rental or move in with one of their kids.

Emma fingered Marcus's engraved name on the door. It'd take a lot more than moving to a new place to heal from his death. Besides, they were barely able to keep up with their bills as it was without having to pay rent on top of everything else, and none of the kids had any spare bedrooms in their homes. Then there was the advice from so many people who warned against making any major decisions in the shadow of recent tragedy. No, she and Otis needed to stay put, at least for the time being. There was no escaping the house or the memories it held.

She opened the door. Although she knew how the bedroom would appear, it still jarred her to see it so spotless. Was the smell of the lemon furniture polish and carpet deodorizer Marcus used to clean the room still lingering or was it only her imagination?

Turning to the mirror where she'd found the note that sent her tumbling into deeper chaos, she studied her reflection in it. She supposed that if someone who didn't know her saw her, they'd wonder if she'd ever been happy a moment of her life. Sadness was carved into her face more deeply than the letters Marcus etched into the door. Her tiredness showed through clearly, too. Had she worked grueling swing shifts at the hospital without a day off for weeks on end, she wouldn't feel as worn out as she did now. Merely doing simple chores like putting a load of clothes in the washer or vacuuming the den drained her. The last few nights, she'd been so exhausted that she fell asleep without needing to take one of Dottie's sleeping pills, but having one dream after another about Marcus made her feel like she'd stayed up all night watching a home video that kept playing over and over. In each dream, she heard him desperately calling for her, yet as hard as she searched, she could never find him. Whenever she thought she was getting close, his voice grew more distant yet more desperate. She woke up in the morning more tired than when she'd gone to bed.

A long yawn escaped from her. She wasn't going to be able to last much longer, but before she went to bed, there was something she had to do.

The disjointed sounds coming from downstairs told her that Otis remained rooted to the couch, flipping the TV from one channel to another. She closed the door anyway. She didn't want to take the chance of him seeing what she was about to do. Guilt swept over her—she didn't like hiding things from him, but she couldn't predict his behavior anymore.

Stepping into the closet, she felt along the top shelf until she grasped the small envelope. She opened it, sat on the edge of Marcus's bed and re-read his note though she could already recite it in her sleep. Otis had never asked what she'd done with it, a clear sign that he continued to believe it had no significance. But what if he found it? Would he destroy it to make sure no one else reached the same conclusion from it that she had? She didn't know. She no longer trusted him, at least not when it came to anything having to do with their youngest child.

She carefully folded the note, slid it back into its envelope, and returned it to the closet shelf. That small piece of paper was her last link to Marcus. She needed to find a safer place for it, but where? After turning the question over in her mind, the answer came—a safe deposit box, one that only she knew of. Yes, she'd go to the bank the next morning and rent one. She had no idea what it would cost, but whatever the fee was, she'd scrape up the money for it somehow.

She left the bedroom and went into her own. It felt odd being there by herself that late at night, but she realized that unless things changed, she'd have to get used to sleeping alone. She washed her face, brushed her teeth, changed into her cotton nightgown and climbed into bed.

From off in the distance, a siren wailed. What had happened? A car accident? A robbery? A shooting? Somewhere out there, she feared that a family was about to get news concerning a loved one that would turn their worlds upside down. She prayed for them, for Dottie, and for Ofc. Rusty Carter until she fell into a troubled sleep.

When she woke, dim light from the waning moon and the coming dawn turned her bedroom into varying shades of gray. For a groggy moment, she wondered why Otis wasn't beside her until she remembered where he was. She slid a hand over to his side of the bed. Its coolness depressed her—it was one more sign that her life was never going to be the same.

Sitting up, she tried to shake off the sadness settling on her like a heavy quilt. She needed to stay busy, to keep her mind off her troubles. She looked forward to going back to work. Being at home left her too much time to feel sorry for herself. Otis had too much time on his hands as well and it was helping to fuel his obsession with striking back against the police department. Thanks to his seldom taking vacations or calling in sick during the thirty-some-odd years he'd worked at a building supply warehouse, he had enough annual leave to last until late fall, and he made it clear that he intended to use every single second of it to fight the police department.

She used to resent the rigidity of both of their work

schedules, however since Marcus's death, she appreciated the steady rhythm and order their jobs had given to their day. The recent chaos made her feel like she was trying to gain footing on shifting sand. What she needed—what everyone in her family needed—was normalcy. And while she realized they'd have to create a new normalcy, she couldn't ignore the possibility that it might be something as bitter as the way things were now. Somehow, she had to make sure that didn't happen.

That thought weighed on her while she watched the sun ease over the horizon. With its rising, her bedroom slowly turned from shades of gray to its true colors. She pulled back the curtains and saw there wasn't a cloud in the sky. The day was bound to be another scorcher and stretch the record for the number of days in a row that the temperatures soared above one hundred. The condition of her backyard forced her to turn away from the window. If she didn't remember where she'd planted things, she'd have no idea that the shriveled things littering the area used to be gloriously lush groups of hostas, asters, verbena, impatiens, marigolds, delphiniums, larkspurs, and black-eyed Susans. That some of the sturdier plants like her roses, bachelor's buttons, coreoposis, and lantana still clung to life gave her little comfort. Too much of what she'd tended to for years was dead.

She couldn't put all of the blame on the heat. If she'd remembered to put on the sprinkler each morning, some of the plants probably would've survived. She sighed. The damage was done—there was nothing to do other than to salvage what was left, including the lavender rosebush near the front porch steps. Better to plant it at Marcus's grave before it got too hot outside. Afterwards, she'd return home, take a shower and do whatever she could to help Dottie prepare for her long journey north. The idea of her elderly friend having to travel so far away worried Emma. All sorts of calamities could strike. Simply riding in a car or on a train for hours on end was dangerous. Emma had heard of people developing deadly blood clots from having to sit for long periods. If anything happened to Dottie . . . .

"Stop it," Emma said aloud to herself. She had too much to do that day to waste time imagining reasons for more heartbreak.

She changed into some of her gardening clothes—an old T-shirt and a faded pair of shorts—and went downstairs. Otis was where she'd left him the night before. He lay on his side, snoring softly, and the remote had slipped from his hand and fallen to the floor. She picked it up and put it on the coffee table, then looked down at her husband. He wasn't a handsome man—his features were so coarse that they made him look primitive—yet that had never mattered to her. It was his goodness that made her love him and somewhere beneath his anger, bitterness, and hurt, she believed that goodness still existed. Careful not to wake him, she kissed him and breathed in his scent. He stirred slightly before his snoring fell back into its steady rhythm.

She rummaged through the drawer of an end table until she found a small notepad and pen and wrote a note explaining she was borrowing his truck to run an errand. He'd probably still be asleep by the time she returned, but in case he wasn't, he'd know that a robber hadn't made off with his precious old pickup. She left the note on the coffee table and went outside.

There was a freshness to the early morning air that seemed to signal God was giving everyone another chance to get things right for once, and it was so quiet, the only thing she heard was distant traffic and the twittering of birds. If only it could stay like that. She knew, though, that it would soon be too miserable to do anything outside and the quiet would be shattered by the noises made by Waverton coming to life.

When she reached the lavender rosebush, she was relieved to see it showed little damage from the record heat wave. Its abundance of blossoms still perfumed the air and flowed down canes onto pine straw mulch. Despite the flowering shrub's hardiness, she wanted to be careful transplanting it. The first step was getting it out of the ground with most of its roots intact.

She tugged on a pair of work gloves and used a shovel to gently pry it from the soil. After placing it on a wide square of burlap, she gathered the fabric around the plant's root ball, secured it with twine, then left it on the ground to load the F-150 with the things she would need at the cemetery. By the time she got a three-gallon bucket filled with rich black soil from her compost bin onto the truck bed along with eight large plastic jugs of water, a bag of slow-release fertilizer and a wheelbarrow, sweat streamed into her eyes. She wiped it away, then set the rosebush amidst the items as gingerly as if it were a baby. And though the cemetery was less than a fifteen-minute drive away, she retrieved more burlap from her gardening shed to completely cover the rosebush to protect it from windburn. She double-checked that she had everything she needed, climbed into the truck and drove off.

Almost at the same time that she parked the truck, the cemetery's groundskeeper parked beside her. Noticing his curious expression, Emma introduced herself.

The slightly-built old African-American man flashed her a smile that revealed gold caps on his front teeth. "Thought you looked familiar. I was there at your son's—" His voice faltered and his smile went limp.

"Yes, thank you," Emma said, though she had no idea why she thanked him. He'd only been doing his job.

He slid on a stained baseball cap. "You out here mighty early."

"I wanted to put a rosebush on Marcus's grave before it got too hot." A thought came to her that shot fear through her. "That's okay, isn't it? I mean, it doesn't break any rules about what can be on graves, does it?"

"No, ma'am, 'specially not for flowers as purty as what you got in the back of that pick-up. Matter of fact, I'd be happy to plant them for you."

"Thank you, but I'd. . ..I'd rather do it myself."

"Okay." Motioning to a utility building near the parking lot, the groundskeeper added, "I'll be in there if you need me. By the way, my name's Jim—Jim Reese."

"Nice to meet you, Mr. Reese."

"And you, too, Miz Jennings. Don't stay out here too long. This heat we've been having is dangerous."

"Don't I know it, but it shouldn't take more than a few minutes to plant this rosebush."

"All right," he said and walked to the utility building.

Emma went to the back of the truck and let down its tailgate. The sweet fragrance from the rosebush's pastel-colored blossoms floated up to her when she put them in the wheelbarrow. To save herself a trip back to the truck for the shovel, she carefully wedged its blade under the roses' burlap-shrouded root ball and then she started up the cemetery's sloping hill. At first, she was so focused on balancing the shovel and not letting any of the flowering canes spill over the sides of the wheelbarrow and scrape onto the walkway that she kept her head down, but when she finally looked up, she froze. Straight ahead of her was Ofc. Rusty Carter sitting cross-legged at her son's grave. He seemed lost in his own world while plucking a blade of the faded grass and studying it like it possibly held the key to unlocking a deep mystery.

She stood gripping the handles of the wheelbarrow, feeling torn. One part of her wanted to go to him and convince him that he bore no blame for her son's death, the other part of her wanted to rush back to the truck to avoid saying anything to him that might stain Marcus's memory and destroy her family.

Consumed by the limbo she'd found herself in, she didn't realize how high she'd tilted the wheelbarrow until the shovel tumbled out of it and hit the concrete walkway with a loud metallic clang.

CHAPTER 10

Startled by the sharp clang, Rusty jumped up and spun around. In his daze, it took him a moment to register the identity of the woman who stared at him while clutching the handles of a battered wheelbarrow overflowing with lavender roses. When the realization of who she was sank in, he felt like ice water had been shot into his veins.

"I'm sorry. I'm so sorry," Emma Jennings said in a rush.

"For what?" he blurted. Her apologizing to him for anything was more shocking than her sudden appearance. Didn't she recognize him?

"For . . . uh . . . um . . . " she stammered, continuing to gawk at him like he'd been the one who had materialized from out of nowhere instead of her. "For scaring you," she finally said.

Her undeserved concern for him deepened his shock. He'd gunned down her son and yet she was apologizing for disturbing him where she had buried the boy. He didn't have a right to be there. Why had he returned? He'd made a silent vow to never return to the property after fleeing from it the day before, so what drew him back in the small hours of the morning? What had made him sit there in the darkness, completely oblivious that it was giving way to dawn and turning heavy with the possibility that she'd find him there again? Hadn't he hurt her enough without inflicting his presence on her at a place where she should least expect it? He swallowed hard then murmured, "Do you know who I am?"

"Yes," she said softly.

"Tell me." He had to hear her say his name. He had to be certain she knew she was speaking to the man who killed her child.

She studied him briefly. Though he was sure his guilt was more visible than a highway billboard, he saw no condemnation in her eyes. "You're Ofc. Russell Carter, Jr."

"That's right." He couldn't think of anything else to say. There weren't any words to undo what he'd done to her and her family. He wished he could vanish.

She seemed to be at a loss for words, too. As if needing something more to do with her hands, she set down the wheelbarrow, picked up the shovel and pushed its blade beneath the mound of lavender roses, then brushed her palm over the blossoms. "If you'd like to stay, I can come back later."

He wanted to ask why she'd do that, why she was being kind to him. It also struck him as peculiar that she hadn't asked why he'd returned, especially so early in the morning. But he was too shaken to ask such questions and since she appeared to be as equally undone, he simply said, "No, that's all right. I was about to leave anyhow."

"Are you sure?"

"Yes."

She clasped her hands together. "Oh, okay."

He heard a hesitation in her voice, like she wanted to say more but was holding back. It was just as well. He wanted to escape as fast as possible before his nervousness made him blurt out something he'd regret. Taking a step away from her and toward the pathway, he said, "Goodbye, Mrs. Jennings."

"Goodbye."

While quickly walking to his pickup, he sensed her eyes on him. It wasn't until he drove out of the parking lot that he was able breathe easily. That had to be his last time visiting Marcus Jennings' grave. He couldn't return. Ever.

He'd hoped to sneak into the house without waking his parents, but no sooner had he unlocked the front door than his mother yanked it open. "Where've you been?" she shrieked. "You've had us worried sick! I was about to call Headquarters to have them start looking for you!"

"Good Lord, Mom," Rusty said with a hand over his pounding heart. "You scared the bejesus out of me."

"How do you think me and your dad felt when we woke up in the middle of the night to find you gone without a trace? We didn't know what in the world had happened to you!"

"I couldn't sleep," he said, stepping around her to make his way in the den. "I thought maybe going for a drive would help me unwind."

"You've been gone for hours. Where'd you go? California?"

He wasn't the least bit tempted to tell her the truth. With a shrug, he answered, "Nowhere special."

His father came out of the kitchen stirring a mug of coffee. "Boy, you got to quit running off without telling anybody where you're going or when you're coming back. Your momma's nearly worked herself into a state."

"You know the strain this awful mess has put me under," she said to Rusty as if her husband's statement needed verification. "And your daddy's blood pressure's probably through the roof."

"Sorry," Rusty said, raking fingers through his hair. "I'd planned on getting back here before y'all woke up, so I didn't think to tell you I was going out for a while."

Doris flopped onto her well-worn place on the sofa and Russ settled into his recliner and put on the TV. She said to Rusty, "I had you at the bottom of Cherokee River. I had you dead and gone."

"Not finding me in the house is no reason to jump to the conclusion that something bad had happened to me."

"Oh, really?" she said. "We discover that you've disappeared in the dead of night and we're automatically supposed to know that you're just out joy riding? You must think we have E.S.P."

"I said I was sorry," Rusty said, growing more irritated with her by the moment.

"For crying out loud, Doris, leave him alone," Russ snapped while flipping from an infomercial. "I told you all along you were probably getting yourself worked up for nothing."

"I beg your pardon for being a concerned mother," she said with her chin starting to tremble.

"Aw, Mom," Rusty said, but he recognized the look on her sharply angled face. No amount of begging or pleading was going to pry her from her martyrdom. It was what she lived for.

The new cordless phone rang with a high shrill. Russ grabbed it, looked at the caller ID, and answered it by saying, "Kick Ass Paint and Body Shop. Can I help ya?"

The prank softened the edges of Rusty's irritability. It tickled him how his dad had started answering calls he suspected were crank calls or from reporters in all kinds of goofy ways to throw them off. So far, their home had been everything from a dentist's office to a barbershop to a paint supply company to a men's impotence clinic. And Russ's ability to conjure up zany business names on the fly was wild, especially since he wasn't naturally a funny guy.

"You wanna speak to Rusty Carter?" Russ asked, like he'd never heard the name before. "Sorry, he don't work here." He paused. "Yeah, this is 555-8712, but we ain't got no Rusty Carter working here. No, this is Kick Ass Paint and Body. You got the wrong number, lady." He punched the button to disconnect the call and grumbled, "That ought to fix that fucking bitch."

"I wish you'd quit doing that," Doris said. "It's only stirring them up more."

"I don't give a rat's ass," Russ said. He turned the volume higher as the local morning news came on.

Rusty found it ironic that despite how much he and

his father hated the media, they watched one TV news show after the other. It was like how people couldn't help but gawk at horrific traffic accidents. He sat on the sofa next to his mother in front of the TV.

"There's oatmeal on the stove in case you're hungry," she said to him.

"I'll fix myself a bowl once a commercial comes on," he replied, noticing that her worry that he wasn't eating enough had trumped her anger over how he'd disappeared during the night. Although she was sometimes irritatingly dramatic about it, he knew her concern for him was real. She loved him. If there was one thing he was absolutely sure of, it was that. Perhaps in an ideal world, she could've been a better mother, but on the other hand, he could've been a better son.

He regretted scaring her by not thinking to leave a note. He'd probably added a few more strands of gray to her hair that was already streaked with them. She was only forty-six, but she appeared at least ten years older. It wasn't so much the gray hair that did it or how the skin beneath her jaw had become slack and finely creased—it was how she radiated a belief that life was something to be endured more than enjoyed. Looking at her brought words like "burden" and "duty" to mind.

The news anchorwoman's mention of Creighton Jones' name forced Rusty to turn his attention from his mother to the TV.

"The civil rights leader will return tomorrow to hold a press conference with Marcus Jennings' family," the anchorwoman said with a file photo of Jones on the screen. "It is expected they will continue their demands that the white police officer who shot the African-American youth be indicted and the city police department be investigated by federal authorities."

"Tell that coon to keep his good-for-nothing ass in California!" Russ hollered at the TV.

Rusty slumped back against the sofa. He shared his father's wish that Jones would stay in California instead of returning to make his life more miserable. What really burned him up was that while Jones had free reign to say anything about him that he wanted, he couldn't publicly speak a word to defend himself. And no telling what else Jones would come up with either. Maybe a few more witnesses to say Marcus Jennings had been surrendering? Who were the so-called witnesses who had told him that in the first place? More importantly, which witnesses would the grand jury believe?

"Earth to Rusty. Earth to Rusty," Josh said to Rusty as he, Rusty, and Scott stood around a pool table at the Silver Spur.

"What?" Rusty asked, shaken from his thoughts. "Is it my turn again?"

"Yeah, dude," Scott said, "but you've been looking like you're a million miles away."

Actually, only about six, Rusty wanted to say. That was how far the honky tonk was from the cemetery where Emma Jennings had found him that morning, and despite having dinner with Josh and Scott before they ended up at the Silver Spur, he still couldn't push memories of the encounter with her from his mind. Why had she been so kind to him? That was the weirdest thing. Sure, there were plenty of nice people in the world but for her to have treated the killer of her youngest child the way she did defied reality. She was turning into as much of a mystery as her son.

Maybe if she spoke during the press conference that she, her family, and Rev. Creighton Jones were having the next day, she'd reveal more about herself. With her compassionate demeanor and quiet gentleness, she could sway more people against him than any of the rabble-rousing her family and Creighton Jones were doing. Her kindness made her Rusty's most dangerous opponent. Goddamn it.

Letting out a heavy breath, he took a shot and sent balls scattering across the table in every direction except the one he needed them to go in.

Josh laughed. "You're hopeless!"

"At least tonight I am," Rusty said while remembering how he usually beat Josh and Scott at pool without hardly trying.

Scott gave Rusty's shoulder a quick pat. "Everybody's entitled to have an off night every once in a while."

Rusty gulped another swig of beer. He appreciated how his two buddies were acting as if everything was normal. Clearly, they were avoiding talking about the shooting and instead, were keeping the conversation to ribbing each other and Rusty about how they played pool.

"Hey, guys!" a fellow cop named Grant Smith hollered to them over a Kenny Chesney tune blaring from the jukebox.

"What's up, Grant?" Josh said as Grant approached.

"Nothin' but the rent," Grant said. "And it just keeps going higher and higher." He turned to Rusty. "How you doing?"

"Good," Rusty said before taking another swig, this one much bigger than the one before.

"I'd probably be a basket case if I were in you right now," Grant said. "I don't see how you can stand it. I mean you can't turn on the TV or look at the newspaper without seeing how they're demonizing you. And that shit they dug up about your family was really below the belt. Whatever your folks did way back when ain't got nothing to do with what you had to do last week."

Rusty felt sweat begin to trickle down the back of his neck. Catching sight of a waitress weaving between tables while balancing a tray stacked high with empty shot glasses, beer mugs, crumpled napkins, and overflowing ashtrays, he decided he needed something stronger than Budweiser. "Ma'am," he said to her, "can you bring me a gin and tonic?"

"Sure thing, babe," she said, not missing a beat in her rhythm as she snaked her way toward the bar.

After casting a concerned glace at Rusty, Scott said to Grant. "You and Ashley still going hot and heavy?"

"Absolutely. Matter of fact, she's moved in with me.

She can't stand how you're being treated either, Rusty. She told me to tell you that."

"I appreciate it," Rusty said, although in truth, he didn't. He wished Grant had left them the hell alone.

"She's like the rest of us with any ounce of sense—she can't believe that they're making you out to be some kind of gun-slinging, dirty cop when the only witnesses at the scene back up what you're saying," Grant went on, apparently oblivious to Scott's attempt to change the subject.

Rusty ran his hand through his hair that was starting to turn damp with sweat. Why was it so hot in the place all the sudden and where was that fucking waitress with his gin and tonic?

"Geez," he muttered while wiping away sweat, "it's hot as hell in here."

Josh shrugged. "Feels fine to me."

"Me too," Grant said.

Scott tugged at his shirt collar although Rusty didn't see even a trace of sweat on him. "Wish I could say the same, but I'm starting to cook too. To tell you the truth, I'm tired of hanging around here."

"We only got here like an hour ago," Josh said. "And the wet T-shirt contest is about to start. Check out those girls leaning up against the bar," he said motioning to four women who only had enough clothing on to avoid getting arrested for public indecency. "They told me they're entering, and I sure wouldn't mind them shaking their bazoongas at me for a while."

"Then stay," Scott said before draining his beer and setting it on the pool table with a firm thump. "But if I were you, I'd make sure that was the only things they shook at me. They look like the type that has cooties."

"They're not that skeezy looking," Grant protested.

"Suit yourself," Scott said. "Rusty, do you wanna go to the river?"

"Yeah," Rusty said, brightening.

"Which one?" Grant asked. "The Cherokee?"

"What difference does it make?" Scott asked.

"It's been a while since I've been down to the

Cherokee," Grant said. "I wouldn't mind going with y'all if that's where you heading."

"Better stay here and keep an eye on this guy," Scott said, jerking his thumb at Josh, "so he doesn't get carried away and start wanting to do more with them girls' bazoongas than look at 'em. He's got a reputation for getting too friendly too fast, and sometimes it hasn't gone over too well."

"Bullshit!" Josh said with a laugh. "You're only jealous because I get more pussy than you do."

"Whatever," Scott said. He gave Rusty a nudge. "Let's go."

Rusty deeply breathed the humid air once he and Scott made it outside. The night was as hot as the other ones that preceded it in the heat wave still gripping the city, but at least there was a slight breeze and they were finally free of Grant. Josh too. Sometimes he got on Rusty's nerves.

"You okay?" Scott asked him.

"I'm better now, and I'll feel even better once we're at the river."

"If the waters ain't too rough, we ought to go swimming."

"In what? Our drawers?"

"You can if you want to. I'm taking mine off so long as nobody's around."

Rusty grinned. "The only time I ever skinny-dipped was on a dare when I was in the third grade. You've never seen a kid get in and out of the water as quick as I did. I wanted to get my clothes back on before one of the hellions I was with hid them."

"Then you're way overdue for swimming with nothing but what you were born with. Ain't nothing like it." Scott pulled his truck keys from his pocket. "See you there."

Rusty climbed into his pickup and maneuvered it behind Scott's onto the two-lane road leading to Cherokee River.

It only took a few moments for the lights in the Silver

Spur's parking lot to disappear and it grew darker still the further they drove.

"But you went away," Miranda Lambert crooned on the radio. "How dare you. I miss you . . . ."

Rusty switched to another country radio station. It wasn't that he didn't like Miranda Lambert. Or that tune, at least he had liked it until he learned that she and her then husband, Blake Shelton, hadn't written it to chronicle the typical story of a lover being dumped, but instead about the grief and shock resulting from the death of Shelton's brother Ritchie who was only twenty-four when he died in a car accident. Ever since discovering what inspired the song, Rusty couldn't bear listening to it.

The appearance of headlights growing closer and burning brighter in his rearview mirror made him forget about the song. If the car behind him got any closer, it would be on top of him. Rusty flashed his high beams to signal to the tailgating driver to back off, but the car remained right on his bumper.

Rusty pressed down on the accelerator, forcing his Sierra to barrel faster on the road that had begun to twist sharply between a thick forest.

The car sped up too.

"You asshole," Rusty muttered to the unseen driver. "If I'm going too slow, just go around me for crying out loud."

As if suddenly yielding to Rusty's command, the car darted across the two solid yellow lines into the oncoming lane and drew evenly with Rusty. In the fraction of a second that Rusty had to look at the car, a flash appeared from it.

"Holy shit!" Rusty yelled as the glass of his driver's side door shattered and pelted his face.

The second bullet smashed his windshield.

Rusty slammed on the brakes and tried to pull onto the road's narrow shoulder, but he hit a guard rail and started flying upside down into the darkness.

CHAPTER 11

"There!" Stephanie said with satisfaction when she applied the final stroke of eye shadow onto Emma and moved so Brenda could see her handiwork.

Brenda gushed, "You look beautiful, Momma."

Emma managed to muster a smile for her two daughters to mask how ridiculous she felt wearing so much makeup and for allowing her hair to be sculpted into a glossily gelled swoop similar to what her daughters sported. She hardly recognized herself as she studied her reflection in the mirror above the chest of drawers in her and Otis' bedroom. Other than an occasional dab of lipstick, she never used any cosmetics and about the most she ever did with her hair was to pull it back into a bun.

"I hate all this fuss," she said, tugging at the silk scarf Stephanie had tied into a fancy bow around her neck.

"Tell us something we don't know," Stephanie said, "but we can't have you looking like something the cat dragged in during the press conference. This is a big deal, and Rev. Jones and reporters from around the country will be getting here any minute."

"Lord, have mercy," Emma groaned. She dreaded the start of the ordeal and wished she had the backbone to return to work that day instead of caving into her family's demands that she stay home and read the speech Denise

Hollingsworth had written for her. She didn't bother to fool herself that the same wouldn't happen the day of the rally. She'd be there too. Despite all of her silently sworn pledges that she'd have no part of it, Otis and the kids made trying to stand up to them harder than fighting against a strong rip tide. She couldn't do it anymore. They'd worn her down.

"Don't worry, Momma," Brenda said while lounging on Emma's side of the bed, "it'll be over with before you know it."

No, Emma thought, that was only true for doing enjoyable things like working shredded leaves into her compost pile, pruning one of her crape myrtles or arranging freshly cut delphiniums in a glass vase. Having to sit beside Creighton Jones in front of a roomful of reporters was enough to make time stop, and only thinking about how much more time she'd be forced to spend in his presence before he found another sensational case to milk for more attention made her head hurt. She rubbed her temples to ease away the dull ache in them.

"Be careful not to smudge your makeup," Stephanie said.

Emma dropped her hands into her lap with an irritated sigh. Her baby girl was getting on her nerves worse than ever. So was Otis. She hated the smug look he had when overhearing her call her supervisor to say she wasn't going to be able to come into work until the next day despite what she'd said earlier. Instead of appearing so smug and full of himself, Otis could've told her how much he appreciated her agreeing to participate in the press conference after all. That would've helped—at least some.

What little they'd said to each other that day had been limited to things like, "Do you have the metro section of the newspaper?" and "Pass the salt, please." They both saved more meaningful conversation for their children. When she left him in the kitchen, he was yakking away with Ed and Otis Lee about whether they'd have any success in getting *Sixty Minutes* to do a story on Marcus's death. Now, as she looked at a glamorized version of herself in the mirror, she wished she were able to force from her mind the possibility of anyone from the famous news program contacting them.

Brenda slid off the bed and went to the window. "Doggone that Justin!" she fumed, referring to her oldest son. "I told him to stay in front of the house to show people where to park and he's nowhere in sight. Shoot, here comes somebody now."

Stephanie joined her. "It's probably Denise and Serena. Sure looks like their Navigator. They said they'd get here before Rev. Jones to do some advance work."

Advance work? Emma was afraid to ask what that meant.

"It is them!" Stephanie said with excitement, apparently watching the two women emerge from their expensive SUV. She raced to the door. "I'm going to go downstairs and help them get everything set up."

Brenda followed her out of the room. "And I'm going to find Justin and whip his behind for not doing what I told him to."

Emma trudged over to her bed. She was tempted to lay down but didn't want to risk ruining her hairdo, so she sat on the edge of the bed, disgusted at how she was letting herself be primped and propped here and there like a stupid show dog. She had no one to blame but herself though. If she ever needed reminding of that, she only had to make another visit to the cemetery.

A jumble of voices from downstairs broke into her thoughts. There were several she didn't recognize, probably reporters'.

She sighed. If only Dottie were with her, it wouldn't be so bad. Dottie had only left the day before, yet that was long enough for Emma to feel completely lost without her. When the Amtrak Silver Meteor pulled out of the train depot with Dottie waving goodbye from a window seat, Emma felt like her last lifeline was being yanked away, especially since there was no telling how long Dottie would have to stay in New York. She called from Albany to report her safe arrival and that her sister was holding her own, though barely. Until Sarah either recovered enough to return home or died, Dottie planned to stay with her.

"Enough about me and my woes and troubles," she said to Emma during the call, "how you doing?"

"Fine," Emma answered, hoping she sounded convincing.

For a moment, only the muffled sound of distant traffic came over the line, then Dottie spoke again. "You don't have to sugar coat stuff with me. How you really doing?"

"I'm fine," Emma insisted while twisting the telephone cord tightly around her fingers. "Honest. I don't want you worrying about me. You've got enough on you with Lunnella being so sick."

"She's in a mighty bad way, for sure, but still, I hate leaving you at a time like this."

"You can't be in two places at once. Yes, I miss you, but Sarah needs you a lot more than I do. I'm okay."

"I hope you take my advice and stay away from the cemetery until this whole mess is over. It won't do you a bit of good to keep running into that cop."

Emma remembered her chance meeting with Ofc. Rusty Carter two days earlier. It was obvious she hadn't reacted to him the way he'd expected. He probably assumed she'd been too shocked by his presence to start yelling and screaming at him or maybe he thought she was such a devout Christian, she was willing to forgive him no matter what. If he hadn't rushed away so quickly, he might've realized he wasn't the one who needed forgiveness.

"I wonder if he's there now," she said, thinking aloud to Dottie, the only person she'd told about her encounters with the policeman.

"Stay away from him," Dottie warned. "He don't need to know nothing but what he does already—that he shot Marcus in self-defense. That's all anybody needs to know, and that's all they will know so long as you don't get to blabbing."

Emma twisted the phone cord tighter around her fingers. What was she to do when there were no good options? Whether she betrayed her child's memory and devastated her family in the process or whether she made a human sacrifice of Rusty Carter, someone had to suffer.

If she were able to go back in time and do just one small thing differently, maybe that would've been enough to change the whole course of events. She might've been able to head off tragedy the same way someone snuffing out a tiny spark prevented a deadly wildfire. What would've happened if after the first time Marcus complained about high school, she'd said, "Honey, I know how you feel. I didn't like school either," instead of only telling him to get his butt on the bus?

"Rusty Carter's going to get cleared no matter what," Dottie said, capturing Emma's attention once again. "Ain't no need to bring up nothing else about Marcus."

"But it tears me to pieces to see that poor young man blaming himself."

"You don't know he's doing that."

The idea that something other than guilt drew Rusty Carter to her son's grave had never dawned on Emma. "Why else would he be hanging around the cemetery then?" she asked.

"Maybe he's like Joe after he got back from Vietnam," she said of the oldest of her five sons. "Killing troubled him, even though he knew he had no choice. It took him a while to get over what he had to do to survive in them jungles. He put up a good front, but when I used to see him staring off into space, I knew it was weighing heavy on him."

Dottie paused and Emma imagined her shaking her head with sorrow over what Joe endured. "He had a tough time of it, all right," Dottie went on. "It was bad enough what he had to go through in Vietnam, but for him to come home and find his whole country turned against him and them other boys who fought with him—well, that almost did him in. He made it through though, with the help of the good Lord, Rusty Carter will too. Just give him some time."

Time. How much of it would it take before he no longer felt the need to visit Marcus's grave? What was going through his mind now? How was he holding up?

Of all the cops on patrol the day Marcus decided to go

into that 7-Eleven with a toy gun, why did he have to be the first one to show up? Why couldn't it have been someone like . . . like his father? Killing Marcus wouldn't have fazed Russ Carter one bit, and it would've been easy to remain silent while he came under attack. He deserved that and more for what he'd done. But his son was innocent. It wasn't fair for both of them to be painted with the same brush.

But for all her thoughts of fairness, what was she doing about them? Nothing except praying Dottie was right in saying Rusty Carter's visits to the cemetery were helping him make peace with what he'd been forced to do to survive. It was the only thing she knew to do.

With a heavy weariness, she rose from her bed, went to the window, and saw Justin directing a slow-moving stream of vehicles arriving at the house. She noticed the logos of all the major TV networks on the sides of vans that were topped with satellite equipment. She also noticed the same stretch limousine that brought Creighton Jones to her home days earlier. He was back. Damn.

Later that evening, anyone watching the news—including Rusty Carter—would believe from her participating in the press conference with him that she agreed with his garbage. It made her sick.

Stephanie reappeared in the doorway. "Come on, Momma, everybody's asking about you downstairs."

"Tell them I've run away from home," Emma said as she turned away from the window in disgust.

Stephanie laughed and gave her a warm hug. "It'll be okay. Trust me."

"I don't like—"

"I know, I know," Stephanie interrupted, "but we need you to do this."

Emma nodded barely enough to signal her surrender—if only Stephanie knew how many times the thoughts of actually running away had entered her mind.

Stephanie held her at arm's length and studied her for a moment as if noticing something different about her that she couldn't quite put her finger on. Finally, she said, "You're a lot stronger than you give yourself credit for."

"What makes you say that?" Emma asked, surprised. The comment seemed to have come from out of nowhere.

"Because it's true."

"I sure don't feel that way now."

Stephanie hugged her again. Tighter this time. "Sometimes you have to go by what you know, not what you feel."

"My daughter the philosopher," Emma said with a bittersweet smile.

"I love you, Ma."

"I love you too, baby." Indeed, the love she had for Stephanie was so powerful she was sure it could take her breath away if she totally gave herself over to it. It had to do with Marcus. What didn't anymore? His death made each of her surviving children that much more precious to her.

"Are you ready?" Stephanie asked.

Emma shrugged. "About as much as I'll ever be."

"All right then, let's go."

They held hands while entering the crowded living room. Through the jumble of people, Emma noticed the furniture had been rearranged to accommodate a long, narrow table draped in white linen with chairs from the dining room set behind it. Everything was out of place. She felt like a stranger in her own home. She heard Ed announce from somewhere in the crowd, "There she is!"

As people turned to look at her and allow her and Stephanie to make their way further into the room, her unease sharpened. *Just keep putting one foot in front of the other,* she told herself. Like she had a choice in the matter. Stephanie was pulling her straight toward Creighton Jones who stood near the long table with his two aides, Otis, Ed, Brenda, and several others from the family. Once again, Emma desperately wished Dottie were with her.

"Mrs. Jennings!" Jones boomed like they were long-lost friends. He came at her with outstretched arms. "It's so good to see you again."

He swept her up in a warm embrace. With her face

pressed against him, she couldn't help but catch the scent of his cologne. It had a rich, masculine spiciness to it. She didn't doubt she could pay her light bill with what a few ounces of the stuff cost.

"How have you been?" he asked. Cameras clicked away like cicadas at dusk.

"Fine," she said automatically. Slipping out of his embrace, she made herself ask, "And you?"

"Couldn't be better! Being back here feels like coming home. Nothing like being somewhere where people need you."

"That's exactly where you are, Rev.," Otis said, clapping him on the shoulder like they really were long-lost friends. "We need you to help us shake up things around here and show the cops they can't keep killing us black folk like we're flies."

"Rest assured, my brother, we're going to put a stop to it," Jones replied.

Otis beamed at him while Otis Lee, Ed, Brenda, and Stephanie acted like they had to pinch themselves to believe the famous civil rights leader was in their midst again. Mindful of her family and the others who filled the room, Emma struggled hard to hide her contempt for the man.

"Exactly how do you plan to do that, Rev. Jones?" a reporter asked with a pen poised over a notepad.

"He'll respond in a few minutes," Denise Hollingsworth said, positioning herself between the reporter and Jones, "once the press conference officially begins."

That sent Serena McMillan into motion. She handed Emma, Otis, and Jones the typed statements that had been crafted for them. Emma thought back to the dry run of the press conference that she, Otis, and Otis Lee had gone through the night before with Otis Lee substituting for Jones who'd been tied up with conference calls regarding the rally. She'd stumbled through her statement that was full of demands for Rusty Carter to be indicted and for the police department to be overhauled and how protests would continue until those things happened. Yet saying again that she doubted she'd be able to read the thing in front of a gaggle of reporters only resulted in her family and Jones' assistants assuring her that she could. They spoke to her like she was a little girl afraid of starting kindergarten.

Now, with camera crews making last-minute adjustments to their equipment, she tried to steel herself for what she had to do. Of herself, Jones, and Otis, she was to be the last to speak, then they would answer reporters' questions. *Lord, help me, Jesus,* she prayed.

Serena motioned for the three of them to sit, and a small ripple of relief went through Emma when Otis chose the chair in the middle, saving her from having to be next to Jones. Sliding into the seat beside Otis, she gave him an anxious glance. He responded with a quick smile and gentle squeeze of her hand. It was the first time he'd touched her in days. Whether it was a faint sign that their relationship would eventually get back to how it used to be or if it was only a remnant of the way it had been, she couldn't say, but she welcomed his touch nonetheless. Too soon, though, he drew his hand away as he focused on Serena who tapped a microphone to get everyone's attention.

"Ladies and gentlemen," Serena said, "thank you for coming this afternoon to. . ."

But the sight of the man positioned behind several reporters suddenly made Emma only dimly aware of Serena. There was no mistaking him, even amidst the thick crowd. His authoritative bearing commanded attention—she'd recognize him anywhere. So what was Det. Larry Entminger doing in her home? And why now for heaven's sake? He knew what time the press conference had been scheduled for. Anyone reading the paper or watching the news lately knew that.

She scanned the room for his partner. Not finding him rattled her even more. Had Det. Entzminger come alone or had he ordered Det. Andy Jamison to snoop around the house while everyone else was packed into the living room?

She reminded herself that even if Det. Jamison searched every inch of the house, the only thing revealing the truth of what happened to Marcus was hidden away in a safe deposit box at her bank, yet that didn't bring her the relief she desperately needed. How could it, given the way the African-American detective kept staring at her? He locked his eyes on her like he could peer into her soul and make the half-truths and outright lies she'd told him become more visible than large, malignant tumors on an X-ray.

She looked away from him and realized Serena had yielded the microphone to Creighton Jones. He was thumping on the tabletop podium to punctuate his words, but she was only able to follow a few of them before her attention shifted back to Det. Entzminger. Was it her imagination or had he moved closer toward her? Good Lord—what if he pushed his way forward and announced in front of everyone he had proof she'd lied to him? What would she do? And wasn't it a crime to lie to an investigating officer? Wasn't that "obstruction of justice" or some such thing that could put her behind bars, not to mention shame her family?

Her mind raced with images of being hauled out of the room in handcuffs like a common criminal while the media captured her and her family's humiliation.

Get hold of yourself, girl, she told herself. Surely Det. Entzminger wasn't that cruel. Or was he? Did he enjoy showing how he dealt with people who dared to lie to him?

Another glimpse at him chilled her. He didn't have a trace of compassion in him. That was clear as day. She'd bet he'd even throw the book at his own mother if she so much as double-parked. Upholding the law was probably his religion, and no doubt he was willing to sacrifice anyone at its altar.

He stood ram-rod straight while scrutinizing her. What was he about to do? Without knowing that, it was impossible to think of how to counter him. She fingered the ridiculously colorful scarf around her neck. It felt like a noose. She hated it along with everything else she wore.

It was all wrong. She should've tried harder to convince her family not to go through with the press conference. It was a disaster in the making. They might as well have set booby traps throughout the house.

She suddenly realized that the room had gone silent and everyone had joined Entzminger in staring at her. In confusion, she looked to Otis.

"It's your turn now, baby," he whispered.

"Oh!" she said more loudly than she meant to, and then, adding to her embarrassment, she repeated herself. "Oh!" What was wrong with her? Why was she acting like an idiotic parrot that only knew one word? How on earth had she not noticed Otis finishing reading his statement? She must be losing her mind.

Drawing in a deep breath, she tried to steady herself. The time for backing out was long gone. She had a roomful of people waiting for her to speak. There was nothing left to do except to take the words Denise Hollingsworth had written for her and claim them as her own. She clasped her trembling hands together, leaned forward and read, "My nightmare began on July 30, the day my child was shot and killed by—" But images of Marcus's body laid out on the stainless steel table at the morgue, Rusty Carter sitting cross-legged in the cemetery, faded silk flowers flapping in the hot breeze, and a kid heaving a trash can through a plate glass window hit her like a sledgehammer and cut her off in mid-sentence. She collapsed into sobs.

As Otis pulled her close and their children rushed to comfort her, the idea of how TV coverage of her meltdown would entertain people while they channel surfed from sit-coms to game shows to the local news later that evening made her cry harder and burn with shame.

Creighton Jones shoehorned his way between Ed and Otis Lee to embrace her and over the rising murmuring, he loudly proclaimed, "See the hell this poor woman is going through? She's heartbroken! She's devastated! Rusty Carter snuffed out her son's life for no good reason. He can't be allowed to get away with it!"

"Oh, God," Emma moaned, sickened by his closeness. He was smothering her. So was her family. She couldn't breathe.

"Momma, are you okay?" Brenda asked.

"I . . . I . . . need to lie down," Emma said, gasping for

air. It was as if someone had wrapped a plastic bag over her head.

The murmuring grew louder.

"You sure you don't need for us to take you to the hospital?" Otis asked. "You look like you're fixing to fall out."

"No, I just need to rest for a while," Emma said, yanking off the scarf and using it to wipe sweat that had started streaming down her face. To hell with her makeup. She couldn't believe how the room had become so hot and stifling, yet why was she the only one wilting from it? Again, she wondered what on earth was wrong with her, although she knew, whatever it was, it wasn't anything that a trip to the emergency room could cure.

"Get Momma some water!" Ed yelled to no one in particular.

"Here, I'll help you up," Brenda said to Emma, looping one of Emma's arms over her shoulders. Stephanie braced Emma from the opposite side.

Emma was grateful for her daughters' aid. She didn't know if she was able to make it out of the room under her own power, and she wanted to leave before she made more of a spectacle of herself. Added to her sudden weakness, a nasty, sour taste filling her mouth made her afraid that she was about to throw up. The only thing worse than having that getting caught on camera was Det. Entzminger confronting her. He showed no sign of preparing to do that, however. Was it wishful thinking or did he actually appear concerned? Maybe he had a bit of humanity in him after all.

A somewhat frazzled Denise Hollingsworth grabbed the microphone. "I'm sorry, ladies and gentlemen, but if you'd be so kind as to excuse Mrs. Jennings. She's . . . um . . . er . . . she needs to rest. In a moment, though, Rev. Jones and Mr. Jennings will take questions."

Emma felt everyone's eyes on her while Brenda and Stephanie helped her shuffle out of the room with her sons following close behind. A neighbor came around the corner from the kitchen with a glass of ice water for Emma.

"Thank you," she said. She took several gulps from

it and instantly felt a little better. Simply having that awful taste rinsed away helped. She was able to mount the steps with only light support from her girls.

Once settled in bed with a washcloth moistened with cold water pressed to her forehead, she told her children, "Y'all go on back downstairs. I'm all right."

"You sure?" Brenda asked. Her troubled expression mirrored that of her brothers and sister. "I'm still wondering if we ought to get you to a doctor."

Emma made a dismissive gesture. "I don't need a doctor. I just need to rest for a while." She added, "By myself—without y'all hovering over me like a bunch of mother hens."

"We're worried about you," Otis Lee said.

"Well, you shouldn't be," Emma said. "I'm feeling a lot better. Honest. And a little nap is all it'll take for me to be good as new." Seeing that they remained unconvinced, she pointed toward the door and gently but firmly said, "Go. Now."

With obvious reluctance, they filed out of the room. Emma rolled over onto her side and remained on the bed for nearly three hours, pretending to be asleep whenever any of her children or Otis returned to check on her. She wasn't up to talking to them yet. They'd either want to keep fussing over her or rehash every tiny detail of the press conference and their excitement about the upcoming rally.

Finally, thoughts of the rosebush on Marcus's grave made her sit up. The plant had to be watered daily for it to have any chance of surviving the heat wave. Wondering if she'd be able to leave the house without having to come face-to-face with Det. Entzminger, Jones, his aides, his bodyguards, or any of the reporters who had packed the living room, she peeked out the window to see if their vehicles were still in the yard. Only her old Skylark and Otis and Ed's pickups were visible. Thank God.

She changed into her gardening clothes, went downstairs, and found Ed softly snoring in the recliner and Otis on the sofa watching CNN. "How you feeling?" he asked her.

"Much better," she said. "Didn't I tell you I only needed some rest?"

"Yeah, but seeing as how you were turning green around the gills, I got to wondering if you had something serious ailing you."

"It was too much commotion, that's all. You know how much I hate having to talk in front of a lot of people, especially when they're poking cameras and microphones at me. I told y'all last night I couldn't read that paper, but you wouldn't listen to me."

"I bet you could've done it if you'd set your mind to it."

"With a heap of folk staring at me like I had two heads?" she said, resentment igniting inside of her. He either had no idea of how hard she'd tried or flat out didn't care. "It didn't help matters to see that black detective who came by here the night Marcus died."

"Jerry Entzminger," Otis said.

Emma didn't bother correcting Otis' recollection of the detective's first name. "You talked to him?"

"Only long enough to ask what he was doing here."

"What did he say?"

"Said he needed to ask you a few more questions about Marcus."

"Did he say why the heck he showed up during the press conference?"

"No, but it don't matter. I don't want you talking to him any time or anywhere. He ain't doing nothing but scheming to clear that cop."

"You don't know that for sure," Emma said, instantly regretting the remark.

"Like hell I don't! I ain't falling for that 'impartiality' bullshit!"

"Don't use that kind of language with me."

"I'll talk any fucking way I want to in my own house!"

She grabbed her purse and marched toward the back door.

"Where you going?" he demanded to know.

"Out."

CHAPTER 12

"You're one lucky dude, Rusty," Scott said as he and Rusty watched a glass technician install a new windshield in Rusty's Sierra.

"Don't I know it," Rusty said, thinking back to the night before when Scott had found him hanging upside down in the Sierra after it flipped over, then landed with its wheels spinning uselessly in the air. It was nothing short of a miracle that the pickup hadn't slammed into a tree and that—other than some cuts on his face from shattered glass hitting him and a bruised chest from his seatbelt restraining him—Rusty had been able to walk away from the wreck without any injuries. That there was no damage to his truck besides the smashed door window and windshield added to the miracle.

"They haven't gotten any leads on the creep who shot at me?" he asked Scott.

"Nope," Scott answered through clenched teeth.

"So he's still out there." Rusty scrutinized the busy street facing the garage. "He could be watching me now for all I know."

"Wish I'd gotten a better look at the car the prick was driving, but all I had on my mind was getting to you."

"I'm glad you did. I didn't get a good look at his car either. I was too busy trying to stay alive."

"Speaking of which, maybe you ought to leave town until things blow over."

Rusty stared at him. "And go where?"

"My aunt and uncle have a cabin up near Hendersonville, North Carolina. I'm sure they'd let you stay there for a while."

"But there's no telling how long this guy will be after me. Even if I'm cleared, there's nothing to say that he won't keep hunting me." Starting to pace from one side of the garage to the other, Rusty went on, "Besides, I can't let him run me out of here. This is the only place I've ever lived." Pacing even faster, he said, "Damn it, though, this whole thing is making me crazy."

Scott grabbed him by the arm. "Stop it! I know it's hard, but try not to let him get in your head like this. That's probably what he wants."

"Yeah, besides killing me."

"There's a way out of this. We've just got to figure out what it is."

"I can't think straight anymore." Rusty swallowed hard. "And to tell you the truth, I'm scared shitless. I mean, somewhere out there, there's some nut who wants to kill me, and I've got a bad feeling that the only way to stop him is for me to kill him first."

He left the garage for home, all the while checking his rearview mirror, scanning the road ahead for anything that looked suspicious, and cursing himself for not being able to remember much about the car the gunman drove. Even its color escaped his memory. Should he ask the department to have him hypnotized? He had heard that sometimes people could remember things under hypnosis that they couldn't otherwise. He rejected the idea as quickly as it came to him. Hypnosis would just be a waste of time; he simply had been too scared to really look at the car, which is why he couldn't remember any details about it.

* * *

When he arrived home, he saw his sister's beat-up minivan parked in the driveway. "Crap," he groaned. After what he endured the night before, he didn't feel like dealing with Charlene and his nephew and niece. Why the hell did they have to come over so often anyway? And stay for so long? Charlene wasn't ever going to find a husband for herself and a stepfather for Blake and Abby if she kept hanging out at her parents' home.

The kids barreled into him as soon as he stepped inside. Abby wrapped herself around his lower left leg. "Mama told us somebody tried to kill you last night, Uncle Rusty!"

Before Rusty had time to answer, Blake clutched him from the other side. "Your face is all scratched up!"

"Yeah!" Abby said. "You look somethin' awful, like a mean cat got hold of you."

"I'm okay," Rusty said while trying to peel the kids off of him.

"I'm gonna kill that nigger who did this to you!" Blake declared.

Stunned, Rusty could only stare at him. He'd never seen the seven-year-old boiling with such hatred. Pure racial hatred, the kind the Carters were now infamous for. Had it played a part in his shooting Marcus Jennings? If Marcus had been white, would he have waited a moment longer before firing—a moment that might have given him enough time to realize Marcus's weapon was only a harmless toy?

"Listen to the big man talk." Russ Carter smirked as he cracked open a beer and flipped the TV channel from his wife's favorite game show to CNN.

She only huffed in protest and went on crocheting a dish rag to add to the teetering pile of them that she would donate to their church's annual fall bazaar to raise money for missionary projects.

"You ain't killing nobody," Charlene said to her son. She unfolded a pair of jeans from some hand-me-down clothes that a cousin, who had a son a little older than Blake, left at the house for Blake. Charlene studied the jeans. "Try these on, Blake, to see if they fit."

"They got a hole in the knee," he pointed out.

"So what?" she said. "That's the style anyway."

"I'm tired of wearing Dylan's old clothes," Blake said.

"Did I ask you what you were tired of?" Charlene snapped at him. When he didn't answer, she said, "Huh? Did I?"

"No," he mumbled.

"No, ma'am," Charlene said sharply. "Keep sassin' me and I'm going to whip your ungrateful little behind."

Go home, Rusty wanted to tell her. Instead, he went into the kitchen for some iced tea.

He began filling a glass with ice cubes as his mother came in. "Have them men from IA been back in touch with you lately?" she asked.

"No," he murmured. The thought of Detective Larry Entzminger and his sidekick, Detective Andy Jamison, made him stop in mid-motion. He hadn't seen the two Internal Affairs investigators since they came by the house the day following the shooting, but he knew they had interviewed other people in the department about him, gone through his personnel file, his school records, even his medical records going back to when he was a boy. In short, they had combed through, scrutinized, and picked apart every aspect of his life. Had they found anything that made him look bad? If so, what was it and how did they plan to use it against him? And had they found out anything more about Marcus Jennings that hadn't already been reported?

Watching the news conference held by Creighton Jones and the Jennings family sure hadn't shed any new light on the boy. It only made Mrs. Jennings appear more sympathetic, especially when she broke down and her children had to practically carry her from the room. What kind of jury would side against her in favor of Rusty? None that he could imagine.

Suddenly, a loud explosion erupted. Rusty dived to the floor. "Get down, Mama!" he screamed in terror.

She ran toward him. "Honey, it's only . . ."

"Get down, I said, before you get shot!" he yelled.

"What the hell's going on?" Russell Carter flew into the kitchen with Charlene and her children screaming wildly as they raced in behind him.

"That guy's shooting at us!" Rusty hollered, his panic nearly cutting off his breath. "Y'all get down!"

His mother grabbed him. "Honey, it's only a bag of popcorn busting."

"What?" he asked, panting.

"The bag of popcorn I was popping for the kids," Doris said. Kneeling beside him, she cradled his head in her lap and wiped away the sweat streaming down his forehead. "It busted. I'm sorry, sugar, that it gave you such a fright."

"You got to get hold of yourself, boy," Russell said with obvious disgust. "Otherwise, you're gonna wind up in the loony bin."

"Jesus Christ," Rusty said. With what little strength he had left, he sat up and wiped away more sweat.

"You want one of my nerve pills?" his mother asked him.

"Yeah, two would be even better," he answered.

She released him and went to fetch the tranquilizers. Abby took her place, cuddling against him. "Don't be scared, Uncle Rusty. I ain't gonna let nobody hurt you."

That got a weak smile from him. If only his four-year-old niece could protect him. "I appreciate that, baby."

Not to be outdone by his kid sister, Blake said, "Anybody tries to do anything to you, I'll stomp the shit out of 'em!"

Charlene yanked him toward her. "What did I tell you about cussin'?"

"Ow!" Blake tried to twist out of her grip, but she held tight as she dragged him toward the sink.

"Maybe this will teach you a lesson." She grabbed a bar of soap near the kitchen sink and tried to shove it in his mouth. He squirmed like an eel caught by an alligator. "Ugh!" he protested.

Rusty forced himself to stand and walk to his bedroom on unsteady legs. Any more commotion and he really was going to end up in a loony bin.

He stretched out on his twin bed and stared upward, trying to make a pattern in the countless bits of popcorn-like plaster covering the ceiling. Of course he couldn't. There was no more rhyme or reason to it than to how his life was shattering. Both were in utter chaos.

His mother tapped lightly on the door before opening it. She set a glass of water on a nightstand and shook out a pill from a prescription bottle.

"I told you that I need two," Rusty said.

She hesitated. "These things are real strong. You might ought to see how one does you before taking another one."

"They don't do you too bad and you've been taking them for as long as I can remember."

"That's 'cause I'm used to them."

He swallowed the one she gave him and held out his hand, which still slightly trembled, for another one.

Doris Carter sighed. "Okay." She tipped the bottle over his palm until another of the small white pills tumbled out. "Be sure not to drink no kind of booze with these."

Doing so hadn't occurred to him, but now that she mentioned it, it struck him as a good idea. He wanted oblivion. That was probably the fastest and easiest way to get there.

He sat up. "We still got some salami?"

"Yeah, you want me to make you a sandwich and bring it to you?"

"Aint' no need for you to go to such trouble. I'll just get a piece, something to soothe my stomach." *While one of Daddy's beers soothes my mind.*

"Oh, Lord, I hate that you're going through all this."

He forced a smile. "It can't last forever." Perhaps if he told himself that enough times, he'd believe it.

Judging from his mom's expression, she was having a hard a time believing it too.

He followed her down the hallway, but when she

veered into the den to help Charlene separate Blake and Abby as they furiously fought over a glow stick, he slipped into the kitchen and grabbed a beer from the refrigerator. He made it back to his room without drawing any notice.

After gulping down the beer, he laid down on his bed and closed his eyes against the bright morning sunlight.

He awoke to even harsher sunlight. He glanced at the clock on his nightstand—four-fifteen in the afternoon. The act of sitting up felt like moving through thick molasses and his tongue nearly stuck to the roof of his mouth. Grimacing, he went to the bathroom, rinsed his mouth and splashed cold water on his face. It was then that he noticed the only sound in the house was coming from the TV in the den. No doubt that his parents were snoring in their respective recliners and Charlene had left with her kids. Finally.

Sure enough, a trip to the kitchen to make a sandwich confirmed his assumptions. He ate a salami sandwich while downing it with a Budweiser. Before he knew it, he'd drunk another Bud, his father's last one, which meant a trip to the corner store to replenish his dad's stock, preferably before his dad woke up.

The heat outside was even more brutal than he had braced himself for, and inside his truck was worse still. He cranked the air conditioner to its highest setting and maneuvered the Sierra onto the street. When in the hell would the heat wave break? It was already into its thirty-eighth day, and had long ago broken the city record for the number of consecutive days that the temperature went over one hundred degrees. Eventually the brutal summer had to end. Surely.

The ten minutes he spent inside the corner store buying a six-pack offered a brief relief from the heat, and thankfully, he'd found a shady spot to park his truck under so it wasn't as bad climbing into it as it had been when he'd gotten in it to drive to the store. He sat for a few minutes, letting the air conditioner blow refreshingly cool air on his face and Taylor Swift croon to him through the stereo speakers. It felt good to be away from home and he wasn't ready to go back just yet, but didn't know where else to go, nor did he have anyone to go anywhere with. Scott and Josh wouldn't finish their shifts until later that night.

He put the truck in gear. He'd just drive around for a while to clear his head, then return home.

In the back of his mind, he'd known all along where he would end up. He couldn't stay away from it, not even for a single day. He was nuts to be there; he knew that. It didn't change anything, though.

He slowly walked up the long, winding walkway, pausing occasionally to read some grave markers that were on either side of him. By the time he reached his destination, sweat dribbled into his eyes and plastered his T-shirt and Levis to his body. He wiped his forehead and knelt beside the grave that Mrs. Jennings had covered with the most beautiful roses he had ever seen. He hadn't known such a vibrant shade of purple existed, and the flowers' fragrance carried him to where no problems existed or ever would.

Gently, he ran a fingertip over a few rose petals. They felt like soft velvet, like something you'd wrap the most precious newborn baby with. Where had Mrs. Jennings gotten this miracle? He studied the flowers longer as a memory struggled to reach the forefront of his mind. When it finally did, he realized he'd seen a rose bush exactly like it near the Jennings' front porch. Odds were it was the same one, and Mrs. Jennings had moved it here.

It was so mesmerizing that it took a few minutes to realize that she'd planted more flowers on the grave. He didn't know what kind they were, only that they were in beautiful shades of pink that complimented the lavender roses. The grass close to them was as lush as they were, and contrasted starkly against the withered centipede in the rest of the cemetery. He thought about the jugs of water Mrs. Jennings had in the wheelbarrow along with the amazing roses when they had first met. Apparently, she was still lugging up the jugs to maintain this miniature Garden of Eden. Should he start leaving large containers of water for her to save her the trouble of hauling them herself?

He ran his fingers through his sweat-slickened hair. What he ought to do was to leave her the fuck alone and allow her to tend to her baby boy's gravesite without worrying about running into him there.

As if his very thoughts of her had conjured her up, he began to hear the rhythmic squeaking of her wheelbarrow matched by the sound of her distinctive footsteps. Shit. What was he going to do now? What was he going to say? If he had to come, why hadn't he picked a time when it was less likely that she'd find him there again? Shit. Shit. Shit.

The sounds grew louder until they suddenly stopped. Then he heard her speak almost in a whisper: "Rusty? I mean, er . . . Ofc. Carter?"

He took a deep breath and turned around. "Hi, Mrs. Jennings."

"Oh, my God!" she screamed and ran to him. "What happened to you?"

Stupid from the shock of her taking him in her arms, Rusty could only say, "What?"

"Your face." She touched a trembling hand near one of his cuts.

Her gentle touch froze his brain. Not a single word came to it. He couldn't believe that she was holding him as if he were . . . Marcus.

"What happened to you?" she repeated.

For a moment, all he could do was look into her dark brown eyes. They were filled with worry. This was crazy—her worried about him, after what he'd done? Why?

Knowing that he had no chance of saying anything coherent while he remained in her embrace, he eased out of it. "I. . .uh. . .got in a wreck."

That only seemed to deepen her concern, which he didn't deserve the least bit of. "Lord have mercy! When?"

"Late last night," he answered while silently cursing himself more for having come when he did. He should've remembered that his face looked a mess and would trigger questions from her.

Taking hold of him again, she scrutinized him all over. "Where else are you hurt?"

"Nowhere." He tried to work his way from her again, but she held him firmly. "Honestly, Mrs. Jennings, I'm fine. It's only these few cuts on my face."

"Did someone run into you?"

He looked away. Why was she asking him all these damned questions? Why couldn't she just let him leave? Her strong grip and piercing questions rattled him so badly that he couldn't think straight, much less come up with any convincing lies. "No," he answered weakly.

"You ran into someone else?"

"No, into a tree."

"What! You weren't trying to kill yourself, were you?"

"No!" he said. His shock caused more words to tumble out uncontrollably. "Somebody was trying to kill me! When he shot at me, he busted the glass on my car door and it cut my face, and when he took a second shot, I lost control of my truck and hit a tree."

"Oh, Lord!" Mrs. Jennings shrieked before bursting into tears and pulling him against her. "This is all my fault!"

Seriously wondering if he had started hallucinating from being in the heat for so long, he asked, "How the heck could any of this be your fault?"

"I . . . I . . . "

"Miz Jennings!" the groundskeeper hollered, causing her and Rusty to jump apart. "You all right?"

"Yes, Mr. Reese. I'm fine."

The elderly man approached her, his eyes darting to Rusty. "You sure you all right?"

"Yes," she said.

He shot Rusty another look, much darker than the one before. "You know who he is, don't you?"

She nodded and gave Rusty's shoulder a quick squeeze. "It's okay. Really."

Clearly surprised by what he'd just seen, the groundskeeper muttered almost under his breath, "If this don't beat all."

You don't know the half of it, Rusty wanted to tell him. He turned back to Emma Jennings. "What were you about to tell me?"

Mr. Reese leaned in closer while resting his hands atop the handle of a straight-edged shovel, signaling he was as curious as Rusty about what she had to say, and Rusty could tell it was draining away her courage to tell him something.

As politely as he could, he asked the old man, "Do you mind giving us some privacy?"

"No problem," he replied. He moved a grand total of about eight feet away before making a show of edging around a grave maker. He wasn't going anywhere out of earshot and obviously knew nothing could be done about it, goddamn him. The moment was gone. Mr. Reese had ruined it. There was no use hanging around any longer. Mrs. Jennings seemed completely defeated. She couldn't even look Rusty in the eye, much less say anything important to him.

"Guess I'll head back home," he told her before adding a lie, "good seeing you again."

"You, too," she murmured, locking her gaze on the gardening gloves she tugged on. She was about as sorry a liar as he was. No doubt their encounter had left her shaken too, and she wished it hadn't happened.

"Hope you don't stay out here in this heat too long," he said. "That could be dangerous."

"You right about that!" Mr. Reese agreed.

Rusty rolled his eyes. The asshole didn't even bother to pretend he wasn't eavesdropping.

"I'll be careful," Mrs. Jennings said. "You be careful, too."

He started walking toward his truck. "Don't worry about me. I'll be fine." Another lie.

CHAPTER 13

"You did what?" Dottie screeched when Emma told her what she had nearly blurted out to Rusty Carter.

"I couldn't help it. I can't stand him not knowing the truth. It's eating me alive."

"Emma Louise, you listen to me, and you listen to me good," Dottie said in a way that reminded Emma of how her mother used to talk to her when she meant business. "You stay away from that fella. Don't be nowheres around him."

"That would mean not being able to go to Marcus's grave."

"Well, then, that's you'll have to do until he's cleared."

"But no telling how long that will be," Emma said, nearly in a wail.

"I don't expect it'll take too long. From what they said on the news, they usually wrap up these kinds of investigations in only a few weeks."

Emma slumped back against her bed's headboard. "Knowing my luck, this one will drag on until Kingdom come, and in the meanwhile, I can't live with myself because of what I'm doing to that poor boy."

"You just making it worse on yourself with talk like that. Stop it, and keep telling yourself that this will be over soon. Carter will be back on the force in no time flat without your having to rip your marriage and your family to pieces by blabbing about what Marcus really did. And there's his reputation to consider too. You don't want folk thinking that he was a nut."

"He wasn't!" Emma hollered.

"I know that, honey," Dottie said in a comforting tone. "But other people won't. You know the stupid things folk say about people who . . . um . . . "

Emma gripped the phone tighter as an uncomfortable silence set in between her and her best friend of over a half century. Finally, after determining that Dottie couldn't find the right words to say, she said them for her. "Who commit suicide."

"Yes." After another uncomfortable pause, she said, "Just hold yourself together, honey, and keep quiet. That's the only way this will all work out for everyone's sakes, especially yours and your family's."

"I'll try, I will, but I don't know how much longer I can go on like this."

"Promise me you'll hold tight until I get back there."

Emma's heart sank. "But there's no telling when that'll be, as bad off as your sister is."

"She is in a bad way," Dottie admitted, "but she's no worse than she was when I got here and that may not change anytime soon. I'm gonna talk to her doctor when he makes his rounds tomorrow morning, and if he thinks there's a good chance Sarah's gonna stay like this for a while, I'm coming home, at least long enough to buck you up some."

"You're too old to be ripping and running between here and New York on my account."

"Don't you worry about me. I'm fine. You the one who needs help, and I'm gonna give it to you. Promise me, though, that you won't do anything at least until I get back there."

Knowing that Dottie wasn't going to take "no" for an answer, Emma wearily said, "Okay."

Early the next morning, she walked along the hospital corridor to clock in for her first day of work since Marcus's death. It was a relief to be in a place unmarked by the chaos that had turned her life upside down. She took comfort in the assurance that some things stayed the same no matter what. Her twelve-hour shifts at the hospital were going to be her oases of normalcy; her escape from being surrounded by people obsessed with avenging Marcus's death. The demands of caring for patients would leave little time to think about anything else. While that used to be a burden, she recognized the blessing in it now. She longed to lose herself in the relentlessly grueling job and considered asking her supervisor, Carol Tyler, to schedule her to work more days that week. The memory of how Mrs. Tyler had gone on and on about how noble Emma was for turning down the offer of an extension of paid leave until after the rally was downright funny. It had taken more than a little effort not to let on to Mrs. Tyler that she'd rather work double-shifts for free than to stay stuck in the house any longer, especially since it had been turned into the central command center for planning that God-awful protest.

And as if Creighton Jones's appearance wasn't enough to guarantee coverage by all the major media, several celebrities had promised to fly in for the event too, including Forty Ounce, a rapper so famous that even Emma knew of him. The crowd was expected to number in the thousands and the idea of having to speak to them made her stomach knot. There was no way she was going to be able to do that, yet despite her meltdown during the press conference, her family and Creighton Jones and his two fashion-plate henchwomen kept declaring that she could if she set her mind to it. If only they'd leave her alone.

"Hey, Emma!" someone called from behind.

Emma turned and saw Mabel Davis and Flossie McDonald entering the hallway from a side door. Like her, they'd been nurses' aides at the hospital since time began.

Flossie was the first to reach Emma. "Welcome back, girl," she said, giving Emma a hug. "We been missing you."

"I don't see how considering how often y'all have been coming by the house," Emma said. She squeezed Flossie tightly, then opened her arms to Mabel. "Did y'all get the 'thank you' cards I sent?"

"Yes," Mabel said, pulling Emma close. "You didn't have to do that."

"I know, but I wanted to let you know how much I appreciated everything you did for me."

"It wasn't no trouble," Flossie said.

"Lord have mercy, y'all have only brought enough food to feed an army," Emma said. "We've still got some of that chicken, macaroni salad, and red velvet cake left. No telling when I'll need to cook again."

"I bet you it won't take long for it to get eaten up with all the folks y'all got coming and going," Flossie said. "Matter of fact, I'll probably stop by Saturday morning with a platter of sandwiches so y'all will have plenty to eat before going downtown for the rally."

Emma's smile wilted. She could've gone a lot longer without being reminded of the dreaded event.

"Oooh, I can't wait," Mabel said. "This is like being back in the sixties with Martin Luther King. My momma wouldn't let me go to none of the marches and stuff back then, but can't nobody stop me this time, nobody that is but Mrs. Tyler, and if she don't let me off, I'm going to raise sand."

"I wish I didn't have to go," Emma muttered.

Her friends gaped at her.

"Why?" Flossie asked. "Seems like you'd want to be there more than anybody."

Emma paused before saying anything else. Her feelings about Creighton Jones weren't something she wanted a lot of folk to know about—even close friends like Flossie and Mabel. If word got out about how she couldn't stand the sight of him, the police were bound to use it to try to play "divide and conquer". It was too high a risk to take so she simply shrugged and said, "It won't do nothing except make the police dig in their heels."

"It'll do a lot more than that," Mabel said. "It'll probably save somebody's life because you can bet your bottom dollar them cops will think twice and then some before they kill another black guy. Maybe if the kinfolk of the fellas they killed earlier this summer had spoke up more, Marcus would still be alive."

Anxious to change the subject, Emma said, "I don't know, but one thing's for sure—if we don't clock in soon and get to work, we'll have all the time in the world to go to rallies because we won't have jobs."

"Yeah," Flossie said and added with a sigh, "Jesus, I'll be glad when I don't have to punch a clock no more."

They swiped their badges on the electronic time clock and got in a nearby service elevator. Emma stepped onto her floor to the greetings of more coworkers. It was clear some of them weren't comfortable being around her. They gave her a quick wave or a brief greeting before busying themselves with tasks that probably weren't as urgent as they acted like they were. Emma understood. She'd run into more than a few people like them since Marcus's death. Afraid of saying the wrong thing, they tried to avoid her as much as possible.

Carol Tyler, however, was thrilled to see her and gave her a printout of information about each of the patients Emma was assigned to for the next twelve hours. Emma noticed that because of an overflow from the trauma unit, there were more young people on the floor than usual. She started the morning by bathing and dressing a frail old man who was scheduled for transfer to a nursing home that afternoon. It wasn't long before she became completely absorbed in her work, and she was doing fairly well until she had to deliver a breakfast tray to Room 4125.

She rapped on the door and waited a moment before opening it. At first, she and the young African-American couple inside the room who were either about to have sex or just finished having it simply stared at each other in surprise. Then the woman scrambled off the man who was lying in the hospital bed with a bandaged chest, and she tried to yank her clothing back into place over her heavy breasts and wide hips, but one side of her denim miniskirt stubbornly remained hitched higher than the other.

The man grinned, flashing Emma a mouthful of gold teeth. "We didn't hear you knock."

"I . . . um . . . sorry," Emma stammered. His lack of concern at being caught by a stranger in what most people would consider an embarrassing situation rattled her almost as much as walking in on him and the woman. She doubted they were married. With his gold teeth and gangsta-style gold necklaces draped around his neck and the woman looking like an extra from one of those trashy BET music videos she used to fuss at Marcus for watching, they didn't seem the marrying kind. However, that apparently hadn't stopped them from acting like they were in a secluded honeymoon suite instead of a hospital room with a door without a lock and a steady stream of staff, volunteers, and visitors.

Remembering why she'd come in the first place, she approached the man with the tray. "Here's your breakfast."

He took the tray from her, lifted its lid and sneered at the bowl of oatmeal beneath it. "You can take this shit back, lady," he said, "and bring me some pizza."

She wanted to tell him to watch his mouth but figured it'd be a waste of breath. She made no move for the tray. "Pizza's not on the breakfast menu. You didn't see it on the menu card, did you?"

"What you talking about?" he asked.

"Didn't they give you a menu card last night to fill out for what you wanted this morning?" Emma asked.

"Seem like somebody left something like that yesterday," the man's girlfriend said while leaning back in a chair next to the hospital bed. "I don't remember what we did with it though."

"I was so fucked up from pain medicine that I don't remember much of nothing from yesterday," the man said, "but I can tell you now I don't want this." He gave the oatmeal another disgusted glance. "I got a taste for some deep-dish pizza with pepperoni and sausage."

Emma pulled out her patient data printout to check if he had any diet restrictions. Before getting to the section of the printout that listed which type of diet he was on, she skimmed over his admitting information: His name was Jahreen A. McMurphy. He was twenty-one. He'd been admitted two days ago. He was a post-surgical transfer from ICU. His diagnosis: gunshot wound to the chest.

She skimmed further down the sheet and told him, "You're on a soft diet. That means no pizza or anything else you have to chew."

"I'll eat whatever the fuck I feel like," he snapped.

Emma glared at him. A four-by-four inch bandage covered the center of his chest. It was the same place Marcus would've been bandaged had he survived getting shot.

"Can't nobody tell me what I can eat and what I can't," Jahreen mumbled while reaching for an overnight bag on the floor. "I ain't no child." He stuck his hand into the bag and pulled out a thick wad of cash.

"Where'd you get all that money?" Emma heard herself blurt out.

"What?" Jahreen said, obviously startled by the question as was his girlfriend.

Without thinking, Emma plunged ahead. "You're dealing drugs, ain't you?"

"Bitch, you need to quit trippin'," Jahreen said with a threatening scowl. "How I get my money is none of your fucking business."

His girlfriend scrambled to her feet. "You got no right to be asking him shit like that! Who you think you are, the police?"

"I'm a mother!" Emma screamed, so furious she could barely see straight. Jahreen A. McMurphy was the kind of vermin that had ruined Waverton, who made it dangerous to walk the streets even in broad daylight, who turned decent people into vicious crackheads who'd rob or kill for their next hit. She hated him.

"You're fucking crazy," Jahreen said. "Get the hell out my room before I knock the shit out you."

His girlfriend charged over to Emma. "I don't know what your fucking problem is, you goddamned bitch, but you don't be busting into people's rooms accusing them of shit like that! Who's the head man in this place? I want to talk to him right now!"

You'd better not come one inch closer to me, Emma thought, glowering at her. The woman was no better than Jahreen. No doubt she lived off of his filthy drug money.

Jahreen extended a twenty-dollar bill toward the woman. "Forget about her, baby, and go get me some pizza—sausage and pepperoni."

Emma whirled toward him and hollered, "How dare you after everything the doctors did to save your life! You sorry, low-down—"

With a wild shriek, Jahreen's girlfriend grabbed her and slapped her hard across the face, blinding Emma with pain.

The door flew open. "What's the devil's going on in here?" asked Wayne Jeffcoat, a physical therapist.

Emma fled past him and the blur of other staff members who were rushing to the room to see what the commotion was about. Ducking into a bathroom, she locked the door, slid to the floor, and buried her face in her hands. She lost track of time as the madness that erupted in Jahreen McMurphy's room replayed over and over again in her mind. Had she really barged in on him, hurled accusations at him, and gotten into a fight with his girlfriend? Had she lost her mind?

She leaned against the door, only dimly aware of Carol Tyler sporadically paging her on the overhead paging system. Although her hatred of Jahreen eased, it still burned within her like a stubborn brush fire. The cruel unfairness of him surviving while Marcus died from nearly the same exact wound fanned the fire's flames. And that no-account thug didn't even have the decency to appreciate how blessed he was.

The sound of people talking and the clatter of hospital equipment being rolled by echoed through the door. Emma checked her watch and was shaken to realize she'd been in the bathroom for over an hour.

She stood and studied her reflection in the mirror. Too bad that looking exactly as she always did hadn't stopped her from acting like a total stranger. God, what a mess she'd made of things. Not only had she probably lost a much needed job, she'd also put the hospital at risk for a big lawsuit. Security was most likely searching for her to escort her from the building and warn her never to return. The image of being led away like a common vagrant from where she'd spent most of her working life filled her with shame, but she should've thought about that before behaving so crazy. Why hadn't she simply walked out of Jahreen McMurphy's room instead of letting herself spin out of control?

She sighed. The damage was done. The only thing left to do was to deal with it.

After steeling herself, she opened the door a little, however spotting some staff members milling around the nurses' station farther down the hallway instantly weakened her resolve. She wasn't up to talking to them. They'd be full of questions, and it was going to take all the courage she had to answer the ones Mrs. Tyler would have for her.

She dashed across the hallway to a stairwell, jogged down two flights of stairs and emerged onto a hallway lined with administrative offices. Half-expecting someone to grab her from behind and handcuff her, she scrambled into her supervisor's office.

Carol Tyler, who was sitting behind her desk with her office door open, slammed down the phone receiver she had pressed to her ear. "Emma!" she cried and sprang from her high-backed, leather chair. She ran to Emma, wrapped her in a fierce bear hug and said, "Oh, my God, I've been worried sick! We've been hunting high and low for you, and I've been paging you like crazy! Are you all right? Are you okay?"

"Yes, ma'am," Emma said slowly, completely dazed.

"Oh, you poor dear! I hate that you had to even be in the same room as those awful people!"

Emma wasn't sure she'd heard right. "Ma'am?"

"Jahreen McMurphy and his slut of a girlfriend, Kenyatta Simmons. She bragged—bragged I tell you!—that she slapped you, and she had the nerve to say she'd beat the you-know-what out of you if she ever saw you again! That woman is despicable! Well, let me assure you, sweetie, you won't have to deal with her anymore. She knows better than to show her face on these premises, and we'll support you a hundred percent if you want to take out a warrant against her! Jahreen's history, too. We've transferred him to another floor and as soon as he's medically stable, we're discharging his sorry behind!"

"But—"

"I know," Mrs. Tyler said, cutting in, "you're thinking I'm being too harsh. You hate to see people getting in trouble, but nobody around here gets paid enough to be physically abused. I won't stand for anyone on my staff to be subjected to that sort of thing!" She pounded her desktop for added emphasis. Another look at Emma made her features soften. "I can't tell you how awful I feel that this happened on your first day back at work. I'm so, so sorry."

Emma didn't know what to say. Her head was spinning from the wild turn of events.

Mrs. Tyler leaned forward. "Are you sure you're okay?"

"Yeah," Emma answered quickly. "I'm fine."

"It's a wonder after tangling with a hell-cat like Kenyatta Simmons. Would you believe that she and McMurphy had the audacity to try to complain about you after how they acted?"

"What did they say?"

"Some malarkey about you accusing him of dealing drugs," Mrs. Tyler said, like the matter wasn't worth talking about.

Emma swallowed hard. The temptation to allow McMurphy and his girlfriend to be cast as the wrongdoers pulled at her, yet so did the need to admit what she'd done to set them off. Another thing troubling her was how little it had taken to pitch her over the edge. Just discovering McMurphy survived getting shot—that was all. That she'd actually hated him despite knowing little else about him bothered her also. Something was wrong with her, terribly wrong.

"It's true," she murmured.

Carol Tyler's over-plucked eyebrows rose, though only slightly. "Oh, yeah? Well, I'm sure he gave you good reason."

"No, ma'am, not really, and even if he did, it wasn't my place to get into that with him. I was there to deliver his breakfast, not a sermon. The truth is—" Emma said, pausing to steady herself, "I deserve to be fired."

"Deserve to be fired my foot! Especially over something like that! You're being way too hard on yourself, as usual."

"I don't think so, and if you'd seen how I'd acted, you wouldn't think so either." Emma slumped in the chair. "I went crazy on him. He did something that made me think of my boy in a way that got next to me and. . .and. . .I started screaming at him. Not even a dog deserved to be treated like that. It was horrible. What's worse is that I can't say it won't happen again. I feel like I've got a bomb inside of me or something, like the least little thing could set me off. I hate to say it, but maybe I'm not fit to be here."

Mrs. Tyler dashed from around her desk, knelt in front of Emma and patted her on the knee. "You don't mean that. It's just that you're upset, and it's partly my fault. I should've insisted you take more time off. Here's what I want you to do—clock out, take another week off, and don't even think about this place while you're gone."

"But how will y'all manage?" Emma asked, although the real question was how would she manage another week at home?

"Don't you fret. We'll find a way. Better that than to lose you. You're worth your weight in gold around here."

A dry laugh escaped from Emma. "That's hard to believe."

"It's the truth! You're the best aide I've got."

"I appreciate your saying that."

Mrs. Tyler stood up. "Okay, then. I'll see you in another week. Until then, your job is to stay home and take good care of yourself."

The hospital's parking lot shimmered from the brutal heat, and by the time Emma reached her car, she was damp with sweat and her mouth was dry. To make matters worse, the Skylark's interior was hot enough to bake a pound cake in. She opened both its doors and ran the air conditioner full blast while she took down the sun shield, folded it and tossed it into the back seat. For all the good it had done, she might as well not have gone to the trouble of putting it up.

She prayed the heat wave would break soon. It had already claimed three victims: a road construction worker who died from a heat stroke while shoveling gravel and an elderly couple whose rotting bodies were found in a single-wide trailer that was a hundred and ten degrees inside. The way Emma saw it, the weather had claimed other victims too, because she was certain it helped trigger the explosive chain of events that had blown the city apart. There was no convincing her that everyone from the police chief on down would've acted more rationally had the vicious heat not pushed them to their breaking point.

With the air conditioning still on its highest setting, she drove out of the parking lot. Going straight home wasn't an option. She wasn't ready to have to explain to Otis why she had another week off. The library. Yes, if there was one surefire way to be able to forget about everything going wrong, it was to dive into some good books.

An hour and a half later, she came out of the library with everything from historical romances to mysteries to gardening books. She needed to see a world beyond her hurt. If she didn't get herself together soon, she'd still be a wreck when she was due to return to work.

The books slid around on the passenger seat as she navigated the Skylark onto a busy avenue. Although it was the most direct route to her house, she regretted taking it when Waverton High came into view. The school's roadside marquee heralded the start of classes the next week. On that day, the campus would be swarming with kids pretending they hated being back at school while they excitedly caught up with classmates they hadn't seen since the end of the last school year. They'd also sign up for various clubs and sports teams, show off the latest in fall hip-hop fashions and debate which rapper had the best CD out. If they spent any time at all remembering the quiet boy who'd been a dim shadow in their midst the year before, it'd probably only be when someone mentioned the riot and upcoming rally. Beyond that, Marcus would be the furthest thing from their minds.

Despite wanting to quickly put the school in her rearview mirror, Emma stopped in its parking lot and stared blankly at the ugly, 1970's-era building that had even uglier portable classrooms behind it. It was best that the students there move on instead of dwelling on what happened to her son. Right, of course it was. She shouldn't resent them for it. Stories of others' tragedies usually didn't stay with her long, any longer than it took for her to read about them in the newspaper or watch them on TV, so why should she expect the kids at Waverton High to act any differently?

She buried her face in her hands. Trying to think logically was a waste of time. What she really wanted to do was smash something—anything—to pieces. The memory of boys pitching a trash can through the plate glass window of a laundromat during the start of the riot returned. The glass's shattering had brought them pure joy.

"Oh, God," she said, alarmed that the idea of vandalizing property had held an appeal for her even for an instant. She put the car into gear and drove home.

CHAPTER 14

As he stirred some butter into the lumpy grits his mother had made for him, Rusty tried to focus his attention on the melting square of pale yellow instead of the morning news program his dad was watching.

"You're not eating enough to keep a bird alive," his mom fussed.

Rusty mashed one of the lumps in his grits. "I'm just not hungry, and having the TV on about that doggone rally isn't helping my appetite."

"Huh?" his father said, momentarily distracted from watching the news about the hugely promoted event that would take place later that afternoon.

The image of Rev. Creighton Jones filled the TV screen and roiled Rusty's stomach. God only knew what that spotlight-hogging, slick-tongued creep would say about him in front of thousands of people and media who had swarmed in from all over creation. Thoughts of what Jones would spew out about him kept him awake most of the night, and what little sleep he did get was tormented by nightmares of Jones and Marcus Jennings. The ones about Marcus were the worst, especially the one in which he had broken into pieces on the asphalt just like his toy gun had in real life.

"I wanna watch cartoons, Granddaddy," Abby said,

swinging her chubby legs from the kitchen chair she sat in next to Rusty.

Blake thrust his fists into the air and yelled, "Transformers!"

"Quit that hollering!" Russell Carter, Sr., hollered at his grandson.

"For God's sake," Rusty muttered under his breath. He pressed his forehead against his palm. It was going to be a long, long day. He knew that to get through it with what little he had left of his sanity, he had to stay busy. He'd start by washing his mom's old Grand Prix, especially since Blake had clumsily written "Wash Me!!!" on the rear of it. With the morning news weatherman predicting another day of scorching heat, Rusty figured he ought to wash the car and his truck before it got too hot to do anything outside.

He had barely washed one side of the Grand Prix before Abby came out dragging the small plastic wading pool Charlene had found for her during a clearance sale at Walmart. The little girl had come fully prepared to use the pool. Not only had she put several toys in it, but she had also outfitted herself in a bubble-gum pink bathing suit and her blue eyes were barely visible behind the bulky "Hello, Kitty" swimming goggles she wore.

"Can you fill up my pool for me, Uncle Rusty?" she asked, positioning it near the dripping sedan.

"Sure, honey," Rusty said reluctantly. It was clear that the kids weren't going to give him a moment's peace, and because their babysitter was sick with some sort of virus, they'd be at the house until Charlene got off work. Rusty sure hoped the virus the sitter had was only the twenty-four hour kind.

Noticing that the wading pool was as dusty and grimy as his mother's car had been, he told Abby, "Take them toys out so I can hose it off first."

She did as he asked, but squealed in protest when some of the water he sprayed on the pool splattered her.

"Girl, why are you carrying on like that about a little

bit of water when you're wanting to get in more of it?" he asked.

"Because it's cold!"

He didn't bother trying to make sense of her reasoning. How could you with a four-year-old? Instead he finished cleaning the pool and filled it. She tossed the toys back in it, stepped into it, and contented herself with stacking the toys on top of each other until the movement of the water caused them to topple over, and then she'd start all over again.

Rusty envied how such a simple thing delighted her. If only he could be a carefree kid again. He had spent many a summer day at his grandparents' place out in the country, whiling away the hours with his Granddaddy Virgil on the banks of a creek, both of them with the long cane fishing poles his granddaddy favored over rod-and-reels. He wasn't one to wear shorts either, no matter how hot it was. He either wore his old Levis or bib overalls along with one of his T-shirts that, despite his wife's best efforts to keep them clean, he kept stained with grease from the Massey-Ferguson tractor he had to continually work on to grow soybeans and corn on his twenty-five acre farm. Rusty couldn't ever remember him wearing tennis shoes either, only steel-toed boots, although he did take them off while they fished.

While Rusty occasionally glanced at Abby's blue eyes behind her goggles, he tried to block the image of how his grandfather's pale blue eyes must've appeared behind the peep holes of his Klansman's hood. What had they seen? Exactly what had Virgil Carter done while cloaked beneath whiteness? Who had he terrorized? Beaten . . . maybe even murdered?

The media was certainly doing its best to answer those questions. Their determination to find anything that could cast him, Rusty, and their family in the worst possible light remained relentless. Lately, they had taken to interviewing family members of Hugh Jefferson to show that their grief and anger over his death had not faded one bit since Russell Carter, Sr., killed him eight years ago. "In cold blood,"

Jefferson's elderly mother said, dabbing away tears. "That evil Carter shot my boy dead in cold blood and he got away with it, and now his son's followin' in his footsteps. They think they above the law, but they's one law they can't get around." She pointed heavenward with a finger made crooked from age and arthritis. "The *man* above. Ain't no getting around His law."

Rusty scrubbed the front of his mother's sedan much longer than he needed to before pausing to splash water on his face. He savored the water's coolness. It reminded him of an early fall day that he'd spent floating in an inner tube on Cherokee River. Although always beautiful, the river was especially so that day as its surface reflected the deep variations of gold, red, and brown of the changing leaves of trees lining its banks. The water also mirrored a dreamy version of two blue herons perched on an outcropping of granite. Rusty lazily watched them until they took flight and soared beyond the forested horizon.

A blast of gunfire shook him from his daydream. "Abby!" he yelled, hurling himself toward her as he spotted an old Honda Accord slowing in front of the house. The screaming child reached out for him.

He snatched her from the pool and shielded her with his body a split-second before another quick burst of gunfire crackled. He gripped her while scrambling behind his mother's car. Shots thudded into the side of it before Rusty heard the gunning of an engine and the squeal of tires as the Accord raced away.

"Uncle Rusty!" Abby wailed.

"Oh, my God." Rusty panted, holding her close against his racing heart.

His dad came flying out of the house with a shotgun. "Where'd that sonuvabitch go?"

Too shaken to answer, Rusty rocked Abby back and forth, trying to calm them both. The next moment he heard the jangled voices of his mother and Blake who ran toward him and Abby.

His mother reached them and peeled them apart. "Are y'all okay?"

"Somebody tried to kill us!" Abby cried.

"I know, baby, I know," Doris Carter said, sobbing into the girl's hair.

"No," Rusty said to Abby. "He wasn't trying to kill us; he was trying to kill me."

"Goddamn it!" His dad clutched the double-barreled Winchester and motioned it in the direction that the Accord had gone. "Had I gotten to this just a little quicker, I could've shot the hell outta that motherfucker!"

"You sure could've, Granddaddy," Blake said.

Still clutching Abby, Doris softly moaned over and over again, "Lord have mercy. Lord have mercy . . . "

The strength to continue sitting upright drained from Rusty. He lay on the grass and stared blankly at the sky. His beautiful, precious, innocent niece had almost been killed—because of him.

A couple of hours later, about a dozen people from the city's police department, including Chief McDonald, still lingered in his living room. Most of them had also been there after news of the first attempt on his life had spread. And not unlike McDonald had done before, he gave Rusty a hearty pat on the shoulder and said, "Rest assured, Carter, we're going to track down this mongrel, and when we do, he'll wish he'd never been born."

"Yessir," Rusty said, hoping that his lack of confidence in Chief Junious McDonald's assurance didn't show.

However, his dad didn't bother to disguise how he felt about his former friend and coworker. "That's a bunch of bullshit, Junie, and you know it. Y'all—"

"Russell!" Doris cut him off. "Please! Don't make a bad situation worse."

He whirled to face her. "How can it get worse? Some maniac's on the loose with our boy in his crosshairs. He almost killed him and Abby, too, and what are y'all doing about it?" He fixed another hate-filled glare at Chief McDonald. "Not a fucking thing."

"I'm sorry," Doris said to McDonald. "He's . . . " She

glanced at her husband, then back at the man who, along with his wife, used to invite the Carters over for barbecues. "He's upset."

The chief stood up to leave. "No, need to apologize, Doris. I'd probably say the same if I were in his shoes."

"This is getting next to all of us," Scott said.

Rusty felt as helpless as he was sure they did. Short of making him a prisoner in a safe house for God only knew for how long, there was nothing they could do.

Det. Ron Baker, who had taken the official report of the murder attempt, made his way back over to Rusty. "If you remember anything else about what happened, call me, no matter what time of the day or night."

"Sure thing," Rusty replied. From the rear of the house, he heard Charlene continuing to comfort her children, especially Abby. How often would she allow them anywhere near Rusty now, and who could blame her?

"You all right, man?" Scott asked him.

Rusty studied him for a moment. "What do you think?"

Scott could only shake his head with sadness.

The sun was high overhead as Rusty sat at the grave of Marcus Jennings. He checked his watch—it was three minutes past noon. He'd killed Marcus at 2:38 PM. It was only another two hours and thirty-five minutes away. He could wait that long. It was only right that their lives should end at the exact same time of day. And as they'd been together when Marcus died, they'd be together when he died.

He breathed in the magical fragrance of the lavender roses and the other flowers that covered the burial site while continuing to cradle his Glock .45 semi-automatic in his lap. Only one bullet was chambered in its magazine, but that's all it would take to end the threat he posed to those he loved and to free himself from the nightmare his life had become. 2:38 PM. It wouldn't be much longer.

CHAPTER 15

With her husband, children, Rev. Creighton Jones, Denise Hollingsworth, and Serena McMillan surrounding her, Emma felt ganged up on, but she was determined not to cave in, not this time.

Jones squeezed her hand with his soft, manicured one. "Please, Mrs. Jennings, this is so critical. Won't you reconsider?"

"Absolutely not." It was all she could do not to yank away from his grasp. God, how she despised him.

"Momma, please for Marcus's sake," Brenda pleaded.

That got to Emma. If only she could tell them why she was acting this way. It was impossible, though, so she would simply have to stand her ground and let them think whatever of her.

"You make me sick!" Otis said.

That drew stunned looks and sharp gasps from his children, but he thundered on, "You could make this speech if you wanted to." He held up the typed remarks Denise had written for Emma to deliver at the rally which would start in only about an hour. The speech was similar to the one that Emma had tried to read during the press conference, but it contained more shots at Rusty. As if that poor boy hadn't suffered enough because of her—he'd nearly gotten killed. There was no way she was going to spew those things about him that were nothing but hateful lies. She felt terrible enough by agreeing to sit on the dais while others vilified him. Even though she wouldn't speak a word, her mere presence would imply that she agreed with what they said about him.

Ed protectively pulled her close to him, but aimed his comments to his father. "There's no point badgering her. If she can't do it, she can't do it. Leave her be."

In response, Otis stomped into the den where his grandchildren were watching cartoons.

"Oh, Lord," Stephanie moaned.

"It'll be fine," Rev. Jones said, radiating confidence. "Even if your mom doesn't speak today, there are plenty of us who will tell the world how Russell Carter, Jr. gunned down Marcus in cold blood, and we'll make sure he pays and pays dearly."

"That's right," Otis Lee said. "We won't let him get away with this and murder somebody else's child."

Emma felt another blinding headache coming on. Though Otis was in the den, there were still too many people jammed into the small kitchen and the blaring cartoons from the next room grated on her nerves that were already at their breaking point.

"Momma, are you okay?" Brenda asked.

"No, I'm going out on the porch for a little bit for some fresh air."

But she found no relief there either. Several friends had showed up early—way, way early—so they could be part of the motorcade to the outdoor arena where the protest would take place.

A few minutes of chit-chat with them was as much as she could take before mumbling something about needing to run a short errand.

She didn't wait until the air conditioner of her old sedan got going good before she drove away. Despite her pledge to Dottie and the little time that remained before they were due at the arena, she knew where she had to go, if only for a few minutes. Perhaps it would be long enough to get the peace she needed to get through the rest of the day. *Please don't be there, Rusty, please.*

* * *

He was, though, and what she saw him gently caressing before he noticed her made her race to him. "Oh, my God, Rusty, no!" she cried and flung herself against his sweat-soaked body.

He started shaking with sobs. "I . . . I can't take it anymore, Miss Emma."

She gripped him tighter. "You can't do this. I won't let you!"

"You don't understand. He came at me again this morning, except this time he nearly killed my niece while trying to shoot me. She's only four years old, for Christ's sake, and she could've got killed because of me."

"No. You're not to blame for any of this. It's all my fault!"

Confusion contorted his features. "What are you talking about?"

She made him sit down next to her, and the fragrance of the flowers on Marcus's grave floated over them as the entire truth gushed from her.

When she finished, she said, "You've got every right to use that gun on me."

He made no response. He obviously needed time to absorb what she had told him. The midday sun broiled her, but she didn't bother to wipe away the sweat stinging her eyes and fusing her clothes to her skin. She would give him all the time he needed. That was the least he deserved.

Finally, after what seemed like an eternity, he said, "You hadn't intended to hurt me—"

"But I did," she interrupted him. "I nearly got you killed, and your niece too. Oh, God, I'm so sorry. I can't begin to tell you how sorry I am," she said, breaking down once more.

"You were only doing what you thought was right."

"But it was wrong! It was the worst thing I could've done. I shouldn't have listened to Otis or Dottie. Had I done the right thing, none of this would've happened."

"You would've destroyed your family though."

Emma had no answer for that. She looked at him through her tears and begged, "Tell me what to do."

He leaned back and studied the cloudless sky as if it held the answers.

After another long period of silence, she added with more desperation, "Whatever you want me to do, I'll do it."

"I don't know. I just don't know. Part of me wants you to tell everyone what you told me, but another part wants you to keep quiet about it. I don't want you to lose your family—you've suffered enough."

"Me! I haven't gone through anything compared to you."

"I haven't lost a son."

"I wouldn't have either if I'd been a decent mother to him."

"You were a good mother to him. Kids act like he did all the time when they first start high school, but eventually, they get over it. How the heck were you supposed to know that he'd be an exception?"

She continued to sob. "I don't know, but I should've. I was his mother. I was the only one he could talk to and when he really needed me, I turned my back on him. In every way that counted, I was the one who shot him, not you."

"No, you would've had enough sense to realize that what he had was nothing but a toy."

"How?" she demanded to know. "How could anybody figure that out in a split-second?"

"I . . ." his voice trailed off.

"That 'toy' looked as real as real could be. He'd terrified the people in that store with it, and they had a whole lot more time to get a look at it than you did, so how were you supposed to know it wasn't real?"

"I guess I couldn't have," he lamely conceded.

"There's no guessing to it. You did what you had to do. Had I paid more attention to Marcus, he wouldn't have been there in the first place."

"Miss Emma, you can't keep blaming yourself. Even I know you well enough to say without a shadow of a doubt that if you realized how bad off he was, you would've done anything to get him help. You would've laid down your life for his without thinking twice about it."

"I would've." She sobbed harder. "I wish to God I could now."

He hugged her. "You and I have got a job to do."

"What's that?" she asked, her voice muffled by his T-shirt.

"To help each other see that neither of us is to blame, and that we've got to go on—somehow."

She rested against him. She was so tired.

He eased away slightly, stuck out his hand and astonished her with a weak smile. "Deal?"

She managed a smile that needed even more strength than his and took his hand in hers. "Deal."

Her six-year old grandson was the first to spot her when she returned home. He raced into the house hollering, "She's back! She's back! Grandma's back!"

A horde came pouring from the house with Otis leading the charge. "Where the goddamn hell have you been?" he yelled at her. "We've torn this place apart looking for you!"

"You had us worried to death, Momma!" Stephanie cried, running behind him.

"Oh, my God, Mrs. Jennings!" Creighton Jones hollered. "What happened to you? Did somebody try to kidnap you?"

"No, I—" With her thoughts swirling in a chaotic jumble, Emma didn't know what else to say.

"Where the hell have you been?" Otis demanded once more.

She looked from him to one of their children to the other. "I had to go Marcus's grave, and I guess I lost track of the time. I'm sorry."

"I'm sick and tired of your foolishness," Otis spat out. He grabbed her and gave her a brutal shake. "There's twenty thousand people waiting on us at the arena. Twenty thousand! And you've had us wasting time hunting for you. You're making us look like a bunch of stupid niggers who can't get their shit together. Why don't you think of somebody else for once?"

Wincing from his words that hurt more than his vise-like grip, Emma choked back tears.

Denise Hollingsworth closed in on her from the other side. "You have to start taking this much more seriously. I realize you've been through a lot, but so has the rest of your family and you don't see any of them behaving so irresponsibly, do you?"

Then Jones launched his assault. "You've got to stay focused on the cause, Mrs. Jennings. We must get justice for Marcus by making that vicious, racist murderer pay for what he did."

Emma jerked from Otis's grip and yelled at Jones, "Shut up! You don't know what you're talking about!"

Her outburst clearly stunned everyone, her most of all.

"Momma!" Brenda said. "What in the world has come over you?"

"Quit acting a fool, Emma!" Otis said and tried to grab her again, but she escaped from his grip.

"There's nothing wrong with me!" she said. "As a matter of fact, I've finally come to my senses about this whole, awful mess. It's nothing but a lie, and I'm not going to stand for it anymore!"

"Don't pay her no attention!" a suddenly panicked Otis commanded everyone. "She's talking out of her head. One of y'all will have to stay here with her while the rest of us go downtown."

"You're not leaving me anywhere," Emma told him. "It's over, honey. I can't keep this up for another second."

"What the blazes are you carrying on about, Momma?" Ed asked.

Otis snapped at him, "I told you not to pay her no attention!"

"It's about something I should've told y'all from the start," Emma said.

"I don't know what you're talking about," Jones said to her, "but whatever it is, it's going to have to wait until after the rally. You've made us late enough as it is."

Emma pointed to his limo. "Get off my property and leave me alone with my family!"

"You don't talk to me like that!" he said in a shocked tone.

"I'll talk to you a lot worse than that if you don't get the hell out of here," Emma said.

Otis whispered harshly to her, "You gave me your word."

"I was wrong."

Her oldest daughter stepped closer. "Wrong about what? What's going on?"

"Your momma is just having a fit," Otis said to Brenda, "and we ain't got time for it. Watch her until we get back."

"I told you I'm coming too," Emma said.

"No, you're not!" Otis said. "And I ain't arguing with you no more about it." Gesturing to the others on the porch, he said, "C'mon, y'all."

"You can't keep hiding from the truth, Otis," Emma said.

"What's going on?" Stephanie asked, repeating her sister's unanswered question.

"Yeah," Ed said to Otis, "what do you know that you don't want us knowing?"

Before Otis had a chance to respond, Jones—who apparently shared Otis's growing panic that the situation was getting out of control—said, "We've got to go! Brenda, come with us. Ms. Hollingsworth will stay here and tend to your mother so we can—"

Brenda cut him off. "I'm not going anywhere until I hear what Momma's got to say."

"Me either," Ed said as his brother and sisters nodded in agreement.

"To hell with y'all then," Otis told them. "We don't need you."

"We're not trying to be disrespectful to you, Daddy,"

Stephanie said. "It's only that you seem to know something that Momma thinks we've got a right to know too."

"And before y'all go digging yourselves down further into a big lie," Emma added.

"The only thing y'all need to know," Otis said, "is that Rusty Carter killed y'all's brother in cold blood."

"That's not true, and you know it!" Emma said.

"What!" Stephanie said as everyone exchanged shocked expressions. Jones began shoving people off the porch. "All right, folks, let's move! Let's move! We gotta hurry!" He turned to his several of his bodyguards. "Keep her here and don't let her out until you hear from me."

Otis Lee barreled toward him. "You can't make my momma a prisoner in her own home!"

One of the bodyguards blocked his way. "Settle down, chief," he said with an ice cold smile.

"Are you going to let your children be treated like this?" Emma shouted above the commotion at Otis who was helping Jones shove people toward their vehicles.

"I'm doing this for them, for you, and most of all, for Marcus!" Otis said over his shoulder.

Emma said, "You ain't doing this for nobody but yourself, and you ought to be ashamed!"

Stephanie burst into tears. "I don't understand any of this! Why is Daddy acting so hateful?"

"He's hurting, and he's got good reason to hurt," Emma said, drawing Stephanie close, "but he's handling it as wrong as can be."

"For God's sake, Momma, tell us what's going on!" Ed said.

"In a minute, baby," Emma said, then she glared at Jones' bodyguards. "Me and my kids are going upstairs, and y'all better not give me any lip about it."

The one who stopped Otis Lee flashed another of his cold smiles. "Of course not, ma'am, as you long as you don't leave this house."

Blazing with anger, Otis Lee said to him, "You got a lot of damned nerve—"

Emma quickly shushed him. She was sure the guards

had guns on them and if Otis Lee made the wrong move . . . . *Oh, Lord.*

She led Otis Lee and the rest of her children into her bedroom, and they piled onto the bed with her like they used to do when they were small. After taking a deep breath, she told them everything, and then fell silent. It was time for them to speak.

For a few moments, none of them appeared able to. They just sat there in a daze. Finally, Stephanie said, "I knew Marcus seemed kind of down, but I never would've thought in a million years that he'd—" She began crying.

"I didn't see it coming either," Emma said as she hugged her. "God knows if I had, I would've gotten him help, whatever he needed to get better." Fresh tears spilled down her face. "There's nothing I can do to change that. What I can do, though, is to try my best to make amends, starting with clearing Rusty's name."

"Not if Daddy and Rev. Jones have any say about it." Ed kicked into the carpet.

"They can say whatever they want," Emma said. "They're not going to keep me quiet. It's not only about doing right by Rusty, but by Marcus, too. If telling what happened to him saves the life of only one kid who is suffering with depression; that will be the best way to honor Marcus. I see that now."

"Doesn't look like you'll be able to do much about it, at least not as long as Jones has his goons guarding this place," Otis Lee said, clearly frustrated.

"I wish I'd never called that man," Stephanie said.

"Don't you go blaming yourself, honey," Emma told her. "You were only doing what you thought was right, and if I'd been straight with you from the beginning, you wouldn't have ever bothered with him."

"I still should've seen through him," Stephanie said. "You were right, Momma, he's nothing but a snake."

"He can't stop me," Emma said. "Neither can his flunkies or anyone else. I won't stand for another day to go by without everyone knowing the truth."

"Surely you're not still set on speaking at the rally, are you?" Brenda asked.

"I most certainly am," Emma said. She was surprised how calm she felt. It was like Marcus was supplying her with the peace and strength she needed. She had to get to that rally—the odds were that it would be the only time Marcus's death was the center of such nationwide attention.

Brenda asked, "How are you going manage that? Those guys downstairs have turned this place into a state pen."

"I've got a plan," Emma said, "but I don't want none of y'all being part of it. Matter of fact, the less y'all know about it, the better, so when fingers start pointing, they won't be in your direction."

Otis Lee said, "You're not leaving us out."

The others firmly echoed his sentiments.

Emma expected as much. They were fine children, every single one of them. And that was exactly why she couldn't allow them to get involved. "I've got to do this on my own," she told them. "Y'all are just going to have to trust me on this."

That brought more protests. If there was a battle to be waged, they wanted to be right by her side.

"If you really want to help," Emma said, "then stay up here and if Jones' people holler for me, tell them I'm sick in the bathroom with diarrhea on account of my nerves being tore up."

"While you sneak out of the house," Brenda accurately guessed. "Well, even if that works—which is a big 'if'—there's no way you'll be able to get by Jones and Daddy, not to mention the bodyguards around Jones who know you're supposed to stay here." She shook her head. "I hate to say it, Momma, but you don't have a chance of pulling this off."

Emma felt her resolve flagging. Although she'd blurted that she had a plan, she realized she really hadn't thought out anything beyond escaping from the house. And even if she managed to do that, how was she going to get downtown? She couldn't drive there. Her car and those of her kids were parked in full view of Jones' men. They'd nab her if she tried to get close to any of the vehicles. Damn. What was she going to do?

Well, if she kept dwelling on the huge odds against her, she'd fail for sure. She'd simply have to tackle one problem at a time.

"Maybe you're right," she told Brenda, "but I've got to try." She quickly brushed her hair, wiped her face and smoothed down her dress. "If I'm not back in ten minutes, you'll know I got away."

Stephanie hugged her. "Be careful."

"I will."

As Emma crept to the stairway, she listened to the voices from below and judging from what she heard, the guards were in the den watching the rally on TV. The very idea of them lounging in her home like they owned it made her furious. She shook away the thought. *Got to stay focused on escaping, girl.*

She began her descent, careful not to step on any of the boards that creaked.

"Hey, all right!" one of the men yelled.

Emma gasped in fright and nearly tumbled backwards. Her heart kept thudding while the guard's companions joined him in cheering something that was evidently happening at the arena. Probably that rotten boss of theirs had just arrived. Or maybe it had to do with one of the celebrities scheduled to give speeches before Jones delivered the crowning one for the day.

Once her heart finally returned to its normal rhythm, Emma continued down the stairs. She reached the bottom and peeked around the corner into the den. Sure enough, the men were clustered around the TV, delighting in what they were seeing.

Emma tiptoed into the kitchen and outside through the back door. She released a sigh of relief. On to the next problem—getting to the arena. The quickest solution was to find someone in the neighborhood to take her there, but that was sure to spark questions about why she hadn't gone with Otis and Jones. She'd simply have to think of something believable.

After scaling the fence that separated her yard from a neighbor's, she rang the neighbor's doorbell. No answer. There weren't any cars in the driveway either. Damn.

She went to the next house. Same thing. She looked around. The neighborhood appeared completely deserted. There wasn't a single person in sight. It was as if all of Waverton's residents had mysteriously vanished. Despite the blistering heat, Emma shuddered.

The realization that she needed to call a cab made her wish she'd thought to bring her cell phone. In all the hullabaloo, she'd forgotten it in her car and she wasn't going to risk being spotted by Jones's bodyguards to get it. She'd have to find a pay phone.

As she drudged down the street in search of one, heat rose from the asphalt in shimmering waves. It radiated through the soles of her shoes; making her feel like she was walking over an endless bed of hot coals. The sun punished her from above without a trace of mercy. It had to be at least a hundred degrees, and it seemed to get hotter with each step. By the time she made it to a telephone booth at the end of the street, she was exhausted and drenched in sweat. So much for the effort she'd taken to make herself look presentable—she'd turned into a soggy, smelly mess.

Worse yet, the pay phone in the booth was gone. Only the scratched up metal panel it had been attached to remained.

The phone booth was in the parking lot of a liquor store, but like the rest of the neighborhood, the place was deserted. She tried its door anyway. It was bolted shut. What the hell was going on? The store was open even on Christmas Eve for crying out loud. Why was it closed? Its tacky portable roadside marquee sign provided the answer: Rally Today!—Meet Us There!!!

"Oh, Jesus," Emma groaned. She wiped away sweat and crossed onto the next street. Downtown was over four miles away. At the rate she was going, by the time she got there, everyone might be gone.

She managed to walk nearly a quarter of a mile before the fierce heat forced her to stop at a boarded-up deli. Sagging against its front that was spray-painted with obscenities and gang graffiti, she mopped away sweat. What she saw when she opened her eyes made her wonder if she'd become so desperate that she was starting to hallucinate, but when a city bus lumbered to a stop in front of her and belched out a thick cloud of sickening exhaust fumes, she knew it was for real.

The vehicle's door clacked open, revealing Dookie Walters who had become a bus driver for the city shortly after he and Emma became friends some thirty-odd years ago.

"Emma! I thought that was you!" he said, gaping at her from his high perch behind the steering wheel.

She heaved herself up into the bus that was empty except for him. "Lord have mercy, am I glad to see you, Dookie. I don't think I could've took another step."

"What the heck are you doing here?" he asked as she flopped onto the seat behind him and began fanning herself. "Why ain't you downtown along with everybody else?"

"It's a long story, but if you can get me to the rally as quick as you can, I'd be much obliged."

Dookie put the bus in gear. "You got it, sister."

"Excuse me, excuse me," Emma repeated while working her way through the packed crowd at the arena. She paused to squint over the shoulder of a man in front of her to make sure she was heading in the right direction. The stage remained straight ahead. Creighton Jones was approaching the microphone. Lord, Jesus, Emma thought. She began closing the gap between them more quickly. As she squeezed between sweat-soaked bodies and dodged a kaleidoscope of umbrellas that people were using to protect themselves from the fierce sun, she half-listened to Jones bringing the crowd to its feet with his demands for justice for Marcus.

"Don't let this rotten, racist police department in this city get away with murder! They must be stopped!" he boomed.

"Yeah!" the crowd roared wildly.

Emma paused again to look over another person's shoulder. She wasn't too far from the stage now. She pressed on.

"It was the Jennings' son this month," Jones hollered, "it'll be yours next month if we don't put an end to this!"

"Yeah!"

Emma reached the cordon that ringed the stage and ducked beneath it, startling one of Jones' bodyguards.

"What are you doing here?" he said, blinking at her as if he must be imagining things.

She pretended that he didn't recognize her. "I'm supposed to be up there," she said, pointing toward the dais and adding loudly, "I'm Emma Jennings."

"Hey, sweetie, it's Marcus Jennings's mother!" a lady in the crowd said to a man while she gestured toward Emma.

Others from the crowd surged toward Emma, wanting to hug her or shake her hand. That flustered the guard even more. More security rushed to his side.

With countless people looking on, Emma smiled at the guards. "If y'all would be so kind as to let me through, I'd appreciate it."

"Well . . . uh . . . " one of the guards stammered.

"Er . . . ah . . . " said another.

"What y'all waiting on?" someone from the crowd yelled. "You heard Mrs. Jennings—get out her way!"

"That's right!" someone else hollered.

The grumbling grew louder with each second that the guards stared stupidly at one another, none of them sure of what to do.

A hugely fat woman cupped her dimpled hands against her mouth and shouted, "Rev. Jones! How come your people won't let Mrs. Jennings up there?"

"They disrespecting her!" someone else yelled.

Creighton Jones glanced down from the podium and at the sight of Emma, his eyes grew wide.

Taking advantage of the moment, Emma pushed her way past the guards and bounded up the steps. Otis came at her. "Don't do this," he said in a desperate whisper.

"I'm sorry, but I have to."

Creighton Jones looked like he was about to pass out. "Well, I declare!" he managed to say to the crowd. "It surely is Mrs. Emma Jennings! Even though she's been so delirious with fever today that she should be in the hospital, she's able to join us after all."

Emma marched to the podium and shoved him aside. "Ain't a doggone thing wrong with me, and you know it."

"I—" he said.

"Shut up and sit down!" she told him.

The crowd watched in stunned silence. People stretched as far as the eye could see. Yet, instead of making Emma nervous, they gave her courage. It had to be more of Marcus's magic.

She grabbed the microphone. "Y'all have heard a lot of talk this afternoon. Now you're going to hear the truth."

An eerie silence settled over the place. "My son—" she paused. There was no turning back now. "Committed suicide by forcing Officer Carter to kill him."

In the next moment, shouts, shrieks, and loud mumbling erupted, and in the next moment, gunfire.

Emma gasped at the sight of the chaos breaking out in front of her as people tried to take cover. She was too shocked to move even though shots continued to crackle.

Something massive slammed into her and knocked her to the floor. "Stay down!" Otis said, shielding her body with his.

She moaned in pain beneath his crushing weight.

After quickly scanning their surroundings, Otis heaved her against the back of the podium and then gasped. "Jesus, no!"

The searing pain in Emma's chest forced her to wince so hard that she squeezed her eyes shut and moaned in agony.

"You've been shot!"

"What!" Her eyes flew open and she looked down at the red splotch in the middle of her chest that was growing wider.

"Help! Help!" Otis hollered wildly. "My wife's been shot! Somebody help!"

He clutched her to him as she gripped her chest. The pain was beyond belief. It made her barely aware of hearing another loud shot and more screams.

The next few minutes were a blur as strange faces appeared above her, strong hands grabbed her, and she felt herself loaded onto a stretcher and then shoved into an ambulance.

"Hold on, baby, hold on," Otis said between sobs as he knelt beside her.

Then everything went black.

EPILOGUE

Emma grinned at Rusty as he climbed out of his cruiser, but he scowled at her. "Miss Emma! Tell me I'm not seeing what I think I'm seeing."

She laughed. "Nope! Your eyes do not deceive you."

"You just got out of the hospital a few days ago."

"And this is the best medicine for me," she said, planting more of the calla lilies she'd gotten from where they had overgrown in the backyard. A cool breeze gently swayed them. She was so thankful they'd survived the horrible heat wave that had finally come to an end.

Rusty leaned against a pine tree near her. "Guess there's no arguing with that. I've never seen you looking better."

"This is the best I've felt since. . ." Emma's voice trailed off and her smile faltered for a moment. She took in a deep breath. It still hurt some to do that, but the pain was easing by the day. The beauty and scent of her flowers helped. Cupping a slender lily and inhaling its soothing fragrance, she said, "Well, in a very, very long time."

"I know the feeling."

"How's your hand?" Emma said, gesturing toward the cast that covered Rusty's right hand and forearm.

He was about to answer, but something behind her caught his attention.

Emma turned around to discover her husband in the front doorway glaring sullenly at the young cop before stepping back into the house and slamming the door behind him.

"I wanted to see how you were doing, but maybe I shouldn't have come." Rusty's gaze stayed focused on the closed door while he massaged his fingers that were still mottled with different shades of blue, brown and gray bruises.

"It's okay. He just needs more time. We all do. We've been through hell. You especially. Your hand is still paining you. I can tell by how you're rubbing it."

He flexed his fingers a few times. "It's getting better, little by little."

Emma hesitated before asking, "And your dad? How's his jaw?"

"Mom says it'll have to stay wired for another month or so."

"You still haven't spoken to him since you . . ." Her voice trailed off again. Despite their growing closeness, there were still some things she had a hard time talking to him about.

"Slugged him," he finished for her. "No, and unless he apologizes for what he said about you, I may never see or speak to him again."

"But he's your daddy, Rusty."

"I don't care. That doesn't give him an excuse to talk about you like that. I explained to him why you did what you did, and although he'd never admit it, he knows he would've done the same if he'd been in your shoes except he wouldn't have had the decency to ever tell the truth. He is my dad, and I do love him, but the fact is he's a racist asshole who got away with murder." As if only then realizing what he'd said, he added, "Sorry for cussing."

"Don't worry about that," Emma said with a dismissive wave. "But please give speaking to him again more thought. What happened to Marcus has caused enough damage as it is. I hate the idea of it tearing you and your father apart."

Rusty rubbed his bruised fingers again. "I can't make any promises."

"Life is short, honey. Remember that. We can't count on having all the time we need to make things right."

"Yes, ma'am."

Emma rested back on her heels. Rusty was not going to budge on the issue, not yet anyway, so she decided to change the subject. "You enjoying desk duty while you're having to wear that cast?"

"Kinda, sorta. It's easy work and I'm glad to be back on duty, but I miss having a beat."

"You're a lot safer there, that's for sure."

"If I really wanted to be safe, I'd never leave my apartment and Gerald Townsend would've ruined my life," he said of the African-American gunman who had tried to kill them both.

"That poor sick man," Emma said, thinking about the images she'd seen on the news of his scrawny, needle-scarred body lying on the arena floor amidst the overturned soda cans, boxes of popcorn, candy wrappers and other trash that people dropped while fleeing from him. It had only taken a single shot from one of Jones' bodyguards to kill him—it had gone straight through his heart.

In the days since his death, the authorities had met with little success in figuring out exactly what had triggered his determination to kill Rusty, and then Emma when she'd come to Rusty's defense. With no known address, job, or close family or friends, he seemed to have been a drifter. Although investigators had tracked down a few of his cousins in Washington, D.C., they claimed to have lost touch with him years ago. None of them had seen him since he'd signed himself out of a hospital where he'd been getting treatment for heroin addiction and schizophrenia.

Emma shook her head with sadness. What if Townsend had stayed longer in that hospital or someone had forced him to return?

"Miss Emma?" Rusty said softly. "You okay?"

"I'm getting there. You know how it is."

"Yeah." He squatted beside her. "Don't push yourself.

In the meantime, it's a mighty nice change to see you gardening here instead of at Marcus's grave."

"It's time to plant flowers for the living." She extended a pot filled with calla lilies to him. "Hope these will do for a housewarming gift."

"They most certainly will," he said with the sweetest smile she'd ever seen.